Trust No Bitch

Ca$h & NeNe Capri

Lock Down Publications
Presents
Trust No Bitch
A Novel by *Ca$h & NeNe Capri*

Lock Down Publications
P.O. Box 1482
Pine Lake, Ga 30072-1482

Lock Down Publications
Ca$h
Email: ldp.cash@gmail.com
Facebook: Cassius Alexander
Like our page on Facebook: Lock Down Publications @
www.facebook.com/lockdownpublications.ldp
Amazon: http://www.amazon.com/Ca$h
NeNeCapri
Facebook: NeNeCapri
Twitter: @NeNeCapri
Instagram: @NeneCapri
Cover design and layout by: **Marion Designs**
Book interior design by: **Shawn Walker**
Edited by: **Shawn Walker**

Acknowledgements

We would first like to acknowledge our fans nationwide. Thank you for supporting our individual careers and this collaboration Trust No Bitch. To our loyal supporters on the social websites, in the book groups, and the distributors, you fuel our drive. To the readers, you make us what we are authors. Thank you Shawn Walker for your boss editing. Keith, we thank you for the cover and look forward to more of your work. Friends, family, associates, and fellow authors we thank you all.

Dedications

CA$H: To the one who prefers to remain anonymous, they can't destroy what they can't see.

Nene Capri: To My beloved daughter Princess Khairah everything I do is for you. Mommy loves you.

Chapter 1
Mentor and Protégé

Kiam was putting the last of his things in the two boxes he had placed in the middle of his bunk. As he lined his things neatly from one side to the other his mind shifted to the work that lay ahead. His blood rushed through his veins as he felt the reality of impending freedom. The thoughts were sweet in his mind but bitter in his belly. He had spent the last eight years living how many would consider beastly.

At age twenty-six the trail of blood he had left behind was long and thick. And honestly it was only going to get thicker. As he turned to check to see if he had everything, one of his boys entered his cell appearing to be all about business.

"Ay, Kiam, one of your homeboys just came on the compound. Some cat who calls himself Supreme. He says he's from the eastside of Cleveland. Isn't that your hood?" asked Philly Cat, a straight up G from South Philadelphia who was serving thirty years behind a snitch nigga's testimony.

Philly Cat was one of the dudes responsible for checking new arrivals' credentials when they first came on compound to make sure that they were solid. The rule stood firm, snitches weren't allowed to live amongst real niggas at Lewisburg.

"Yeah, that's my hood," Kiam attested. "But the name Supreme don't ring no bells. Did you check out his papers?"

"Nah, he says he sent them home." Philly stood, rubbing his hands together.

"Well, you know the rules, if the homie can't prove who he is, he has to get off the compound. It don't matter where he's from. He's not my muthafuckin' homie." Kiam wasn't claiming nobody that couldn't prove their officialness.

He stood contemplating for a minute then rendered his verdict. "Take me to that nigga."

Philly Cat led Kiam outside on the yard where other solid men were questioning Supreme. Kiam walked up and studied the newcomer. He didn't recognize the nigga's face so he kept quiet and listened to his responses.

It was obvious that if Supreme wasn't from that city once dubbed The Mistake by the Lake, he had at least lived there for a while. He knew the names of all the shot-callers, and he knew all the hoods. He claimed to have once had the notorious Garden Valley projects on Kinsman Avenue on smash before they were torn down and rebuilt, but something didn't seem right about ol' boy.

"Fam, what's your government?" Kiam cut in.

"Michael Gresham," Supreme replied, mean-mugging, with his thick arms folded across his chest.

Kiam ignored the weak intimidation tactic. Instead he entertained him with a small chuckle which was his signature stamp of death. Instantly Supreme knew he had stepped through the gates of hell and Kiam appeared to be the devil himself.

Supreme was a big muthafucka, but size doesn't determine a man's gangsta. His biggest mistake was he hadn't looked Kiam in the eye. That in itself hinted at a flaw in his get-down. Boss niggas could match a man's gaze with one better.

"Homie, I'm gonna make a few calls and check out your street cred. If you're not who you claim to be, you better check off compound now," he warned Supreme.

Kiam didn't stay a second past his words; he turned his back on Supreme and walked away. *That nigga frontin'. I can see fear in his eyes. If it turns out he's a rat, hiding under a different name, I'm gonna send him up out of here in a body bag.* It didn't matter that his release date was upon him, his gangsta was never on hold.

Kiam used his celly Pop's contraband cell phone to reach out to the streets. It only took a few calls to find out that Michael

Gresham was indeed a thorough dude. But the nigga that also called himself Supreme was not that Michael Gresham.

By evening Kiam had learned that the Michael Gresham that had Kinsman on smash got thirty-five years and was at ADX Florence, the super max federal prison in Colorado. The description nor the reputation fitted this clown down here. What the fuck is this nigga hiding? wondered Kiam.

The question rang strong in his mind, but he damn sure didn't have time to figure it out. Kiam hated fake niggas with a passion. He believed that they all should be killed. Weak, fake niggas had cost a lot of good men their lives, taking the stand to testify and selling their souls. In that moment the decision was made. Supreme's fate was death. In fact, Kiam felt that he deserved the most gruesome death just for calling himself some real shit like Supreme when he was not anything close to it.

Late that night he pulled a homemade ski mask over his face to hide his identity in case the wrong nigga saw him moving. He eased out of the broom closet, where he had strapped up, and crept up behind Supreme in the television area. "Welcome to the grave muthafucka," he gritted, shoving a knife between the imposter's shoulder blades.

Warm blood poured down Kiam's arm as he stabbed Supreme repeatedly. The surge of testosterone that filled his body as he took another man's life was priceless. And even with the victory of maxing out on his bid holding in the balance, nothing felt better than the kill. Kiam had well-established that he would stand on principle regardless of the consequences.

The next morning...

Kiam stood in front of his celly and mentor with a heavy heart that contradicted the beast that lied within. In the three years that they had bunked together, Alonzo, whom he affectionately called Pop, had become his surrogate father and his only trusted friend. As anxious as Kiam was to return to the streets and apply all the things that Alonzo had instilled in him, he still felt some kinda way about leaving Big Zo behind.

"Pop, you know I would give anything for you to be able to walk out that door with me." Sincerity covered his face as he looked his guru in the eye.

Big Zo showed no expression. He appreciated the love but the reality was that he wasn't walking out of that door with his protégé. As things stood he wasn't ever walking out of those prison doors, he had life in the feds and that was that.

"Don't worry about Pop, I'm built to last. My life is in here now. That's the bed I made, and that's the bed I'm going to sleep in."

Kiam nodded his understanding. He admired the strength that Pop had in spite of his predicament. Big Zo hadn't let the sentence break him. At fifty years old, he worked out every day to stay in top shape, and he was impeccably groomed. His mind was a vault of knowledge and wisdom that extended far beyond street life. But Pop was about that life too.

He put a fatherly hand on Kiam's shoulder and spat a jewel in his ear. "I see how you're looking at me. You're feeling bad because you're leaving me behind. But there's no time for that. You have to forget about what's on this side of the fence, including that business of last night, I'll handle that. I need for you to focus on what's on that other side. Do you understand me, son?"

Kiam just nodded because he did not trust himself to speak. It wrung his heart to be leaving him behind.

"Go out there and put your hustle and murder games down like I've prepared you to do," Pop continued. "I have schooled you to become the strongest street general to ever fuck with the game, and I expect nothing less of you."

"Failure is not an option," Kiam intoned.

"It is not." Big Zo put the other hand on Kiam's shoulder. Standing at about 6' 2 they were the same height. He looked at his understudy and implored, "Remember, you are to leave no enemy alive or they'll rebuild then come back to overthrow you. Never forget that the only people that can hurt you are those closest to you. No matter who it is—family, friend or foe— if they show one glint of treason you must execute them with extreme prejudice. You bury the muthafucka, let Allah worry about forgiveness."

"I understand, Pop. And you already know how I live."

Indeed Big Zo did. He quickly reflected on the countless sacrifices Kiam made on his behalf. In the past three years there had been several incidents that tested Kiam's loyalty and his gangsta; he had aced each test.

Big Zo's mind returned to the present. He tightened his grip on Kiam's shoulder and continued to drop jewels on him. "Son, you're a throwback. There's not many dudes your age that honor the code. Self-preservation is the only code that still stands today. Fuck anything else you heard."

Pop's brow furrowed, he wished that he had known that when the feds began snatching up his comrades and pressuring them to flip on him.

"Real men like you and me always suffer the greatest penalties because we won't compromise our principles to save ourselves." Kiam's voice almost broke. He knew Big Zo's story well; he had read the trial transcripts more than twenty times.

"I let certain men live because I thought that they were built like me. Death before dishonor is what we were all taught. But at the end of the day, muthafuckas saved themselves and left me for dead. Don't let them do that to you. Do you understand?" Pop questioned needlessly.

"Yes, sir."

"Now you must remember, you can trust yourself and you can trust my daughter. Lissha has been taught by the best. She is just as comfortable carrying a Glock as she is carrying a Gucci bag. She is to be your conduit to the top, but she is not to be your woman. You can have everything that I left out there but my daughter. She is beautiful and any man will be tempted to want more from her than a business relationship, but you are not to fuck her. Is that clear?" He studied Kiam with intensity that was as hot as burning coals. Kiam did not blink. His loyalty was concrete.

"Temptation befalls many. If you succumb to it, I will not be forgiving. I will use everything that I have to reach out and touch you – by any means possible," Pop warned.

"On everything that I love, I won't betray you. And if any amount of money can bring you home, I'll be back to get you," Kiam promised.

"Death before dishonor soldier."

"To the grave," Kiam vowed. He saluted his mentor then walked toward freedom, prepared to conquer the game.

What he was not prepared for was Lissha's beauty.

Chapter 2
Home Coming

Lissha was posted up against her apple red 2012 Dodge Magnum in the parking lot of the prison at nine o'clock sharp. She reflected on her specific orders from Daddy as she awaited the man of the hour. Forty minutes later, Kiam emerged from the front doors of the penitentiary. Lissha noticed that the pictures she had seen of him did not accurately reflect what he looked like in the flesh.

"Got damn," she fidgeted as he drew near. His chocolate, well-chiseled, frame moved swiftly toward her. Instantly she felt the kitty tingle as his eyes met hers. She crossed her legs at the ankle to slow the pulse that was beating fast below.

Kiam put some stride in his step as he looked up and saw Lissha waving him over. Her pretty pecan tan glowed in the sunlight. Her sandy brown shoulder length hair draped the sides of her face accentuating her high cheek bones. His eyes moved all over her 5'8" 135 pound figure, enjoying the journey.

Her breast sat up like two ripe melons and the curve of her hips in those skinny jeans had his dick asking him questions that he damn sure wanted to answer. Then Big Zo's words echoed loudly, *Temptation befalls many. If you succumb to it…*

Damn, Pop, he shook his head. Sensing that Lissha was probably picking up on his vibe, he quickly threw a little smile on his face.

"Look at you, all cheesed up." She smiled and extended her arms to receive him.

"What's up, ma?" He reached in and hugged her tightly.

Kiam felt the magnetism between them as the heat from her body embraced him. Her scent caressed his nostrils as her silky skin melted in his hands. It had been years since he held a woman in his arms and her perfect frame was the welcome he needed. He inhaled deeply, wanting to grip tighter, but Pops warning rang in his ears as if they were being shouted out on a mega phone. *"Don't fuck my daughter."*

Kiam abruptly pulled back.

"Why you acting all scary? Did Daddy threaten you?" She flashed him that pretty smile of hers, then giggled.

"Nah. None needed. His instructions were clear and I'm going to carry them out or die trying." He got real serious erasing the smile completely from his face.

"Well, let's go," Lissha popped the locks with the remote, and headed to her side.

Kiam hopped in and sank into his seat. He knew that everything from this point on would be a test and he intended on passing with flying colors.

Lissha and Kiam drove for hours before they reached Cleveland, Ohio. Kiam was looking out the window taking in the many changes that had been made to the city since he last set foot on its soil. Traveling down Superior Avenue he saw that some of the hoods had received a facelift, but he knew without a doubt that those grimy streets were the same cesspool that they had always been.

The laughter and conversation that filled the vehicle was cut short when Lissha pulled into the 7all apartments, looked up and saw her right hand, Treebie, coming toward them at a rapid pace.

Lissha threw the car in park and jumped out.

Kiam watched as the intense conversation between the two went back and forth. He reached over to the driver's side and let the window down to get a better idea of what was going on.

Kiam eyed the female Lissha was talking to. There was a slight resemblance between them, but not a strong enough one for him to mistake them for family. Like Lissha, she had soft brown skin and high cheekbones. Her hair was a little shorter than Lissha's and a small dimple in her left cheek stood out. Even though she was rocking baggy clothes Kiam could see she was well put together.

"What the fuck you mean the spot got hit?" Lissha questioned vehemently.

"I know that nigga Finch was behind that shit. Bayonna called me about an hour ago and said that nigga is holed up at his girl's house on 144th and St. Clair. I'm ready to do this." Treebie pounded her fist in her hand.

Lissha angrily about faced back toward her vehicle. She gripped the steering wheel tightly as she calculated her next move.

Treebie retrieved a black bag from her truck and passed it to Lissha. "The *whistles* are inside," she instructed before she peeled off.

Lissha quickly unzipped the bag and handed Kiam a 9mm German Luger, a Glock .40 and two silencers. Kiam didn't hesitate accepting them. He hadn't even set his feet on the ground yet, but that didn't faze him anymore than the shit he did to Supreme last night. He instinctively began to assemble his new toys.

Lissha pulled her custom-made pearl handled .380 from the bag, checked the clip, and then slid it between her legs. Satisfied that her "baby" was ready, she threw the car in gear and mashed out.

The ride was silent as Lissha zipped through the streets. Kiam asked no questions. No words were necessary; he wasn't new to the game. He was set to killah mode. A nigga had fucked up and a strong example was about to be set.

Twenty minutes later, Lissha pulled up a block away from Finch's girl's house. She surveyed the area, spotting Finch's red BMW 6 Series in the driveway. She grabbed her sneakers out of the back seat, tossing her heels aside. Kiam stood watch as she laced up, rising to her feet with her heat in hand.

"What this nigga look like?" he grimaced.

"Medium built, short afro, and he has a tattoo of a diamond under his left eye."

"Let's go."

Lissha turned toward the house and Kiam was right on her heels. He moved with the stealth of a panther. As they approached the driveway Treebie, who had already been waiting, emerged from the side of the house. She moved low-key with her fo-fifth at her side.

"You know what to do," Lissha whispered between pursed lips.

"If that nigga buck out the back I'ma put his insides on the outside," Treebie spat with flared nostrils and squinted eyes before disappearing.

Lissha and Kiam moved to the door and she gave the secret knock. Seconds later a knock came back. She hit the door twice more then it opened.

Her gut filled with disgust when she looked at the lineup that painted the living room. It was Finch, his number one, and one of her young boys that ran weight from one side of town to the other. Apparently there was some fishy shit brewing because all of them had guilty looks on their faces as if they had gotten caught with their dicks in some underage pussy.

"What's up, LiLi?" Finch's speech slurred with nervousness pitted from his belly.

"You tell me?" Lissha positioned herself near the door leading to the kitchen. "Do you know what happened at my spot today?" Her voice was real calm as she studied Finch's body language.

"I don't know what the fuck you talking about." Finch reached forward, grabbed a cigarette and lit it. He then sat back in his chair, crossed his legs and blew smoke in Lissha's direction.

"Who the fuck is this?" Finch's boy questioned, pointing at Kiam. "We ain't talking business in front of a fucking stranger," he spat.

"Don't worry about who the fuck I am," Kiam gritted, pulling both bangers from his waist and resting them at his sides.

"What the fuck is going on, Lissha?" Finch roared. "You got this nigga being all disrespectful in my house."

Kiam's head tilted to the side. The nigga fit the description of the one Lissha had said violated, plus he was talking reckless. That was two strikes against him and Kiam didn't even allow one. Without hesitation, he shot Finch in the stomach.

"What the fuck is wrong with this muthafucka?" Finch clutched his gaping wound, buckling over in pain.

Beebop put his hands in the air and began to plead his case. "LiLi. Hold up, let's talk this shit out."

She shook her head no, rejecting his plea. "The only thing I want to talk about is the whereabouts of my shit?" She waved her piece in the air.

"I know where it's at." Her little runner panicked. Sweat beaded across his face as tears threatened to fall from his eyes.

"Shut the fuck up." Finch squawked. He was folded over at the waist, holding his stomach. Blood gushed between his fingers and anguish filled his face.

Just as the young boy started to reveal their hands, the three men began arguing back and forth.

Kiam and Lissha looked back and forth before Kiam got fed up and shot Beebop in the face. He flew back in his seat and his brains hit the wall behind him hard and slippery.

The young boy hit the floor covering his head and begging for his life. "Where is my shit?" Lissha repeated with finality in her tone. She pointed her .380 and aimed it between youngin's eyes.

"It's in the closet," he speedily rushed his words as he pointed across the room.

"Get up and get it. Punk muthafucka." Kiam growled, gripping both gats so firmly his hands ached from the clench.

The boy returned apprehensively, dropped the bags at Kiam's feet while raising his hands all in one swift movement. "I don't want no trouble y'all." The words trembled off of his quaking lips. But trouble is what he declared when he got involved. Lissha shot him in the back of the head causing him to fly onto the coffee table, shattering glass in every direction.

She picked up the bags as Kiam headed over to a dying Finch who was breathing short and heavy. Leaning in, Kiam placed the gun in Finch's mouth and forced eye contact. He wanted to make sure he stole his last minutes by filling them with fear and torment.

"Oh god, please. Have mercy. I wasn't trying to cross her," he stuttered.

"Prayer ain't acceptable at times like this. God don't love niggas like us. Make it up in the next life because you leaving this muthafucka. And the next time around, be loyal nigga."

Kiam shoved the gun to the roof of Finch's mouth and let off several shots, spraying the top of Finch's head, decorating the ceiling.

He stepped back, looked at his work, and smeared the blood from his face onto the back of his hand. His breathing was steady but his adrenalin moved rapidly through his body. It was official he was home, back on the killing field. This first taste of blood was merely a catalyst to the terror his return would cause in the hearts of many, and the conflict it would cause in the heart of one.

Chapter 3
Welcome Home

Over the next few hours Lissha drove through the streets, taking Kiam to several of the trap spots to see how shit was moving. Things were gravy at her spots up and down 30th, 55th, and out in EC on Hayden. On Euclid Ave, where it first turned into East Cleveland, on up past Shaw High School she had things on smash. There were other spots in the city under Lissha's control, but she would show him those another day. She figured that he was tired from his long, eventful, first day home and was ready to kick back and cool his heels.

After placing a few calls, she headed to the Ritz Carlton downtown. She had reserved the Presidential Suite for Kiam and a little treat to go along with it.

Lissha pulled up to the valet. She got out, tipped the young boy a c-note, popped her trunk and grabbed a medium sized Louis Vuitton bag. She closed the trunk, then headed toward the entrance. Kiam slid out of the passenger side with his own bag slung over his broad shoulder. He took in the opulent exterior of the hotel, it was a welcome sight after spending almost a decade in a prison cell.

Looking up the block, he saw the new casino that was due to open its doors next month. Downtown was blossoming. There were lines of newly built skyscrapers that sprouted up from the ground toward the sky, helping Cleveland to live up to its new moniker Tower City. Kiam was going to capitalize on the city's growth from the underworld's view.

With an easy stride he caught up to Lissha at the front desk. After getting the keys they walked to the elevators in total silence.

Kiam was worn out, the long drive from Pennsylvania had taken a toll on him. Then, as soon as Cleveland greeted him like a snaggle toothed relative, he had made his first kill of freedom. With the smell of death still in his nostrils, he had toured the city collecting Intel. Now all he wanted to do was take a hot shower, get some rest, and plot his takeover.

When the elevator stopped on the 14th floor, Lissha stepped out, looked down at the key card then walked to the left where the room was located. The moment the doors to the suite opened, Kiam immediately became relaxed. Deep shades of olive green, tan and blue surrounded the expansive living room. The carpet was plush and on key he took off his boots just as he had been raised to do.

He walked over to the floor to ceiling windows and looked out over Lake Erie. The view was breathtaking if one were a romantic, which Kiam wasn't necessarily. He chuckled because he had dumped his first body in that same muthafuckin' lake that now represented something tranquil.

Lissha walked to the wall and flipped the light switch. It beamed a little too bright so she dimmed it.

"This is you for the next couple weeks, player," she stretched out her arms in a behold manner."

The luxurious 1,065 square foot suite offered a view of the city, partial view of the river and lake, one king bedroom with sitting area, one and one-half bathrooms, Jacuzzi tub, expansive living area, a formal dining area with seating for eight, and a kitchen with full-size refrigerator.

It was a far cry from a prison cell.

Lissha walked to the back of the couch and pulled out several bags. Kiam walked over to her and took a quick look inside, there was an assortment of high end labels.

"Thanks, ma," he responded.

Lissha just smiled, then handed him the Louis Vuitton bag.

Kiam unzipped it and to his surprise it was filled with neatly stacked hundred dollar bills.

20

"Daddy said this is just the beginning." She looked up at Kiam's expressionless face and slowly ran her hand up his arm.

Kiam took a deep breath as he battled to control himself, there was a full war going on with his conscious and his duty.

"I have something for you," Lissha mentioned above a whisper.

"What's that?" he asked, unsure if he really wanted the answer.

"Come with me." She took his hand and led him to the bedroom.

Kiam was conflicted. His mind was saying, Nigga you better not! But his dick was tapping against his zipper and screaming *eight years, nigga.*

"Lissha." He called out her name in an attempt to gain control of the situation but his feet didn't get the message because them muthafuckas kept on moving. "Ma, hold up," he protested.

Lissha didn't respond, she used her free hand to open the door and again Kiam was taken by surprise. In the middle of the floor was a huge Jacuzzi with a sexy brown skin honey wearing nothing but a smile and bubbles.

"Didn't I already tell you about acting all scary?" Lissha asked while looking over her shoulder, giving him her sexy low-eyed glare.

Kiam just shook his head.

"Her name is Donella, she is to do whatever you want. For as long as you want it." She let go of his hand. "I gotta go. A bitch needs a shower and a long ass nap. Stupid niggas are tiring as hell," she said, referring to the Finch situation, then she hugged Kiam tight.

"Tell Pop, I send my greetings." He broke their embrace.

"I got you. Now worry about getting that nut off your back. I know if Daddy was in some pussy he would not be thinking about you." She laughed then headed toward the door.

Kiam took inventory of the bad ass female before him.

"You gonna stand over there all night?" Donella slowly lifted her leg from the water and draped it over the edge of the tub.

He didn't utter a sound. He used only his eyes to communicate. Pulling his shirt over his head, Kiam moved closer to where she was.

Once he was completely nude, he stepped into the tub leaning his back against her chest. Her soft breast and the hot water relaxed every muscle in his body except one; that soldier was at attention and doing a full salute.

She pulled his head back onto her shoulder as she ran the sponge over his neck and chest. When she got to that rock a smile came over her face. She took all of him firmly into her hand and began to ease his pain. Slowly she stroked and squeezed. "You are such a beautiful man," she cooed in his ear. "I know your sacrifice." She squeezed harder as her wrist rotated to his pleasure. "It's your time. Make this city bow to you," she encouraged as she ran her tongue inside his ear.

Kiam closed his eyes and enjoyed her handiwork. Just when he was on the edge Donella released him. "Stand up, I want to taste you." She commanded.

Kiam rose to his feet, towering over her. Water and suds ran over his chest and abs as she took him in her mouth. The tightening of her jaws sent chills up his spine. Slippery wet moans filled the room as she slurped and stroked. Kiam placed his hand on her head for balance and watched the show. In and out her mouth his dick disappeared and flutters formed in his gut as he threatened to release what felt like tons.

Grabbing his ass she took him to the back of her throat causing a low hiss to leave Kiam's lips. He grabbed a fistful of her hair and prepared to let go. Pulling back a little, Donella sped up her movements until he released long and hard to the back of her throat. She cupped her tongue allowing him to see the thick white evidence of her effect on his soldier. Then she smiled up at him erotically and swallowed every drop.

Licking her lips Donella moaned, "Mmmm. The taste of power."

Kiam slid down in the tub, put his head back and recuperated. Donella straddled his lap ready to feel all that thickness.

"Nah, we good." Kiam shut her down.

Donella leaned back and made eye contact. "You don't want none of this?" she asked while seductively grinding on him.

"Nah, you put in work. I'm good. Lift up." He pushed her back so he could get up. Wrapping a towel around his waist he walked into the living room and snatched a few bills from the Louie bag that laid on the couch.

"Did I do something wrong?" Embarrassment dripped from her question just as the water slid down her body and dripped from her flesh before she quickly dressed in the complimentary robe.

"You straight. I need to get some rest." He handed her the stack.

"No," she waved it off, "Baby, I'm good." Things were much bigger than that. Donella grabbed her things and got dressed. "If you need anything just let me know."

She wrote her number on the note pad, walked over to him, stood on her tippy toes and kissed his cheek. "You official." She looked down then back up. "The woman that gets all that is going to be a lucky bitch."

Kiam didn't reply, he was the type that kept his words at a minimum. Muthafuckas didn't know what you were thinking until you opened your mouth. He knew nothing about Donella to trust her with his thoughts no matter how trivial they were.

She smiled at him understandingly. "Rest well."

Kiam walked her to the door, locked it, and then headed for the shower.

A different type of man with less control would have been balls deep in baby girl, but Kiam was of a select breed. He needed to get his shit right first, plus he didn't know her. *Fuck around and my dick fall off.* He had got his nut; he was satisfied. Now he needed to get focused.

As the water ran over his head and down his face, Kiam began to plot. First, he wanted to make sure he took care of all the business he had pending. Second, hit the long list of shit Pop needed him to do. He knew he was indebted to Pop, but he also had some unfinished business of his own to settle. He needed to make sure he wasn't under no one's thumb and mercy.

Kiam walked out the bathroom with a foolproof plan in the front of his mind. He lotioned his skin before throwing on the hotel robe and lay across the king sized bed. It had been a very long time since he laid in such comfort. It felt like the bed had grown arms and was hugging him.

He tucked the fat goose down pillow under his head and began to doze off. *This city is like a fat pussy and I'ma fuck her hard until she cum. When she pass out, I'ma grab her purse and be out. They will never know what hit 'em.*

Lissha pulled up in front of the hotel and picked up Donella twenty minutes after receiving her text. Quickly, Donella jumped in the car and fastened her seat belt.

"What happened?" Lissha asked as they drove off.

"Only what he wanted to happen. Pussy will not be a problem," Donella reported.

Lissha didn't respond. She knew that if Dee said it then that's what it was, because Donella had the type of sexiness that could tempt God. She thought back to when Big Zo first recruited Donella to the team. He had met her in a strip club up in B-more where she was wasting her beauty and talents popping her ass for a little bit of a nigga's trap.

24

"What do you want with that trick bitch, Daddy?" Lissha questioned him.

Big Zo laughed. "I don't want the pussy, I want the power she possesses with it. When you look at her, you see a stripper. What I see is a bitch that can lure a muthafucka into the gates of hell. Trust me, she'll be a valuable asset to us."

As usual Big Zo had been right. Before the feds came snatching him and his people up, Donella had seduced and led three of Big Zo's enemies into his hands for execution. Not once had she failed. If Kiam could resist that sweet chocolate candy between Donella's legs, pussy most definitely wouldn't be his downfall.

Lissha phoned Big Zo.

"Hello." His deep voice rang in her ear.

"It's confirmed," she said with satisfaction in her voice.

"Um. Go to phase two."

"Got it. Love you, Daddy."

"Love you, too."

Chapter 4
In Search Of Answers

Kiam was awakened by a soft but persistent knock at the door. He sat up, rubbed his eyes, and swung his legs over the side of the bed savoring the plush carpet underfoot. Looking up, he squinted his eyes against a beam of morning sunlight that peeked through a part in the cream-colored blinds over the main window.

He slid the German Luger from under the pillow and walked bare-footed to the door with the strap down at his side.

"Who's there?" His deep baritone was a little coarse from sleep.

"Room Service," came the feminine reply from the other side of the door. Which was a shock to him since he hadn't ordered anything.

The mention of food caused his stomach to growl. He suddenly recalled that he hadn't eaten since he and Lissha had grabbed a couple of Philly steak sandwiches before leaving PA yesterday.

"Leave it outside the door," he directed.

He allowed a few seconds to pass, then pressed his ear against the door just in time to hear soft footsteps patter away. Cautious by nature he waited a half minute longer before opening the door. He stuck his head out and peered up and down the hallway. Satisfied that everything was good, Kiam pulled the cart inside and relocked the door.

When he uncovered the trays on the cart, the aroma of a decent breakfast wafted up his nose. Kiam licked his lips and inspected the meal more closely. There were egg omelets, hash browns, turkey sausages, toast, cereal, milk, coffee and orange juice. As he began to move the dishes around the tray he saw a folded small card. He flipped it open and quickly read the accompanying message.

Welcome home, Kiam, Please enjoy your breakfast. I'll see you in a couple days.

Lissha xoxo.

Placing the note back on the tray, Kiam cracked a little smile. He pushed the cart over to the dining area, sat at the table as he wasted no time digging in.

An hour later he had fed his belly, showered, and threw on one of the outfits that Lissha had purchased for him. The cream and brown True Religion gear graced his frame like she had gotten it tailored for him. He checked his reflection in the mirror on the wall in the bedroom, pleased with what he saw. His features had matured while he was on lock but his cold black eyes hadn't changed one bit. They made his youthful face appear unreadable.

"Kiam, what's going on in your mind that causes you to look so serious all the time?" The lady that raised him had often asked when he was growing up.

Kiam could never quite answer the question. At least not honestly, because the truth might have sent Miss Charlene to an early grave.

He rested his thoughts on her. She had been murdered in her home a year after he began serving his bid. Somebody had to pay for that, and he already knew where to begin looking for answers.

That nigga DeMarcus better have some names on the tip of his tongue when I find him or it's gonna be a bad day for Cuz.

He sat on the side of the bed and reached for the phone on the nightstand to hit up his dude Czar. He finally picked up after his phone had rung a half dozen times. Surprise rang from his voice when he realized it was Kiam.

A short while later, with the April sun kissing the back of his neck, Kiam slid into the passenger seat of Czar's black 2010 Mercedes Benz GLK 350.

"What's good, Bleed?" Czar greeted him with a genuine smile. He skipped the routine gangsta hug because he remembered that Kiam wasn't a touchy-feely type of dude.

"I see you did the time instead of letting the time do you," observed Czar.

"Anything else would have been asinine, right?" replied Kiam.

"True. Damn, nigga, welcome home. You lamping at The Ritz so you must be good."

"I'm alright."

"Man, I know I didn't send you nothin' on your books but—"

"You don't owe me any explanations," Kiam cut him off. Czar didn't owe him anything which meant Kiam didn't owe him a damn thing either.

"Where that nigga DeMarcus at? He still around?" he inquired.

"Is he? Hell yeah, he's still around. And he has Miles Road turned up from 93rd all the way up to Lee Road. Man, that lame ass nigga has gotten rich since you've been gone. I know he was looking out for you, wasn't he?"

"Something like that." Kiam's response was evasive.

Czar, who was five years older than Kiam, had known him since he was a little badass, so he recognized the bitter tone in which Kiam had replied. He didn't know what DeMarcus had done, but he knew that boy wasn't built to beef with a goon like the one in his passenger seat.

Czar wasn't a groupie type dude, but he had no qualms with giving props to those that deserved them. Although he had never witnessed Kiam take a man's life, he knew what he knew— Kiam's murder game was prolific. Czar knew that just as he knew a pig's pussy was pork. Every dude that had beefed with Kiam had ended up with his shit pushed back— that wasn't a coincidence.

Before he went away on gun charges, at eighteen years old, the streets trembled when Kiam came on the block. Established hustlers had him pegged as a growing force to be reckoned with if his quick trigger finger didn't take him down first. More than a few ballers from over his way secretly rejoiced when Kiam caught time in the feds. They had peeped that he was a hungry lion that would not have been content until he was King.

Czar had peeped the same thing. He wondered if the bid had changed Kiam any.

"So what's up, nigga? You gon' turn it up or are you all rehabilitated and shit?" He asked with a chuckle in his tone.

"I'ma do me." Kiam kept it brief.

"Meaning what?" Czar pried.

"Meaning nothing and everything."

Czar couldn't figure that shit out and it made his head hurt to even try. "I hear you, nephew," he steered the conversation back to DeMarcus. "I'm not tryna plant no seeds because I know you and DeMarcus grew up drinking out the same cup, but it seem like he didn't bubble until Miss Charlene died."

"And you said that to say what?" Kiam put him on the defensive.

Czar turned right on 116th and Union heading toward Miles Road.

"I hate to spread rumors dawg, 'cause that's not my get down but I fuck with you hard so I gotta keep it one hunnid," Czar went on. "Word on the street is that DeMarcus killed Miss Charlene and used the life insurance money to sponsor his come up in the game"

Kiam said nothing. He knew from Miss Charlene's own mouth that any money left over from the policy after her burial went to the church. DeMarcus would have known the same thing.

"I raised y'all to be men, y'all can take care of yourselves when I'm gone," she had explained before that day ever arrived.

So what Czar was saying meant nothing to Kiam. He didn't discount the possibility that DeMarcus had killed Miss Charlene for money, but it damn sure wasn't insurance money.

Kiam was silent, contemplating, preparing. He looked out the window at the changes that had taken place since he went away. Some apartment buildings had been demolished, and empty lots stood where corner stores once thrived. Houses were boarded up and the streets were littered with potholes. Destruction and despair was as visible as a dark, gray cloud filled with rain. But the city hadn't witnessed nothing yet, what he was going to do would surpass the darkest imagination.

Chapter 5
The Foundation

Lissha was comfortably seated in her black, white and silver living room flipping through an Essence magazine. There were several Hawaiian glaze candles burning, and the sound of Trey Songz Passion, Pain, and Pleasure CD was playing in the background. She reached forward, grabbed her huge mug of green tea, and brought it to her lips. As she placed it back on the coffee table her doorbell rang.

She removed her legs from their folded position and rose to her feet. She walked to the door, rested her eye against the peep hole then clicked the locks.

"Damn, bitch. What you got some ass up in here?" Treebie barged past Lissha headed to the living room looking around with a suspicious eye.

"Good Morning, Lish," Bayonna said as she followed Treebie.

"Hey ma, and why is this bitch always so loud and ignorant? This bitch would fuck up a good nut right on the brink."

"Whatever." She palmed her hand in the air. "What you got in this cup?" Treebie inhaled deeply.

"Put my shit down. Who the fuck walks into someone's house and sticks their nose in cups and shit?" Lissha twisted her mouth, walked over to Treebie and took her cup out of her clutch.

Bayonna took a seat in the high back chair, crossed her legs and shook her head.

"Is this bitch drunk?" Lissha turned her question to Bayonna.

"No, I am not but I'm about to be," Treebie announced as she walked to the kitchen, snatched a bottle and three glasses from the cabinet, then sashayed back into the living room.

"Alright, let's get down to business." Lissha watched Treebie pour their glasses of wine as they took a seat across from hers.

"Okay, so Kiam is on deck," Lissha began. She paused to look at both ladies. "We need to introduce him to Gator so he can take over that operation and reinforce our power on the streets. Then we need to set up a meeting for him with the drug connect so he can take that shit over and we can turn down and handle all this other shit we got on the table."

"So, Gator is not calling shots anymore?" Treebie curiously raised her eyebrows.

Lissha cut in. "No. Daddy wants Kiam to take charge and we're gonna back him one hundred percent."

"I'm not comfortable with that. We don't know this nigga." Treebie was getting agitated.

"Hold the fuck up. Don't forget your place in this shit." Lissha turned to Treebie with a wrinkled brow. "This nigga is official. Daddy sent him to us and if you got a fucking problem with that, address it to Daddy and see how that turns out." Lissha stared directly in Treebie's eyes and did not blink.

Treebie glided her tongue across her teeth then sucked them. "I ain't got no problem with Big Zo's decisions. I'm just saying we been working with Gator for years. I know his get down. I ain't got time to be holding no new nigga's hand and then have to worry about him turning on us when shit get tight."

"Have I ever crossed you? Have. I. Ever. Crossed. You?" Lissha emphasized each word waiting for her to say the wrong shit.

"No, and hopefully you never will," Treebie got up. "I gotta pee." She headed to the bathroom.

Lissha's heart began to pick up speed, she was heated. For the first time her right hand and most trusted confidant was challenging her authority. If Treebie's rebellion was a sign that she no longer wanted to take orders she would be wise to order herself a casket because that's how it was going to play out.

"Lish. You know it's not you she don't trust. None of us knows anything about Kiam, so of course Treebie is a little uncomfortable," intoned Bayonna, breaking Lissha's train of thought.

Lissha studied her like maybe she was Judas in disguise. Bayonna felt the burn from her intense gaze and correctly interpreted it. But she knew that there was no flaw in her loyalty so she was unfazed by any uncertainty that might have crept into Lissha's mind.

"Let's just follow the script and put Kiam to the test so Treebie can see what he is made of." She tried her hand at reasoning with Lissha who had a look on her face like she was getting ready to do something to somebody.

Treebie emerged from the bathroom drying her hands with a paper towel. "Look, Lissha. I apologize if I was out of line. I'm not trying to oppose you or Big Zo. It's just that I have sacrificed a lot. We have been through the trenches." She pounded her fist in her hand.

They had indeed been through it together, going back to when it was just the two of them holding down the fort for Big Zo, trafficking blocks up and down the highway to keep lawyer money coming in as he fought a futile effort to win an acquittal.

The day that Big Zo was convicted and sent away, Lissha and Treebie had gone out and gotten drunk, then went back to Treebie's place and cried on each other's shoulder vowing death to everyone that turned informant on him. Together they had murked three of those faggot ass, snitch muthafuckas and to this day they were hunting for the others.

Lissha couldn't overlook Treebie's sacrifices; she had walked away from her husband, Wa'leek, in New Jersey to get down with Big Zo. But had time begun to eat away at her loyalty?

Lissha studied Treebie's face as her mouth continued to move. "Li Li, I love you to the death of me," she proclaimed with sincerity in her eyes. "I will give my life for you, but I will tell you this—if Kiam is foul, Big Zo ain't going to have to touch him. I'm going to put heat all over that ass. That's my word."

Treebie looked in Lissha's eyes searching for approval. Lissha thought long and hard about Treebie's words. If nothing else she was genuine. She had to admit that they had run hard together. Many had folded when things got hot, but Treebie had always stood firm. However, Lissha needed to reaffirm that regardless of all that, they were not equal in authority.

"Apology accepted. But I need you to understand something that should already be overstood. This shit right here belongs to me and Daddy. He makes the decisions and I carry them out." She paused.

Treebie waited for her to continue.

Lissha wet her lips with her tongue then went on. "As far as Kiam goes, you won't have to worry about him crossing you. Because if he does I will kill him myself. But if I find out you stood in the way of him carrying out Daddy's orders, we gonna have a serious problem." The warning was subtle but unmistakable.

Lissha got up, walked to the door and opened it. "Y'all can bounce. I got some shit to do. I'll get up with y'all at the spot in two days," she said.

Treebie headed to the door and Bayonna followed. As they passed by Lissha, Treebie stopped and said, "Either you about to come on your period or you need some dick. But I still love you." She kissed Lissha on the cheek.

Lissha just curled her lips and watched her go by. She wiped her face with the back of her hand as she watched the two ladies walk down the driveway. *That shit felt like the kiss of death.*

She stood staring at them until they drove off.

Chapter 6
Suspicions

The car turned left off 116th Street onto Miles Road. They were headed toward 131st then on up to Lee Road. Trees were barren of leaves because winter hadn't decided to bow completely to spring yet, but the early morning 70 degree temperature lent hope for a beautiful day.

A small group of people were huddled at the bus stop on the corner, in light jackets, waiting on the slow running #50 bus to come. A pair of teenaged girls eyed the whip like they wanted to fuck the grill. Czar honked the horn at them and they waved.

"Lil' hot asses," Kiam remarked with a grin.

Czar pushed on up the street, pointing out all the spots that DeMarcus had on lock.

"I'm telling you, Dee done got his weight up out here. I don't know who put him on but that nigga is doing it. He got runners handling weight and selling steezies for him all up and down this bitch," lamented Czar.

Kiam just listened. There was no reason to comment because he knew that before long the streets would be his. DeMarcus damn sure wasn't built to stop him.

"Who else is gettin' serious money on this side of town?" He questioned his man.

"You got those Gore brothers off Princeton Avenue eating good. They've been locking down a lot of spots, chasing other nigga's off corners up and down East 116th, from Buckeye Road all the way to Harvard Road."

"Greg and Fat?" asked Kiam. He had heard their names mentioned a few times when he had reached out to the streets.

"Yeah. They rock these platinum chains with MBK across the pieces in diamonds. It's supposed to stand for *My Brother's Keeper*. Wherever you see one of them, you see the other. That's how they roll. I figure they're touching about ten whole ones a week."

They'll either get down or get laid down, Kiam decided.

"How many bricks you touching?" he asked Czar.

"Oh, I do a'ight," he replied.

Kiam didn't press him, in time Czar would reveal his hand or get it chopped the hell off. *Take no prisoners,* Pop had lectured Kiam every day. *You'll be able to exert your will over most dudes. Kill everybody else that stands in your way.*

As they drove on up Miles Road, he directed Czar to make a left on 123rd. Czar followed his directions and without being told stopped in front of the house where Kiam had grew up.

Memories came rushing back through Kiam's mind.

"Baby, Miss Charlene is going to watch you while I run downtown to see these white folks about my damn food stamps," his mother told him, handing him a quarter so that he wouldn't act up when she drove off.

Five year old Kiam took the quarter and kissed his mother on the cheek. "I ain't gon' cry, Mama. I'ma go play with DeMarcus until you get back."

"That's my little man. Mama loves you," she said, hugging him tightly.

When she let him go, tears ran down her face, ruining her makeup. "Why you crying, Mama?" He looked at her curiously.

"Mama just got a whole lot of problems." She wiped her eyes and sniffled.

Miss Charlene came outside and told Kiam's mother to be back for him by 7 o'clock. "I gotta go to Bingo tonight. I feel lucky," she said.

"I'll be back way before then," his mother promised. But something in her eyes made Kiam cry as he watched her leave.

When they got in the house Miss Charlene gave him some cookies and told him to go and play with DeMarcus.

He was still crying when he reached the basement where DeMarcus was located, kneeling beside his toys.

"You a sissie," DeMarcus teased.

Whap! Kiam punched him dead in the nose. "Fuck you talking to, bitch?" he snorted.

Now DeMarcus was crying harder than him. "I'ma tell my grandmother," he whined.

"And I'ma fuck you up."

DeMarcus told anyway, and Miss Charlene scolded Kiam something fierce, threatening to beat the skin off his behind. But she was all bark. She loved children too much to do more than pop them once or twice.

"Boy, why you so bad?" she asked, giving him another handful of cookies.

Kiam hunched his shoulders and sat at the window looking for his mother to return. Hours passed and she hadn't shown up. Then hours turned into days and days turned into years.

"You alright, nephew?" asked Czar looking at him quizzically.

"I'm good. Who lives here now?" The house looked ready to fall down.

Czar didn't know so Kiam got out the car and walked up to the door. He had to get inside the house and check something out. That would determine his next move, and whether or not DeMarcus would be the next nigga he killed.

The six raggedy wooden steps strained and squeaked under his weight as Kiam walked up on the porch. At the top of the steps he paused and took in the exterior of his childhood home. The paint had long ago peeled from the banisters, and they sagged like the shoulders of an old, tired man.

In one corner of the porch sat a worn couch with different sized bricks for legs; a rat strolled fearlessly across the back of the soiled piece of furniture fearing no consequences. The rodent suddenly stopped and looked at Kiam, then quickly scurried away.

Instinctively it had recognized the presence of a killah. Kiam liked that. Now niggas needed to do the same.

He proceeded up to the front door and stuck his hand out in search of the doorbell. In its place was nothing but a small gutted out hole. The door frame was freshly painted, like makeup applied on the weathered face of a hundred year old woman, in a futile attempt to disguise the wear and tear that life had taken on her soul. Miss Charlene had to be rolling over in her grave at what had become of the house that she had kept up with a loving hand.

Kiam brushed those melancholy thoughts aside, he had no time for sentimental trips down memory lane until he had the answer to the question that was most prevalent in his mind.

He knocked on the door and waited for someone to answer.

The rap of his knuckles against the cheap wooden door brought no response. He knocked a second time, much louder than the first, but still no one came to the door.

The years of incarceration had trained his ears to pick up the slightest sound or movement. Without pressing his ear to the door he could hear voices coming from inside and they weren't the recorded sounds of a television set. These were live voices. Hood villains talking.

So bring y'alls asses to the door. He pounded on the door like he had some business up in those people's spot and it could not wait.

The door was snatched open and Kiam stood eye to eye with a tall, reedy dude whose melon head was way too big for his rail thin body and pencil neck. Slim's lips looked to be permanently puckered and his jaw twitched. "Fool, why is you banging on my door like you's the goddamn police?" he gritted.

Kiam looked him in the eye, he had already sized ol' boy up just that fast. "Calm the fuck down, nigga, before you get smashed on your own front porch."

"Say what?" Slim asked, adding bass to his voice

"I said what you thought I said," Kiam restated. "But I didn't come here for that. I need to come up in here for five minutes and I'll be out." He reached in his pocket and pulled out a band.

The fiend's eyes bulged at the sight of that fat $1,000 rubber banded knot in Kiam's hand.

"It's either this," said Kiam, indicating the stack. "Or this, nigga." He lifted the bottom of his shirt to reveal the butt of his uncompromising negotiator.

"Man, who are you? You not the police, are you?" asked dude. One eye was on the money and the other was on Kiam's strap.

"Never mind who I am, but I'm not the rollers. I don't care what you have going on up in here. Five minutes is all I need and I'm out," Kiam reiterated.

"A'ight." Pencil Neck licked his dry lips as he accepted the mula from Kiam and stepped to the side.

As soon as he entered the house, the strong pungent smell of burning crack cocaine assaulted Kiam's airway. He walked through the living room toward the back of the house. In the kitchen he encountered another man, and a frail, pock marked face woman, sitting at a cheap card table passing a crack pipe back and forth between them. The card table and the chairs that they occupied were the only pieces of furniture in sight.

The two smokers were in their own world, they didn't even look up and acknowledge his presence. Slim was on his heels.

"Fall the fuck back," commanded Kiam, stopping at the top of the stairs that led to the basement.

"Five minutes," Slim reminded him, then scurried off like the rat.

The old rickety stairs squeaked as Kiam descended them. In the basement memories rushed up on him like a gust of hot air. This was where he and DeMarcus, as little boys, spent most of their time playing. This was also where Miss Charlene had been beaten to death, he had been told.

Kiam ducked under several exposed pipes that hung from the ceiling as he passed by the hot water tank. He recalled the day that he and DeMarcus had tussled and he had rammed DeMarcus's head into that same appliance. They were kids back then, now they were men. If DeMarcus had violated like Kiam suspected, he wasn't gonna ram his head into anything, he was going to cut it off.

He stood back up to his full height once he cleared the last overhead pipe and reached the storage room. It was dark and dank. Kiam left the door open to allow in a little light. He stepped over small puddles of water on the floor as he proceeded to the rear of the storage room where the answer to his question lied.

Kiam ran his hands along the cold concrete wall, feeling for an indentation that was imperceptible to the eye and the touch unless you knew it was there. He had built this stash spot himself yet it took several attempts before he was successful in locating the groove that he was searching for in the wall.

He pressed his weight on the spot and a door that had been camouflaged as a section of the wall opened with a squeak, revealing the hidden wall safe. Its own door was shut and locked.

Kiam didn't have to search his mind for the combination to open it; those numbers were indelibly etched in his memory like his birth date. Besides himself, Miss Charlene had been the only one that knew of this clever stash spot. But DeMarcus would have figured that Kiam had left a bank with her. And he was the type of thirsty dude that would brutally murder his own grandmother for a come-up. Well, Kiam was the type that brutally murdered, period.

Squinting his eyes in the dimness of the light that shined through from the outer room, Kiam unlocked the safe then hesitated before opening the door and peering inside. He knew that the contents would be gone, but he needed confirmation. Proof that his surrogate mother had been murdered over what had been inside.

He opened the door to the safe and reached inside. His hand came into contact with what he was feeling for. He grabbed ahold of it and pulled it out, surprised that it was still in there.

The backpack was musty from years of sitting, but its weight told Kiam that it had not been bothered even before he opened it and looked inside. Stacks of money threatened to spill out onto the floor. Kiam stood there in a daze. If DeMarcus or someone else hadn't beaten Miss Charlene to death while robbing her for the money, what the fuck had happened?

The answer came to him almost instantaneously. Miss Charlene had died because she wouldn't give up his stash spot. In that moment his love for her doubled and his anger quadrupled.

"What you got there, man?" The question came from behind him.

Kiam whirled around and in one smooth motion the banger was off his waist and in his hand. He stepped toward Slim and stuck the Nine in his gut. "You wanna know what I got, nosey muthafucka?" he snarled.

"Nah, not really," dude reconsidered, but Kiam told him anyway.

"I got your muthafuckin' epitaph right here if you don't fall the fuck back." He raised his arm and slapped the curious ass fool across the head with the burner, drawing blood.

"Nigga, you don't have to follow me around. I told you five minutes. Five goddamn minutes! But you on some nosey shit." He pistol whipped the white meat out of the smoker's head.

Standing over the fallen man, he reached inside the backpack and grabbed a stack. He tossed the money on the floor beside the bloodied dude and gritted. "Nosey people get it too. Dark Man X. Check him out sometime."

Inside the car, Kiam was quiet as Czar drove off. He stared out the window at nothing in particular while his emotions tested the strength of his mind.

"Did you find what you were looking for, nephew?" asked Czar, glancing down at the backpack that sat between Kiam's legs.

"Nah, man, I didn't find nothin'." His answer was the truth; the backpack raised more questions than it provided answers.

"You still wanna hit Lee Road and try to catch up with DeMarcus? He has a car lot out in Cleveland Heights."

Kiam thought about that for a minute. If he ran into DeMarcus now he would act on emotion and push the nigga's hairline back. Wrong or right, he didn't give a fuck. But Pop had schooled him to be a thinker and he refused to let those lessons be in vain.

"I wanna put that on hold for a minute. DeMarcus isn't going anywhere." He left it hanging in air, because Pop had also stressed that you never let your right hand know what the left one is thinking.

Changing tactics, Kiam said, "Take me on Benwood. I want to check on somebody and see what she's been up to."

Czar didn't have to ask who lived there, he already knew. She had been Kiam's little wifey before he went away.

The Past...

Faydrah Combs had been a tomboy all of her early life, playing ball and stealing out of stores right alongside of Kiam, DeMarcus, and the other little bad ass boys. When those same knuckleheads put their basketballs down and started slinging rocks, she was down with that, too. Running up to cars and slushing through the snow for that next sale.

Back then she was just one of the homies. Then around thirteen years old, her titties started sprouting out and she grew a little bump for an ass. Those jeans that used to sag started fitting tight. That's when things changed, because that's when those same boys that she used to shoot ball with, and now hustled with, started trying to cut something with her. Every one of them except Kiam.

The funny thing was, that's what made her want his mean, black, skinny tail. One day she had built up her courage and walked right up to him and kissed him in the mouth. "Nigga, you're taking my cherry," she regulated.

Kiam shoved her up off of him. "Fuck you doing, girl?"

"You're going to be my man," she declared, stepping right back in his space and wrapping her arms around his neck.

He shoved her back away from him, harder this time. "Eyez, you trippin'. You're my homie, I'm not tryna get with you like that," he spat.

She loved when he called her Eyez, but she hated that he still saw her as one of the boys. He had crushed her little feelings. But she hadn't let him know it.

"Boy, I was just playing with you anyway. Don't nobody want your little boney ass," she shot back, throwing the bit of booty she had as she walked away.

She left the block, went home and cried in her pillow. She cursed God for not blessing her with the type of ass and femininity that Kiam would not have been able to resist.

From that point on she hid her feelings from him, but whenever they were out hustling and his body came close to hers, her virgin flower begged to be watered.

Two years later, she was still hustling with him. Not because she was as hooked on that street shit as Kiam and them were, but at least hustling alongside of him kept her in his presence. But it was pure torture for her to have to watch him push up on other chicks.

One night seeing Kiam caked up with a female at a party they had attended, Faydrah abruptly left and trekked three miles home, tears running down her chin.

When she got home, she walked in the house and slammed the door behind her, awakening her mom who was asleep on the couch.

"Do you have to make so much noise?" Rebecca complained.

"Sorry." Faydrah ignored the crack pipe on the end table. They had already had it out about that more times than either of them could count.

She sat down on the couch, laid her head on her mother's shoulder and screamed, "Ugh! I swear I hate him."

Rebecca put an arm around her only child. "Okay, tell me what Kiam has done now." She was well aware that he was the source of all of her daughter's frustration.

"He won't notice me unless I'm flipping a brick with him or busting a gun beside him. I could walk butt naked in front of that boy and he wouldn't even look twice." Faydrah poked her lips out.

"Honey, how do you expect him to notice you when you dress and act just like he does?"

"I don't care," she mumbled.

"Tomorrow I'm going to dress you up and do your hair, and if Kiam doesn't notice you I'll quit getting high."

Faydrah laughed. "You should quit anyway."

The next day when Faydrah went out on the block, all the homies mouths were on the ground. Her jeans hugged her booty like leotards, and her breasts commanded notice. Her hair, which she had religiously worn in a ponytail, flowed loosely down her back. Her lips were glossed and her nails were painted in a girlie design.

The block huggers were transfixed.

"Uh, put y'alls tongues back in y'alls mouths because there's only one nigga out here that I want," she announced with confidence.

"Who, me?" said DeMarcus.

46

"Nigga, you wish." She shut him down. *Then walked up to the one she so desired.*

Kiam was posted up on the hood of his Yukon. He had been watching her since she walked up. She was looking all the way sexy.

"Hey, baby," she said in a sultry tone that she had rehearsed all morning long.

"What's good, Eyez?" He spoke back.

"You," she said. *"When are you going to quit playing and be my man?"* She threw her hand on her hip, feigning confidence. But inside she was so nervous she was about to pee on herself.

"Just like that, huh?" He flashed a cocky smile.

"Yep, just like that."

"Girl, go on home." He quickly extinguished her hope.

Faydrah bit down on her lip to keep from crying. Then she turned on her heels and held her head high. She would break down when she got home, but not out there in front of all of them.

"I'll be over to pick my woman up when I come out the trap."

Faydrah stopped in her tracks! She couldn't trust her ears. She slowly turned around and stared at Kiam, afraid to ask him if she had heard him correctly.

"I said what you think I said," he clarified. *Then he walked up to her and kissed some of that lip gloss off of her lips.*

Faydrah almost fainted.

Kiam felt her legs weaken. He held her close and kissed her again. *"Go on home, baby. I'll be through around nine."*

When he took his arms from around her, she didn't walk home, she floated.

Later that night, she drifted to the sky as Kiam tenderly deflowered her. That was the beginning of a young love that lasted until Kiam went away.

Kiam recalled it all. He had thought about her many times during his bid, but he still felt he had done the right thing by telling her to go on with her life. He had heard that she was in corporate America now. That proved that letting go had been best for her.

Kiam was out of the car as soon as it came to a stop in front of Faydrah mother's house.

"I'll be right back," he told Czar.

Ten minutes later he returned with a glint of light in his coal black eyes. He had Czar to drop him back off at the hotel so that he could stash the backpack and change clothes, then he hailed a taxi over to the address that Rebecca had given him.

Chapter 7
Long Time No See

"Excuse me, Miss, can you tell me where the rest room is?" Kiam's voice boomed at Faydrah's back.

For a brief moment she was frozen in her spot. Even though time and circumstances had separated them physically, the connection that they once shared made his voice feel like water to a thirsty soul.

Turning slowly and barely able to breath due to the excitement that rose up in her chest, Faydrah pulled her glasses from her face to make sure that her eyes weren't fooling her just in case her ears were.

"Kiam?"

"Who else you letting get up behind you?" Kiam jokingly stated.

Faydrah turned completely and gasped at the beautiful sight before her. She put her arms around his neck, closed her eyes and hugged him tightly. "Oh my god, when did you get home?" She asked breathlessly.

"A few days ago," Kiam nuzzled his face against the crease in her neck. "You act like you missed somebody."

"I did miss you," she whined. She secured her hold around him.

After a few more seconds of body to body embrace, she backed up and looked him up and down as she ran her hands over his chest. "Look at you, all buff. I guess I can't call you skin and bones no more," she teased.

"Nah, I got my weight up. Been eating my Wheaties." Kiam blushed a little as the warm memories of their knee-high days flooded his mind.

"So, what's up? How did you know to find me here?" She asked as her eyes kept wondering all over his body.

Kiam stood there letting her soak him up.

"Never mind, you don't have to answer that. I already know who told you where I work. Mama still loves you," she added, unconsciously running her tongue over her lips.

"Damn, Eyez. Why you keep looking at me like that?" He affectionately called her by the childhood nickname he had given her due to her pretty diamond shaped light brown eyes.

Faydrah blushed.

"I can't believe you're standing here that's all."

"When is your lunch break? I need to sit and talk to you."

Faydrah looked at her watch. "I had my break already, but I get off at 1:00. I came in early. Let me go up and get my things, then we can go."

"Hurry up, a man is hungry," he said, rubbing his stomach.

"That is the story of your life. Just sit down, I'll be right back." She pushed him toward the seats in the lobby.

"You still think you can beat me," Kiam joked as he sat down.

"Whatever. Just don't leave."

"I'ma wait right here,"

Faydrah giggled as she headed to the elevator.

Kiam's eyes wondered over her curves as she moved away. Everything was swollen in all the right places. *Damn she ain't a teenager no more.*

Faydrah's stomach filled with butterflies as she rode to the seventh floor. When the elevator came to a stop she damn near ran off.

"Damn, girl. What the hell happened in the lobby that got you showing all thirty-two?" Gina asked from behind the receptionist's desk.

"I ran into an old friend. Cover for me, I need to clock out," she replied, whizzing by. Quickly, she moved around her office grabbing her briefcase, cell phone and keys. Cutting off the light she took one last look then shut the door. "Alright girl I'll call you tonight if I can," she said to Gina as she headed to the staircase.

"That must be a hell of an old friend. He got you taking the steps," Gina yelled out.

"Shut up," Faydrah laughed as she entered the stairwell and moved swiftly down to the lobby.

Reaching the last flight, she took a few deep breaths to calm herself. Then she reached in her pocket and popped the other half of her mint in her mouth and exited the hallway. When she got to the seats Kiam wasn't there. She immediately went into panic mode. Her eyes moved all over the lobby in search of him. Damn, she hadn't even gotten his number.

Just as disappointment set in, Kiam came up from behind and put his arms around her. Faydrah jumped, he had a chick's nerves scrambled with excitement.

"Stop, you play too much." She hit his arm.

"You still scared of me? Damn, you a grown woman. What you afraid of?"

"I'm not scared of you," she said in a low voice.

"You ought to be," he teased.

Faydrah sucked her teeth "Whatever. Come on, I thought you were so hungry." She wrapped her hand in his and pulled him toward the exit.

Kiam didn't respond, he was hungry alright but not for food. He was ready to feast on what she had under that skirt.

They walked a few blocks, laughing and talking, and bumping shoulders with the many pedestrians that crowded downtown as she led him to the warehouse district where the good restaurants were. It felt like they were sixteen all over again and had skipped school to hangout. When they arrived at the Blue Point Grille, the city's best seafood restaurant, he opened the door for her and they walked inside.

"You ate here before?" He looked around.

"Yes. I eat here all the time. Come on." She walked over to the hostess and requested a table for two.

Once seated, Faydrah flipped through her menu. Kiam picked his up and scanned the different selections. It had been years since he had sat and ordered from a menu and it felt like he was reading a foreign language.

Picking up on his slight insecurity, Faydrah took control. "I got you, baby."

Kiam just smiled. Faydrah was always very attentive to him and he appreciated that about her.

When the waitress walked over to the table Faydrah ordered for Kiam and herself, keeping in mind that he loved seafood. "The gentleman will have the Shrimp and Scallop Sauté, and I'll have the Lobster Chicken Pasta."

"And what will you be drinking today?" asked the young blonde-haired waitress with a toothy smile.

Faydrah glanced back at the menu, then she looked up and replied, "I'll have a Strawberry Daiquiri." She looked over at Kiam. "Do you still abstain from alcohol, sir?" She teased.

"I don't know what I do anymore." he answered with a slight chuckle. "But I damn sure ain't gonna sit here and sip on no damn daiquiri."

Faydrah and the waitress laughed, "Can you bring him a Coke please."

"Put some Rum in it," he requested before the waitress left the table.

"So, when did you get home?" Faydrah folded her hands and stared in his eyes.

"I been home a few days."

"Okay, taking it into consideration that we haven't been in contact with each other, I'm not upset with you for not finding out where I was your first day home."

"I didn't have to find you, you've always been right here in my heart." He tapped his chest.

"Good answer. Now, what are you doing with yourself? What are your plans?"

"I'm not sure yet. I'm just trying to get adjusted."

"Well, if you need anything just let me know."

Just as Faydrah was getting ready to ask her next question the waitress came to the table placing their drinks down.

Faydrah grabbed the stem and slid it close to her. Taking the straw, she swirled the whip cream around then brought it to her mouth, closed her eyes and slowly ran her tongue down the length of the straw.

Kiam looked entranced as a bit of enticement rose in his gut. "Damn, maybe I should have gotten one of those."

Faydrah opened her eyes "This is the bomb. You want to taste it?" She swirled the straw again and slid it toward him to try.

"Nah, I want to sample it from your lips," he countered in a smooth as butter kind of way.

Faydrah brought it to her mouth and ran it over her tongue. She leaned across table, meeting him halfway, and they their mouths became one.

Faydrah released a faint moan as Kiam greedily kissed her, this time melting under the command of his passion.

A rush of emotions moved through her body like a current.

Pulling back, Faydrah covered her face, allowing her hair to fall forward and shield her eyes. Those almond-shaped windows to her soul threatened to rain tears down her cheeks.

"Many days the memories of your smile and your kindness got me through," Kiam said as he reached out and gently ran his hand along her cheek. Her skin was as soft as crushed velvet.

"I never stopped thinking about you, Kiam." Her eyes reverted back to the table, blinking back a cadre of emotions. "I'm sorry I didn't write or visit. Even though you told me to go on with my life, I should have did something to—"

"Shhh." Kiam interrupted. "It's all good. I'm happy that you were able to go forward and become someone."

"I needed to hear that," she responded looking up into his eyes. "I never stopped loving you."

"I know." he said with understanding that eased the moment.

Just as he pulled his hand away the waitress approached. "Here you go." She sat the plates down in front of them and the aroma instantly filled their lungs, causing Kiam's stomach to growl.

"Damn, this look good," he unwrapped his silverware from the linen.

"It is good," attested Faydrah, placing her napkin on her lap.

"Do you need anything else?" The waitress smiled politely.

"No, we good. Thank you," Faydrah answered as she watched Kiam put his fork to work. She savored watching him take his first bite.

Kiam was unable to say a single word. As soon as he sunk his teeth into the shrimp his taste buds exploded. He forked a second one and chewed with delight.

Setting his fork down for a moment, he looked up at Faydrah who was delighted in his enjoyment. "So what you doing for the rest of the day?" He asked.

"You." Faydrah was now wide open from that kiss.

"So, I don't have to worry about nobody blowing up your phone, or having to look over my shoulder?"

"No, I have had it on lock for months. I'm willing to give you the key." She paused. "Or is there somebody I have to worry about?"

"Yeah, there is somebody you have to worry about," he replied with a smirk on his face. "But, I'll make him be gentle."

Faydrah smiled. "You so nasty."

They talked comfortably back and forth over their meal. The food was delicious and the conversation was even better. They declined dessert, but enjoyed a few rounds of drinks before he paid the tab, called a cab and headed to Kiam's hotel.

Anticipation...

Kiam opened the door and hit the lights. Faydrah sat her brief case down next to the couch and looked around.

"This is nice," she complimented, continuing to peruse his temporary pad.

"It'll work for now." He located the remote and turned on the radio. Maxwell came through the speakers, crooning lyrics that were perfect for their situation.

I should be crying but I just can't let it show/ I should be hoping but I can't stop thinking/ All the things we should have said but we never said/ All the things we should have done but we never did...

Kiam walked over to Faydrah and pulled her close to him. "You're so beautiful," he said, moving her hair back so he could look right into her eyes.

"Kiam. I don't want to be your drunken desire," Faydrah lightly protested as his hands began to roam all over her body.

"I'm not drunk. I'm in total control. And only what you want to happen is going to happen," he said, leaning in and kissing her collar bone.

She purred like a kitten. Kiam reached up and ran his hand through her hair. Pulling her head back, he traced the outline of her neck with his tongue. Gently he pulled her blazer off of her shoulders, allowing it to drop to the floor.

Faydrah simply closed her eyes and allowed him to have every part of her. When he unzipped her skirt it fell to the floor effortlessly. She placed her hands on his shoulders and stepped out of it giving him full access. Kiam slowly unbuttoned her shirt and dropped it on top of her skirt and jacket.

Faydrah felt as shy and nervous as the little blooming flower that had given him her bud years ago. The difference this time was that she was no young girl. She was all woman. No more baggy jeans and hoodies. Her grown woman was on full display in bra and panties—titties perky and pussy fat.

Kiam's dick rocked up at the mere sight of her silky skin. It was as if he was seeing her for the first time, and he was pleased with what he saw from head to toe.

"Eyez, you good?"

She nodded her head, unable to speak.

Kiam released one of her breast from the bra. Placing his mouth over her nipple he sucked lightly, sending heat waves through her body.

Clutching him tightly, she leaned in and bit into his neck.

Kiam reached down and lifted her up slightly, fitting her against his waist. Faydrah wrapped her legs around him and held him between her thighs. Her soft breast pressed against his chest as he walked into the bedroom. He laid her down and stripped out of his clothes.

Faydrah looked on as he released his steel from its enclosure. Her eyes widened slightly; he definitely was not the sixteen year old boy she first gave it to. He was a man in every sense of the word.

"I want to feel you," she whispered while pulling off her panties, allowing him a view of her pretty rose.

"You sure?" He asked, stroking his growing erection to full potential.

"Yes," she responded, reaching out and pulling him to her.

Kiam slid between her legs and rested his dick at the base of her throbbing opening. Her wetness seeped from her lips, kissing the head of his thick rod. Kiam slid back and forth stimulating her clit, causing her to squirm under him.

"Baby, I've missed you so very much," she whined.

"I missed you too," he whispered, tracing circles around her pleasure button.

"Let me have it."

"You want it?" He teased, licking and sucking her breast.

"Yesss," she moaned.

"Get it," he responded as he flicked his tongue across her nipple.

Faydrah took him into her hand and brought him to her moist opening. Slowly he entered her inch by inch, breaking down the tension between them. Faydrah inhaled as he went deeper. Her moans began to fill the room as he stroked faster.

Kiam closed his eyes and tried to focus as her grip became hypnotizing. He stroked from side to side, going deeper with every thrust, causing her to tense up and try to escape.

"Kiam," she moaned as he picked up speed.

"Mmm, yes?"

"Baby, slow down," she panted.

Kiam held back and began giving it to her slowly. "This how you want it, ma?" His strokes became gentle and her muscles tighten around him.

"Ooh, you feel so good," she moaned.

"Go ahead baby, cum on this dick." He steadied his pace as Faydrah pushed the pussy at him so he could hit the spot just right. Her breath quickened as she dug her nails into his back.

"Oh, my god," she cried out in ecstasy lashing her head from side to side. "Put this fire out."

"I'ma put it out, baby girl. Damn, your pussy feels so good. This is how you fucked my head up way back then." He spoke softly in her ear causing her fire to burn more intense. "I used to dream about being inside you again, but even in my dreams it didn't feel this good."

Kiam threw her leg over his shoulder and went to work. She was getting ready to feel the hardness and the raw passion of the years that he longed for her.

"Ohhhh...baby, baby, baby," she cried biting down on her lip.

"You wanted it, now let me get it," grunted Kiam. He grabbed her other leg and placed it on his other shoulder.

"Yes, get it Kiam. Get it all," she cried out as he went deeper than she knew existed.

The room was filled with loud moans and the slippery sound of every stroke. Kiam held on as long as he could. When he couldn't hold on any longer he stroked faster and deeper until he released months of pressure and years of pain. She felt his thick muscle swell up inside of her and spread her wide open just as his hot seeds began to spill out within her buttery cup. Her own love rushed up upon her and caused her back to arch off the bed. "Kiam! Oooohhhh baby, I'm coming!" she screamed.

Kiam kept stroking and his semen flooded her as her body went into pleasurable convulsions. Faydrah's honey spilled down warm and plentiful on his engorged shaft, and she panted as his strokes induced multiple orgasms from her, one right behind the other. "Oh my god. Oh my god." She tried to catch her breath.

Releasing her legs he looked down into her face, then placed soft kisses on her lips. "I never stopped loving you," he whispered.

"I know," she responded on short wind."

Laying there between her legs was his refuge, loving her was easy because she made him feel like a man. With her there was no pretense. She didn't care about the money or the murder, she only saw him.

Faydrah held him tight as he rested against her. Tears ran down the side of her face as she released all the agony of the years she had spent missing him. Through her tears there was happiness; she relished in the pleasure of having him between her thighs.

Kiam was insatiable. Her breathing had barely returned to normal when he flipped her over and began sucking on the back of her neck. In an instant she caught fire again and her legs automatically opened themselves for his desire. She was slippery inside from both of their cum, so he slid right in. "Let me give it to you slow," he crooned huskily as he nibbled her ear lobe and gave it to her gently.

"Anyway you want, baby, I'm yours." She submitted her body to his needs.

Kiam took her to the Mountain Top, and then higher. As orgasm after orgasm rocked her inner soul Faydrah felt like she had soared to Heaven. "Come inside me again, fill me with your essence," she breathlessly moaned.

Once they had exhausted the pleasure of every position possible, they showered and just laid next to each other. Within minutes Faydrah was fast asleep. Kiam watched her as she rested. Tracing his finger along her back and legs, he embraced the silence and cherished the moment he had prayed for nights on end. He lay his head upon his pillow, took a deep breath and began to doze off.

Today was a blessing but tomorrow he was back into killah mode. His only hope was that he never caused Faydrah another day of sorrow or pain.

.

Chapter 8
The Introduction

Lissha got on the elevator and hit the up button. As she rode in silence her mind turned while processing the meeting that was about to transpire between Kiam and Gator. She had been given the instructions from Big Zo weeks ago to inform Gator of the impending change in command.

Gator definitely wasn't going to like being stripped of his power, no matter how good the change would be for the family. He was going to take things real personal, then do something about it. Lissha hoped that whatever that something was it wouldn't be betrayal, because that would get him much more than a demotion. If he bucked on Kiam, that would be just another test of his mettle, and she already knew how that would play out. Gator had proven that he would bust his guns, but was he built to defy Big Zo and go up against his handpicked protégé? That was the million dollar question.

Lissha hadn't acted on Big Zo's instructions because she had decided to wait until Kiam was on the scene, to feel him out for herself. The fate of that decision would soon be revealed.

Exiting the elevator she quickly put on her game face. After about five knocks Kiam still hadn't come to the door. She pulled out her cell phone and dialed the number to his room. After three rings the door came open. The mood was calm and Kiam had a semi-smile on his face.

Lissha looked at him with her nose scrunched up. "What you doing? Why it took you so long to let me in?" She looked around the room with a caution.

Kiam didn't have to reply because Faydrah emerged from the bedroom answering the question with her presence; she was wearing a three piece business suit and a wide smile.

"So, will I see you later?" she shyly asked as she leaned in and kissed him sweetly.

"You can see whatever you want, whenever you want."

"Time will tell." She leaned over and grabbed her brief case. "Enjoy your day." She flashed him a look that confirmed that he had handled his business. She looked at Lissha and held her gaze briefly before walking past her as if she wasn't there.

Kiam walked behind Faydrah. At the door he tapped her butt lightly. "Be good," he warned.

She looked back over her shoulder at him, then preceded out the door. No response was necessary, her body language told the whole story.

Kiam looked on until she disappeared. Lissha stood back watching the interaction between the two and a bit of jealousy brewed within.

"You ready to take care of this business?" Kiam's demeanor altered.

Seized by unexpected feelings of envy, Lissha delayed feedback, but her hustle mentality quickly resumed. "I was born ready. Get ya shit and let's roll."

Kiam picked up on her slight attitude, chuckled as he positioned his gun and collected his thoughts. "Why you acting all salty?" He toyed with her.

"What?" Lissha folded her arms and shifted her weight. "We got shit to do and you all late, up here fucking around with these ho's." She avoided eye contact as she headed for the door.

Kiam's suspicions were confirmed. "You want me to smack your ass too? Maybe that will help you get your shit right." He followed Lissha to the elevators.

"I don't think so," she replied with heavy sarcasm and sucked her teeth.

Emerging from the lobby of the hotel, Lissha handed the valet her ticket and he hurried off to get the car.

"I'm driving," Kiam yelled out as he came up behind her, ducking his head against a suddenly cool spring wind that came off of Lake Erie.

"What makes you think you're driving my shit?" Lissha tossed her long brown hair over her shoulder and gave him the side-eye as she stepped to her silver 2012 Lexus LFA.

Kiam didn't even answer. He opened the passenger side door for her, then headed to the driver's side. The young valet rushed up and gave Kiam the car keys. Lissha accepted that the issue was not up for negotiation. Kiam was driving and that was it.

Huffing, she settled in her seat.

"What happened to the whip you was pushing the other day?" he asked.

"It's at the house. Why?" she questioned him back.

"I hope you're not out here flossing and shit. Fuck the shine, it's about the paper and the power."

Lissha felt like she was being scolded. Within the few days she had been away from Kiam his whole attitude had changed. It was evident that he was settling into his new role and was not tolerating games. This only made her more nervous about the interaction he was about to have with Gator.

Kiam cruised through the streets with her directing the way. He took a careful eye to every block. Different faces, same game. The streets he had left had not changed at all. His intentions were not to come in shaking things up all at once. He was going to make a few good examples and the mouth pieces he would leave behind would spread his reign of terror.

Pulling into the condos out in Beachwood where Gator rested his head, Kiam parked and slid down in his seat. "Sup? Is this nigga going to be a problem?" He asked.

"Not really, but he may resist a little. Daddy told me to tell him a few weeks back about the change in power. But I figured I would let you do that so I could see where this nigga's heart is at. A man can't hide under the element of surprise."

"I hear you. But do me a favor and don't try to figure shit out. Me and Big Zo already did all the figuring. Just do what we tell you." He looked over at her.

Lissha was literally biting down on her lip to keep from responding with something slick. She knew how to play her position but she was not a punk. Gauging her body language, Kiam added, "No disrespect, its business, not personal." He popped the locks and got out.

Lissha checked her guns and got out, lightly slamming her door. For the first time she was caught off guard. She knew she had slightly fucked up and would probably have to deal with Big Zo later, but for right now she had to get into character. In the time it took for them to walk up on the porch the transformation was complete.

Gator opened the door bare chested with the butt of his fo-fifth peaking up from the waistline of his jeans. His shoulder length dreads were tied back in a ponytail.

"Hey, LiLi."

He looked over her shoulder at Kiam as he reached in and gave her a half hug.

"What's up Gator?" She reciprocated. Breaking the embrace, she introduced, "This is Kiam, the brother Daddy told you about."

"Welcome home, little bruh." Gator extended his hand.

"What's up?" Kiam shook his hand but maintained an icy face.

Gator picked up on Kiam's coldness and adjusted his attitude as well. His brows became one and his mouth morphed into a tight line.

"Damn nigga, move back and let us in. It's windy as hell out here. And you need to put a shirt on before you be laid up in somebody's hospital with pneumonia," Lissha chastised.

Gator gradually backed up allowing them to pass him, keeping a careful eye on Kiam as he closed the door. "So what brings you to my neck of the woods?" he asked Lissha.

"You know me, always about this paper." She took a seat on Gators all white couch.

Every time Lissha came over it always boggled her mind how this blue black gorilla had all white furniture throughout his whole house.

Gator flexed his chest muscles before snatching his t-shirt off the back of the sofa. He sat across from Lissha while Kiam chose to stand behind her.

"So what's good?" Gator took a few swigs of his drink.

"Daddy told me to come out here and make the introduction so you can get Kiam familiar with how shit is ran. I'm stepping back," she announced, leaning forward in her seat and looking Gator right in his eyes.

Gator looked at her, then up at Kiam, then back at her. He moved his glass in a slow circle causing the ice to clink from side to side as his face hardened. "Let me get this straight. So Big Zo told you to bring him to me and for me to show him how shit go?"

"Yeah," she replied.

"Then, what?"

"Don't answer that shit, Lissha," Kiam broke in, taking over the meeting, and changing the whole tone of the conversation. "He heard what the fuck you said, and he can figure out what it means. As a matter of fact, wait for me in the car. Let me holla at this man."

One of Gator's eyebrows went straight up. "She ain't gotta go no fucking where. This is my shit. I say who goes and who fucking stays." He tried to flex his dwindling authority.

Lissha stood up. "I'm good. I'ma let men do what they do. I'll hit you later." She exited.

"Yeah, you do that," Gator spat, now heated from his first interaction with the man that Big Zo had spoken so highly of. He hadn't known Kiam a full five minutes and he was ready to kill him.

Once Kiam heard the door shut he went into beast mode.

"Let me explain something to you. I ain't no bitch made nigga. I don't make friends and I don't have time to fucking babysit. Big Zo gave me a mission and I'ma handle it. Period." He sliced his hand through the air in one swift motion to finalize his declaration.

Kiam paused briefly to let his words sink in and to scale Gator's reaction. He looked him in the eye and spoke clearly. "Now this is how this shit is going to go. I'll call you later tonight with a time and a meeting place. We're about to set the tone amongst our own. Don't get held up in traffic, I hate a late muthafucka. Secondly, everything from here forward goes to me and comes through me. Last, but definitely not least, it's business as usual. Handle your end and don't come up short."

Kiam stood staring into Gator's eyes as if he was reading his soul. He had heard that the nigga had a few notches on his belt, but he wasn't impressed because if Gator was truly about that life, Big Zo wouldn't have needed him to step in and run things.

Just as he suspected, Gator had the scent of pussy on him. He knew that there was no way a real thug would let another man stand in his house and talk noise without making the ten o'clock news real interesting.

Inside Gator bristled, he thought about wetting Kiam's shirt, but he figured he needed to go along and see where things would end up. At the end of the day he held a trump card. He intended on holding, then slamming it on the table when it was time to collect. But still, he wasn't about to get chumped off.

"Bruh, you come up in my shit talking real breezy, like you think I wear a thong. If Big Zo didn't tell you, you better find out some other way—I'm not that nigga to handle like a pussy. Now we can make this transition smooth or we can make it bloody. Really, I don't give a fuck, I do or die for mine," Gator let it be known. His hand was inches from his tool.

"You talking but I ain't felt no heat, so what you saying?" Kiam disarmed him with words that did as much damage to a man as hollow points.

As Gator looked at Kiam he fought back his rage and pasted an accommodating look on his face.

"You done?"

"For now." Kiam left.

When Kiam got to the car, Lissha was sitting with her legs crossed, smoking a Black. "Put that shit out," he ordered.

"Hold the fuck up. This is my shit," Lissha quickly responded.

Kiam cut his coal black's over at her. "Don't make me ask twice," he said real calmly as he pulled out the parking spot.

Lissha looked back at him and wrinkled up her nose. The tables had turned and the change of power was now in Kiam's hand. His air of confidence and leadership was sending a surge throughout her body. Daddy had warned her about Kiam but he did not prepare her for the feelings that would develop once she saw him in action.

Lissha took one last pull, blew the smoke in the air, then plucked the Black out the window.

Coming to a stop at a red light, Kiam calmed the situation a bit. "Thank you. You're too pretty to be smoking anyway."

Lissha pouted her lips and looked out the window.

Kiam put his hand on her leg. "We got a lot of work ahead of us, you need to be focused and on point. There is no place for weakness on this level. I interpreted a look in your boy's eyes back there that don't sit well with me. If he shows the slightest sign of shade I'ma get him a headstone, so I hope you haven't been fucking with the help on the side." The strength of his voice commanded that she look at him. When she did, he looked directly into her eyes.

Lissha saw in his face that he was sincere. Just as she was about to respond he flashed her that sexy smile, causing her mouth to turn up at the corners. "I'm just saying," he stated, leaving it hanging out there.

When the light turned green, he removed his hand and placed it back on the steering wheel. The sexy smile evaporated in a flash, as if it had never existed. Lissha frowned again.

"Don't take shit so personal," said Kiam, observing her expression. "It's not even like that with me. I'm on some business shit, point blank. I don't have time to fuck around or to cater to anybody's feelings.

"Shit is about to get serious real fast, so either you're built for this shit or fall to the side. I'm not placating you because you're Pop's daughter, you're in your feelings or on your cycle. So get that in your head right now." He glanced over at her again.

Lissha remained monotone.

"Do I make myself clear?" he asked, returning his eyes to the road.

"Humph."

Kiam didn't acknowledge her grumble; he allowed silence to make his point.

"I understand," she replied through tight lips.

"Good, because I'm going to need that for something. I don't know what y'all have been doing out here but apparently it's not good enough or Big Zo wouldn't have asked me to step in and take over. As I understand it, business has leveled off. A few of our spots have started coming up with short money, and other squads are out here feeling themselves. All of that is about to change."

She wondered if he was insinuating that because she was a female she couldn't handle the business. If that's what he thought, he had the game twisted. She had just shown him the other day that her gun popped off just as lethal as his.

He was pissing her the hell off. But at the same time he turned her on. She had always been attracted to a nigga that knew how to take command of things.

"Who is our fiercest competition?" he asked.

"Wolfman," she answered without hesitation. "He has the biggest name in the city right now?"

"He had the biggest name," Kiam corrected.

Lissha nodded her understanding. She had wanted to get at Wolfman for the past two years but Gator forbade it.

"Tell me everything you know about him, and watch me make the nigga disappear."

Kiam's confidence was music to Lissha's ears. She eagerly dispensed with the information that she had compiled on Wolfman, the city's largest drug dealer. When she had reported all that she knew about him she outlined the rest of the hierarchy.

Some names were already familiar to Kiam through Big Zo. These were people that had come into hood prominence after Big Zo's demise. Dontae, Money Bags Carter, Frank Nitti. He knew their names but the only one of them whom he knew personally was Frank Nitti and he had never liked that bitch.

Kiam listened in silence until they pulled up to Lissha's condo out in South Euclid. He had already made up his mind that he was going to rearrange everybody's position. Muthafuckas could accept it or get wiped out completely.

"What time you need your car, I got some shit to do?"

Lissha cocked her eyes at him as if he was crazy. "Hold up. So you just gonna talk shit to me all day," she counted out on her fingers, "boss me around then take my car? Where the fuck they do that at?"

Kiam didn't budge. "You didn't answer the question."

"You know what; I'm not doing this with you right now. Just bring me my shit in the morning." She hit the locks and got out.

She closed the car door and leaned in the window. "That ho must have fucked you good last night. Because you up this morning with an S on your chest. Today was free; the next one will cost you." She stood up to walk away.

"LiLi," Kiam yelled out. "Be good."

Lissha turned to watch him drive away.

Kiam went right back into game mode; he could feel his adrenaline pumping. Wolfman and all the others that sat below him were about to have their worlds shook up.

Kiam's first stop was at the Verizon store. He bought himself a prepaid cell phone then hit the important people with the number. Afterwards, he cruised his old stomping grounds up and down Miles Road. He wanted to see things through his own eyes, without Czar's commentary.

He stopped at the tire and rim shop on the lower end of Miles Road to holla at some other homies that were hanging out there. Most of them were the same faces from years ago. They were still stomping the hood and hustling the blocks.

Everyone told him that DeMarcus was doing it big. Kiam took that information in and pondered its implications. DeMarcus hadn't shown him any love while he was away, that didn't bode well for him at all.

Back at the hotel, Kiam mapped out his strategy. He was sure that word would get back to DeMarcus that he had touched down, but he was not stepping to the nigga until he had decided his fate. He was going to let him shake in his boots while trying to figure out what state of mind he was in now that he was back.

Kiam undressed and got a few hours of rest because starting tonight he was putting niggas to sleep.

Gator pulled up at the meeting spot with a few minutes to spare. That was a good look because Kiam was in beast mode and wouldn't have excused tardiness. As soon as Kiam saw him pull up in the black Nav' that he had described, Kiam walked up to the passenger door and slid in.

"Where we headed?" Gator asked over the thump of the music coming out of his speakers.

"Wherever the first problem is that needs to be fixed." Kiam turned the music completely off.

"What kind of problem are you talking about, cuz?"

"I'm talking about in-house problems. The situations with the short money. We have to take care of home before we can regulate anything outside of it. Big Zo told me that we have a spot on 102nd and Sophia that constantly comes up short. Either those niggas can't count or they're on some grimy shit. What's your take on it?"

"I don't think the dudes that run that spot are stealing from us, if that's what you're asking." Gator pulled out of the lot and the dark truck blended into the murky night.

"Big Zo does."

"No disrespect to Big Zo, my nigga, but he can't see what's going on from where he's at. Losses are part of the game. I've known the niggas that run that house for ten years, they don't get down like that."

"Well, explain to me how the trap is coming up short five and ten racks a week?" Kiam countered testily.

"Mistakes happen," Gator defended.

"Oh yeah?" Kiam wasn't buying it. A nigga that couldn't count cheated himself; if he cheated you, he could count damn good. "Take me over there so I can have a talk with these fools."

"Alright, but I'm telling you before we get there that Vic and Cantrell has been loyal to the team from day one. You can ask Lissha."

"Lissha's not calling the shots anymore, and neither are you. So just drive and shut the fuck up before I start thinking that you got something to hide."

"Hold up, Bleed! Fuck you talking to? This Big Zo's shit so I play my position, but ain't nothing soft about me. Check my street resume."

"I already did."

The statement left Gator wondering if it was a compliment or a slap in the face. He knew that he had put in work but for some reason Kiam didn't seem to respect his gangsta. It was all good; the cemeteries were full of niggas that had slept on the next man's G.

They rode on in silence until they reached the crack house. Gator called inside and they were let in as soon as they reached the side door. They followed Vic into the kitchen where Cantrell was whipping crack in the microwave. Two of their young workers were seated at a round glass table bagging up rocks.

Gator made the introductions all around. "Kiam has something he wants to talk to y'all about. Whatever he has to say is not to be contested."

Cantrell looked at his cousin Vic. They both had the same question in their eyes. *Who the fuck is this nigga? And why is Gator acting like this muthafucka run something?* Kiam was about to answer that question real soon.

"Rest your feet," he charged.

Vic sat at the table with the two younger boys, but Cantrell chose to remain standing. He leaned against the refrigerator and folded his arms across his chest.

"Fam, you hard of hearing or something?" Kiam grilled him. Cantrell looked at Gator, but Gator looked away. "I don't like to have to repeat myself." Kiam said.

Reluctantly, Cantrell took the last empty chair at the table.

Gator leaned back against the sink and watched Kiam in action.

"I'm already in a foul mood so don't nobody test my patience or this meeting is gonna end with some bodies sprawled out on the floor," he began. His hand went to his waist as he looked from man to man. Nobody said anything but their expressions spoke loud and clear.

"I don't know how things have been done up until now," Kiam continued. "But from this day forward a short trap is unacceptable. Anything missing comes out of your pay to make it right. I don't tolerate stealing or disloyalty. Is that clear?"

Vic waited to see how his cousin was gonna play it. Cantrell spoke his mind.

"Bruh, I have a problem with you walking up in here talking to us like we're your do-boys. Up until five minutes ago you didn't even know me, and you damn sure don't know what's been going on over here. I mean, who the fuck is you? How in the fuck you gon' just pop up out of nowhere giving orders and shit?"

Kiam chuckled. That hinted something real ugly was about to go down, but those boys didn't know his ways so they were at a disadvantage that they couldn't even fathom.

Kiam's chuckle was followed by a half smile, he liked Cantrell's heart. Maybe in the next life the little nigga would be a shot caller, but not in this one.

Kiam's Nine came off his waist spitting something real hot. Cantrell's head exploded in a spray of skull and blood. His body toppled over in the chair and crashed to the floor.

Vic shot up out of his chair, dashing to the counter where he had placed his trey-eight on top of the microwave. Before he could reach his strap, Kiam aimed his nine milli and opened up his back.

Vic's face slapped the floor and he groaned in pain. He tried to crawl but his legs no longer worked.

Kiam walked around the table and stepped over Vic on his way to the counter. He searched the drawers until he found what he was looking for.

Walking back over to Vic, Kiam tucked his banger back down in his waist and knelt down beside the paralyzed and dying man. He rolled Vic over on his back and plunged the butcher knife in his heart. Blood squirted out three feet in the air.

Kiam stood back up and looked at the two young workers who were still seated at the table frozen with fear. "I don't do insubordination, either," he stated. "Remember that, and what happened to them won't happen to you. Do I make myself clear?"

Their heads bobbled vigorously up and down.

"Alright. From now on y'all are in charge of this trap. Get the dope out and torch the house. We can open another spot down the street somewhere. And remember what I said about my coins," Kiam reemphasized. Then he turned and looked at Gator.

"Pick ya mouth up off the floor, homie. It's just another day in the life of a G," he said, strolling toward the door with his nuts hanging low.

Across town, his female counterpart was on her G shit too.

Chapter 9
Blood Money

Lissha moved around her three bedroom apartment preparing for the arrival of her Blood Money Crew. When the bell rung, she had just taken the last piece of chicken out the pan and placed it on a platter. Wiping her hands on the dish towel, she moved to the door and she opened it wide.

"What's up, ladies," she asked as Bayonna, Treebie and Donella piled into her living room.

"What's up, momma?" Bayonna returned the greeting, giving Lissha a half hug.

"It smells good up in here." Donella placed her purse on the coffee table and headed to the sink to wash her hands.

Treebie did her usual. "Damn bitch, I see food but nothing to drink," she remarked.

She pulled two bottles of 1800 from her oversized Gucci bag and started laughing.

"This bitch," Lissha sighed, closing the door and shaking her head.

"Put some music on so we can make this meeting both business and pleasure," suggested Treebie as she strolled to the kitchen to grab four shot glasses.

Lissha attached her iPod to the Bose Sound Dock, it was on and popping. Beyonce's *Love on Top* came blasting through the speakers.

Honey, Honey/ I can see the stars all the way from here/ Can't you see the glow on the window pane/ I can feel the sun whenever you're near/ Every time you touch me I just melt away...

Everybody's head started bopping and their hands and feet were moving to the beat.

Bayonna put chicken wings and potato salad on everyone's plates and brought them to the living room. Donella grabbed the ice bucket and filled it up. Minutes later the Blood Money Crew was seated Indian style around the coffee table in the living room. Treebie poured the first round of drinks and held her glass in the air, offering a toast. "To the takeover."

Lissha and the others clinked glasses and took the shot to the head. Slamming the glasses on the table in unison, they all did a little shake with their bodies, then poured and downed another.

Once they felt that first buzz they began attacking their food.

"This shit is good as hell," Treebie said, showing her chicken no mercy.

"You know how I ride for my bitches, I got you." Lissha snapped her fingers and did a dance in her seat.

The crew joked back and forth as they devoured the food. After they finished eating and cleared the table, Bayonna pulled a Ziploc of weed from her purse and started rolling.

Treebie hummed along with the music and went back to pouring. Within minutes they were good and fucked up.

"So what's on the menu?" Treebie asked, sitting back and lighting up her third blunt.

Lissha grabbed the remote and turned the music down a little. "Well, I introduced Kiam to Gator. That shit was craze."

"What you mean?" Treebie blew out smoke and passed the Kush. Then she listened attentively.

Lissha took a couple hits and then continued. "That nigga, Kiam, ain't shit to be played with. He put Gator on point, which was the first time I ever saw that nigga reaching for a clue."

"Damn," Bayonna gushed as she took the blunt and started pulling hard on it. "So, is it going to be a problem between them or what?"

"I don't think so. But we gotta make sure that Gator falls in. We gotta have Kiam's back no matter what. Daddy says he needs this transition to be smooth." She reached for her drink, and took a few sips.

"And on our end, if Kiam can take over and put the streets under his foot, that will free us up to do this other shit we got cooking outside of him and Daddy," Lissha explained.

"Have we made any progress?" asked Donella, leaning in for Bayonna to blow her a gun. When that hot smoke hit the back of her throat she started coughing and choking.

"See that's why I don't fuck with you. You can't hang. Bitch, you act like you just started getting high yesterday, silly ass rabbit." Treebie said, shaking her head.

"Fuck you, she tried to blow my head off. Fucking around with y'all I'll leave up out of here with my lungs in my purse."

They all burst out in laughter.

When the clowning ceased, Lissha turned serious and answered the question that Donella presented to her. "Yeah. We real good. I got with Spank and he told me about a few card games coming up with some intense money. If shit is like he says, we can hit them muthafuckas and be in and out." This was their thing outside of the business with Big Zo.

"What's Spank's cut?" Treebie shot back.

"He don't want shit from one of the spots. That one is personal. Spank got wind that them niggas be running some card tricks, they beat his ass outta fifty bands. He want them niggas put on they ass. But if we hit the other two, our split is sixty/forty."

"Fuck outta here! We going in, we taking all the risk, then that nigga want forty percent to sit at home and scratch his nuts? Nah, fuck that." Treebie wasn't feeling it at all. She poured herself another drink.

"I agree. Maybe thirty but not forty," said Donella, who usually just went with the flow.

"I don't have a problem with it, he's doing the ground work," Bayonna reasoned.

Treebie cut her eyes over at her. Bay was the least tenured of the crew, and she was the only one of them that Big Zo hadn't recruited himself. LiLi had brought Bay in three years ago after recognizing that she had what it took to be down with them. As far as Treebie was concerned, Bay was still on probation so she often discounted the young girl's opinion.

"Yeah, but Spank ain't gonna be the one standing there with his dick in his hand if them niggas get active," Treebie hotly contested.

"Look, I already approved the amount." Lissha cut back in. "We gotta show them it's real, then we up the price on em'. Let's do these couple jobs and then we can have something to bargain with. Right now we just riding on our word."

"You're riding on your word. I'm riding on my rep. We do one job— the free one. We kill everything moving except one witness to tell the tale after it's over. Then we make that nigga bow to our demands or he can get it too." Treebie looked at Lissha seriously. When it came to the money she didn't play.

Lissha took a few sips of her drink. She kept her eyes fixed on Treebie. "Why you always want to kill somebody?" Lissha asked. "I think you need counseling and some fucking Prozac."

They burst out laughing again.

"Nah, on the real I feel you. And you're right. One on the house and the rest will cost him," Lissha agreed. "The first lick is going down Friday night so everybody be ready to roll. Salute." They brought their glasses together.

Just as the glass left Lissha's mouth her phone started vibrating on the table. When she looked down at the caller ID, it read Daddy. She grabbed the remote, paused the music and put her finger to her lips, gesturing for them to be quiet.

"Hello," she answered in an eager tone.

"Hey, baby girl," Big Zo's voice flowed into her ear.

"Hey, Daddy." She tried to perk up from her drunken state.

"What you up to?" he asked trying to feel her out.

"Nothing much. Just sitting here chillin' with the girls."

"Hey, Daddy," Treebie yelled out teasing Lissha.

Lissha kicked her under the table and waved her hand.

"Is that Treebie?" asked Big Zo.

"Yes, and as you see, she's loud as usual."

"Tell the girls I said hello, then excuse yourself and go somewhere private so we can talk."

"Okay." She dropped the phone to her waistline. "Daddy said hello ladies." She relayed the message as she got up and went toward the bedroom.

"Hey," Bayonna and Donella chorused as she walked away.

Closing the door, she dove on her bed. "Okay, go ahead. I'm alone."

"So what's up with Kiam? Is he getting around the city good?" Big Zo went right into code talk.

"Yeah, I took him on a few job interviews. You know all this application shit is new to him, but he met all the right people," Lissha related.

"Okay, good. Make sure he gets the wardrobe he needs. Tell him I said 'shop around' and don't just go with the first thing he sees."

"Okay."

"We just need a couple more months and everything should line up."

"I know, Daddy. I'm doing everything in my power to make sure I keep shit in line for you."

"First of all, watch your mouth. Second, I heard different. You know ol' boy called and said he was caught off guard by your surprise party." Big Zo was speaking of her not telling Gator about Kiam.

"I know, but I wanted to make sure everybody was legit," she explained.

"I understand. But don't grow a fucking brain in the middle of progress. Do what I tell you. I got this. I need you to hear and obey. Save judgment calls for real important shit like when you can't reach me. Other than that, do what I tell you."

Lissha was quiet. She already knew she had rocked the boat but she was not in the mood to hear his mouth.

"LiLi," he called out.

"Yes," she answered feeling like she was five years old and had wet the bed.

"I know I put a lot on your shoulders, but I need you to be my eyes, ears and hands. We have to be on the same page or none of this shit is going to work. You got me?"

"Yes. I got you."

"I love you, baby girl. Be careful. And make sure that you come to visit me soon. I need to put something in your ear."

"I love you too, Daddy. I'll be down next Saturday," she promised.

"Alright. Good night." He disconnected the call.

Lissha put her phone down on the bed and rubbed her hands over her face. She had to quickly regroup so she could go back out there to the girls without looking like she had just gotten chastised. When she emerged from the room she had a big smile on her face. She got the remote, pumped the music back up and grabbed the bottle and took it to the head.

"Well, damn," Treebie remarked with her head cocked to the side.

"Let's get fucked up. I don't want to know my name in the morning," Lissha said, taking the bottle up once more.

Treebie knew that the sudden change in Lissha's attitude meant that Big Zo had got in that ass. She suspected that he had something cooking. It was only a matter of time before he had Lissha doing sneaky shit that might put them all in a jacked up position. But one thing was for sure and two things for certain, Treebie was not that bitch. She was already making moves to separate herself from Lissha and Big Zo's operation. She just needed to sit back and let her tactics materialize.

Chapter 10
The Heist

Friday night came fast. The Blood Money Crew was in Treebie's basement getting suited up. Lissha stepped into her third pair of sweat pants while Treebie pulled on her second hoodie. Bay and Nella was already geared, lacing their boots. Thick, loose-fitting clothing helped disguise the girl's weight and gender.

Lissha, Donella, and Treebie pulled their hair back into tight ponytails and tucked it under fitted skull caps. Bay wore her hair in an extremely low cut that only a cold broad like herself could rock without looking butch. She covered her hair with a skully too, and they all pulled their head gear low over their brows. The bottom half of their faces was covered with black half-face masks. Nothing showed but the slits of their eyes.

Lissha strapped on a bullet proof vest and waited for the others to do the same. There was no way to predict how marks would act once you run up in their spot so the girls covered all angles.

Treebie walked to the lock boxes and spun the combination. Every time she opened the door to her arsenal chamber, a smile came across her face and her nipples stiffened. If she had a dick, that too would've been rocked up.

"These some sexy bitches," she stated as she reached for her Carbon.

She picked it up and caressed it before swiping her bullets and loading up. A twinkle of anticipating danced in her eyes as she looked to her left at Bayonna and passed her a Calico.

Two months shy of turning twenty-three years old, Bay was the baby of the crew. She was a diminutive chick but her heart was colossal. Her method of operation was no words, only action. The others called her the silent killah because when it was time to rock, she grew a pair of big balls; she didn't let air slide when they threw down on a spot. And if a nigga uttered one wrong word, Bay's Calico made it his last without reasoning.

Donella was next to Bay, tightening up her vest. Amongst the crew she was known as The Negotiator. Whatever information she couldn't get with words and her sex appeal, she negotiated with her banger. Her Glock .50 made a muthafucka spill his guts in one form or another.

Treebie was the live-wire of the crew. She would much rather bust her gun than talk shit out. It was like she was more turned on by the killing than the hustle. When Treebie ran up in somebody's spot their futures weren't longer than the time it usually took her to click clack one in the chamber.

Lissha, on the other hand, was the most level-headed. With a team of women that weren't afraid to bust a gun then come home and drop a grand on the Mac counter, she knew she had the deadliest crew on the streets. By day, they were the baddest by the coldest definition. But by night, they were the wrong bitches to fuck with. And tonight would be no different.

"Check your weapons, ladies," Lissha said. "Make sure they're cocked and locked."

Once everyone affirmed that their guns were ready, she passed them each a voice distorter. One by one, they fitted the contraptions around their throats. After a quick check to make sure everything was in place they moved to the counter and opened the four small containers.

Each woman carefully placed a pair of blood red contacts in their eyes. They allowed a moment for them to adjust, and then they looked each other over.

"We go in this muthafucka as four and we come out as four," said Lissha. She had given this short pep talk dozens of times before. It was part of their ritual but it was not to be taken for granted.

She looked around and read her crew's body language. Satisfied with what she saw, Lissha said, "Let's get it."

"Blood Money!" They chanted in unison.

When they got to the spot they were targeting on Wadepark, they rode by to make sure everything appeared to be as Spank said it would be. From what they could tell, it was legit. They parked a half a block down, eased out of the car, and then moved in the shadows of the night.

Moving up to the door they all went into beast mode. Treebie did the secret knock. A minute or so passed before they heard the door locks click open.

It was on!

They forced their way inside. Treebie pulled her gun and blasted the first two fools to stand up. She watched their bodies drop, then planted herself firm in the middle of the room.

Donella went to the left and Bayonna went to the right. Lissha took up the rear, closing the door.

The startled doorman opened his mouth to say something and got his face blown off. Lissha popped two more in his chest and watched him slide down the wall. She stepped over the man's body and planted her back firmly against the door.

The card players were in clear murdering range. They sat stock still, staring at the red-eyed intruders.

"I need all that shit on the table in a big bag, or I'ma put me a muthafucka in a black one." Lissha's distorted voice commanded respect.

"Hurry the fuck up. Donella yelled out. She waved her gun around the table, daring someone to test it.

"Hold up, nigga, do you know whose game house this is?" A fat yellow skinned brother at the head of the table yelled out.

Without pause Bay let off in his chest sending him hard to the floor. "The next sound I hear better not be anything but paper or plastic. Get that shit packed the fuck up!" she barked, tossing two large shoe bags on the table.

"These niggas think we playing," Treebie spat. Her eyes peered and her breathing thickened. The evil in her soul beamed through those red contacts making her appear bizarrely unnatural.

"Hold up, nigga. We got you." The dude at the other end of the table shouted. He and the two cats next to him began clearing the money off the table and shoveling it in the duffel bags.

When they had given up all of the dough in sight they sat there thinking that they had played the robbers. "Now let's take a walk over to the wall safe, and if you don't have the combination you can start praying," said Treebie.

A look of surprise flashed in the eyes of one of the dudes left breathing; he wondered how in the hell did they know about the safe? Common sense told him that they were going to kill him whether he opened the safe or not, so he might as well have taken the combination to the grave with him. But even a man that's facing imminent execution holds on to hope until the very end. "I can open the safe, just don't kill me," he blurted out like his dick had turned into a clitoris.

Treebie put her gun to the back of his head and marched him to the real prize. He shook like a stripper on a Friday night as he opened the safe and filled the duffel bags.

"Now walk that shit to the door. And if you make a wrong move it will be your last," Lissha said as they kept the guns focused on their targets.

Once the money was safe by Lissha's side the delivery boy turned to walk away with his hands in the air. When he passed Treebie he mumbled something under his breath. Lissha caught a syllable or two, and sent heat to the back of his head. His body flew into the card table, tumbling it over.

"What the fuck?" cried an older gambler. "We gave y'all what you came for. What else y'all want?"

"I need one more thing," Lissha said in a calm deep voice.

The man looked at her and hesitantly asked, "What's that?"

"Your soul," she responded.

Treebie stepped up and served his ass up something hot and heavy. Another gambler reached for his waist and Donella made that his final act in life. Her sistahs chopped down anything else that moved.

When they were done there were only two men left standing. One was a bald older man with a thick gray beard. The other one looked to be in his early thirties. They both had their hands suspended in air with fear enveloping within their hearts as they sat awaiting their execution.

"This nigga shaking like a stripper?" Treebie chuckled, placing the gun on the bridge of the younger man's nose.

Narrowing down at him with unforgiving eyes, she saw the color literally drain out of his face. "Nigga, loosen your ass cheeks. This is your lucky day. We need a mouth piece and you've just been nominated."

Sweat beads ran from his race as the cotton in his mouth made it impossible for him to swallow.

In one move Treebie shot the older man in the face. She looked back down at the young dude who was trembling in his seat. A smell assaulted her nose. She couldn't tell if it was pussy or shit, but she knew it was fear.

Bayonna and Donella moved closer to the door, keeping their weapons focused on him. Treebie shook dude down for weapons, ran his pockets, then handcuffed him to his chair.

Her crew members looked on as she reached in her pocket pulled out a dollar bill. She rubbed it the dead man's blood next to him.

"Make sure you tell them niggas this is Blood Money," she said, stuffing the bloody dollar in his mouth.

The young dude gagged. Easing backwards she lifted her gun to his face so that his eyes were level with the barrel.

"Be easy, nigga," she spat.

She raised up and they formed two lines, back to back, to make their exit.

Within seconds they were gone. The die was cast and the word would go out. *Don't fuck with Blood Money.*

Chapter 11
Business is Business

Lissha opened her eyes slowly and looked around the room. Stretching her arms and legs she prepared to get out of bed but was stopped by the strong arm and leg of the man lying next to her.

"Don't get up yet. I need you to ride this morning wood," he said, placing that hard muscle against her butt.

"Nah, I got some shit to handle," she said, removing his arm from her waist.

"Damn, why you always ready to jump out a nigga's bed and get into the streets?" Gator spat.

"It's not like that. We laying in the middle of a war zone and you wanna cuddle. I fucked you real good last night, you should be straight," she said, rising to her feet and wrapping a towel around her naked flesh.

"Last night is over. I'm trying to get you to make this tent go down." He was laying on his back with his dick holding the sheet in the air.

"You so crazy," Lissha chuckled as she crossed her arms over her chest. He had been her way of winding down after the job she and the girls had pulled off last night.

She stared down at Gator. He had his hands behind his head on the pillow and he was looking up at her invitingly, with his dreads splayed out all over his head. He slowly ran his tongue over his lips, reminding her how he could make it pleasure her.

Lissha weighed her options. She had to meet her bitches in an hour. They were going to celebrate last night's successful caper by hitting the malls. Later they were driving to Akron, Ohio for dinner at The Diamond Grill, then they would come back home and cap the night off downtown at The Horseshoe Casino, gambling and getting buzzed. But right now she had some fire head and good, hard dick just a few feet away. Another orgasm sounded good to her ears.

Walking back to the bed she grabbed a condom off the nightstand. "Strap up, nigga, and consider this the fucking Lottery— prime pussy back to back."

"I ain't mad at you," he laughed, humored by her audacity. He ripped open the pack and strapped up.

She dropped the towel to the floor and straddled Gator's lap backwards. Easing down on all that hardness, she let out a soft moan and went to work. Her ass began to bounce and jiggle, and her moisture slid up and down his rigid length. Gator grabbed her hips and closed his eyes.

When she heard those familiar groans leave his lips she rode harder and faster. She closed her eyes and imagined that the thick, hard, muscle inside of her belonged to someone else—someone she should not have been fantasizing about. Thinking of him immediately took her over the top. She bit down on her bottom lip to keep from crying out his name as her body trembled and she began to release.

Gator felt her walls contract around his dick and he gave up the fight to hold back his seed. He grunted and filled up the Magnum. Lissha rose up off of him, allowing his dick to ease out of her.

"Goddamn, you know how to make a nigga relax in the morning," he whined in a deep, raspy, and satisfied voice.

"I always handle my business, player. No matter what it is."

"Yeah, you do. And I handle the hell out of mines. I love to hear you moan when I'm running pipe all up in your stomach. I'm telling you, ain't no better feeling than fucking the boss's daughter and making her come." He reached out and patted her ass.

Lissha slapped his hand away. "Hold up. Let me clarify something because you're really feeling yourself this morning. You don't fuck me. I'm fucking *you*. It's a difference."

"So you say," Gator lightly disputed.

"Fuck up and you'll see. Don't confuse what we do with what has to be done. Because if you slip up with what Daddy is doing, it won't matter if you make me quote scriptures when I cum, your ass will fall just like the rest."

"What, you gon' replace me with Kiam? Is that why you're so slick out the mouth lately? If so, fuck that nigga. I don't know why Big Zo trust him over me anyway. The way he's coming in wanting to crush everything, we'll all end up in the feds," he fumed.

With a scowl on his face he sat up and fired up a Newport. He blew smoke rings toward the ceiling and recounted to her what Kiam had done to Cantrell and Vic.

"So what? You wanna dig them up and apologize to 'em?"

Gator's expression hardened. "While you joking about that shit, those niggas had been down with the team from the onset. Kiam just killed them for no reason. That shit ain't cool at all. I think Big Zo made the wrong call on this one," Gator objected.

"Well, if you want to question Daddy's decisions, you can do that the next time he calls you. Let me know how that works out for you," she hurled over her shoulder as she headed to the bathroom to jump in the shower.

Gator sat pulling hard on his cigarette. His forehead was creased as he thought about everything that had happened lately. Anger resonated in his gut. He was still caught in his feelings about the way Kiam was moving. He was on some real gorilla hustling. This whole transition didn't sit well with Gator. But he was going to sit back and watch, and when Kiam failed Big Zo, he was going to be the first one to put that shit all in his face.

Chapter 12
A Boss Move

Lissha was lying comfortably in her bed; it was 3:00pm the next day. The rain beat a soothing melody on her windows, welcoming her slumber. She had been up all morning hugging the toilet and calling Earl from the night out at the casino with her girls. Now her stomach and head were paying for her over-indulgence in the free drinks that had been provided to her and the crew. The only relief was in the fact that she had won seven bands at the black jack tables. How she had made it home without wrapping her car around a pole was a mystery to Lissha.

She had just dozed back off when her phone began to ring. She didn't look at it, she merely pushed it to the side, turned over and put the covers over her head.

The phone rang back to back four times before she decided to answer. Pressing the send button on her phone to accept the call, she had already made up her mind to cuss out whoever was on the other end.

"Yo, why the fuck you keep ringing this number?" Lissha growled at the caller.

"Why the fuck are you hollering into the phone?" he replied, remaining smooth and unfazed by her grouchy attitude.

"Kiam?" Lissha asked, pulling the phone back and checking the number.

"Yeah, who did you think it was blowing you up?"

"I didn't recognize the number," she said as she pulled the cover back over her head. "What's up? Where in the hell is my car? You were supposed to return it three days ago."

"Don't sweat that, I got you. Anyway, I'm on my way to pick you up. I need you to take a run with me real quick."

"Nah. I can't leave the house right now. Maybe later."

"Ain't no later, I'll be at your house in twenty minutes. Get your shit together." He hung up.

"That muthafucka gonna be mad as hell when he get here." She huffed, tossing the phone on the nightstand and closing her eyes.

Thirty minutes later Lissha's doorbell chimed loud enough to wake the dead. She felt like her head was about to explode.

"Is this nigga serious?" she mumbled.

Turning over on her back, she stared at the ceiling while contemplating if she should move or just lay there. Just when she was about to get up, her phone rang again. She snatched it up, checked the ID, and then threw it back on the night stand.

"This nigga is crazier than I thought!" She slipped on a t-shirt and walked to the door.

Her pressure went straight to the roof when he began pressing the bell like the jump out boys was after that ass.

Lissha snatched the door open and gave Kiam the dirtiest look she could muster.

Her appearance shocked him. Her hair was wild, her nostrils were flared, and the bags under her eyes looked like you could throw some clothes in them and take a trip.

"Damn. You look fucked up," Kiam remarked as he walked into her house like he was invited.

Lissha stood holding the door knob tight in her hand in an effort to not go ham on him. "What do you want, Kiam?"

"Fuck you mean what do I want? You act like I didn't call and tell you I was on my way," he casually stated as he took a seat on her couch. "It's nice up in here," he said, looking around.

"Thanks," she muttered insincerely.

Kiam snorted. "Too bad, you fuckin' up the good vibes with all that nasty attitude."

"I told you on the phone, I am not going anywhere. I don't feel well. So if you could kindly raise your ass up off my couch, you can catch the door on the other side just as I'm slamming it," she spat.

"I'm not paying you no attention. Get your shit together and pack a small bag, we're taking a trip."

Lissha stared out the door at the rain showering down her walkway. She wanted to go off. Instead, she took a deep breath and closed the door. "Where we going Kiam?" She asked dryly.

"I need to meet that connect," he announced, trying not to watch Lissha's sexy legs as she passed him on her way to the loveseat.

"We are not scheduled to see him until next week."

"There has been a change of plans. I need to see him tomorrow."

"Tomorrow? He's in New York. That means we have to drive all night."

"Exactly, so get your shit together like I said ten minutes ago and come on."

Lissha just looked at him. She took his smug ass in real good. He had on crisp jeans, a black Ralph Lauren pullover shirt and fresh kicks that she had not purchased as part of his welcome home package. He was rocking a fresh haircut with a razor sharp line. Even when he was trying to piss her off, he was still sexy as hell.

"Why you still sitting there?" Kiam lifted his eyebrow. He pointed toward the bedrooms for her to get it moving. Every time he spoke it gave her body a jolt of energy.

The movement of his hands crossed Lissha's line of vision and broke her train of thought.

"Whatever." She tsked, then slowly got off the couch and headed to her room.

"Hurry up," he yelled out behind her.

Lissha's response was to slam the bedroom door behind her.

Unfazed, he called Faydrah.

"Hey, baby," she answered with excitement in her voice.

"What's good, ma? You miss me or what?"

"Boy, get out of my thoughts," she giggled. "I was just going to tell you how much I miss you."

Kiam settled further back on the couch and rocked his foot. "What you miss, me or what I did to you the other day?"

"Both. Humph, I'm not going to lie. Matter of fact, I'ma need you do it again real soon."

"I got you, baby," he promised, looking forward to that replay just as much as she was. "I gotta go on a short trip out of town but I'll be back in a few days, and when I get back I'ma blaze it for you real good."

"You promise?" She sat behind her desk clamping her thighs together.

"Yeah, and my shit already boned the fuck up. I can't wait."

"Ooh, me either baby. I wish I could feel you inside me right now." She closed her eyes and imagined him moving in and out of her with long powerful strokes. "Damn. Why you gotta get me all wet and I have a meeting in five minutes?"

"I thought you stay wet?" he said.

"I do for you," she replied in a sultry tone.

"Don't make me come down there and bend you over your desk."

"Don't be teasing me, Kiam." He had her kitty purring. Unfortunately she had to get off the phone. "Baby, can I call you later?" she asked with regret.

"That's cool," he said. "I'll talk to you later, bae."

"Love you." She blew him a kiss.

Kiam ended the call and sat back silently hurrying Lissha.

Lissha showered and got dressed. Sitting on her bed, she tried to get her mind right for the long drive and the unexpected drop in on their connect. Riz could be real extra sometimes, and Kiam was certifiable. She needed to be mentally prepared for the reality that she was about to put two beast in a cage and the outcome just might be death.

Tucking a few pairs of jeans and tops in a tote bag, she released a long sigh. She then grabbed her toiletries, underwear and bras, and placed them inside the bag as well. She took a jacket out of the closet to carry along in case the weather up in New York was ugly. Finally she placed her Prada sneakers in a shoe bag and set it down on the bed beside the tote bag.

She hit the closet safe and grabbed a couple bands and two credit cards, and put them inside her purse. She retrieved her .380 from the nightstand, checked its clip to make sure it was fully loaded, tucked it inside her purse and headed for the living room.

When she emerged from the bedroom, Lissha was looking refreshed in a pair of light blue jeans, Fendi sneakers and belt to match. A brown tight fitting shirt that hung long in the back and was high in the front showed off a section of her flat, toned stomach. A double piercing accentuated her navel.

Kiam's eyes wondered over her frame. Her facial features where more pronounced with her hair pulled back in that neat ponytail and the loose fitting material of her shirt clung to her chest allowing him to see her pronounced nipples right through the bra.

"Damn, nigga, take a picture it'll last longer," Lissha spat as she noticed him looking a little too long and hard.

"Well, shit, when you left outta here you looked like a deranged killah, now you look more like America's next top model."

"Shut up," Lissha chuckled. She walked toward him and tossed the tote bag in his lap.

Kiam stood up and moved to the door.

Lissha followed behind him, set the alarm and headed to the car.

The rain had stopped and the sun was attempting to peek through the clouds.

Lissha sank into the seat, slipped on her shades, and reclined back.

"We need to take 70 all the way over then get on 78. It's pretty much a straight route," she said, preparing to take a nap.

"Yo ass ain't going to be sleep." Kiam looked over at her.

"Why not?"

"You're a co-pilot. You better recognize," he made known as he pulled off en route to the highway.

Lissha just stared at him for a few minutes then looked away. She could see this trip was going to be pure torture. Before it was over she might have to choke the shit out of him.

Temptation...
When they got to the Holland tunnel Lissha almost did a happy dance in her seat. She was ready for some good food, a hot shower and a long slumber.

Kiam pulled into the Trump Soho hotel, Lissha got out to get the room keys while Kiam secured the car with the valet and gathered the bags.

When he got to the front desk he walked up on Lissha arguing back and forth with the receptionist. He sat their bags down on the floor and asked what the problem was.

"They messed up the reservation, that's what's wrong," Lissha huffed, talking with her hands flying all over the place. She accidently slung the debit card that she was holding.

"Shit," she fumed. She was tired and in no mood for bullshit.

"Ma'am I'm sorry for the mix up, but like I told you we can upgrade you to a suite with two king size beds."

"We requested two rooms, you need to make that happen."

"Look, we good. Let us have the room," Kiam cut in. He picked the debit card up and calmly placed it on the counter.

"I need my own room, I'm not trying to shack up with you," Lissha said, looking to the side at Kiam like he had the coodies.

"Why? Are you scared?" he asked flashing that sexy smile.

"No. I just need my own space." She turned back to face the receptionist who was smirking at their banter.

"Don't worry it's only for two days. Trust, you're not that goddamn irresistible," Kiam affirmed.

Lissha turned up her lips.

The receptionist ran the debit card then returned it to Lissha who was in a tiff.

"Here's your card, ma'am. We will be sending up a complimentary bottle of champagne, and your dinner is on us for the trouble. Is there anything else I can help you with?" asked the young woman as she passed them the room key.

"That will be it for now," Kiam said. He reached down and grabbed the bags. "If you have anything for a bad attitude please send that up immediately," he joked.

"Yes, sir. Enjoy your stay," the woman answered with a chuckle.

"Ya' ass ain't funny," Lissha snorted, heading to the elevators.

When they got to the room the décor took their breaths away. The white and tan room was spacious and airy. There was a living room, dining area and kitchen. Lissha walked through the huge glass doors out onto the balcony. By itself, the view was worth the thousand dollars a night they were paying.

Kiam placed their bags next to the dresser and joined Lissha on the terrace. Together they stared out over the New York skyline.

"This might be the last bit of peace we get. Hold on to it, we're going to need it," Kiam said as he left Lissha to enjoy the view.

After laying out his sweat pants and t-shirt, he grabbed the menu from the side of the bed.

"What you want to eat?" he called out.

Lissha returned inside. "What they got?" She took the menu from his hand and plopped down on the bed.

Scanning the pages she made a few mental choices then picked up the phone.

"Hello. Yes, I would like to place an order. Can I have an order of Shrimp Alfredo with extra shrimp, a side of asparagus and a salad with blue cheese dressing?" She paused to listen to the woman read back her order. "That's correct. What you want, Kiam?" she asked.

"I want a T-bone steak, medium well. A baked potato with sour cream and cheddar cheese, string beans, and ice tea." His mouth watered with anticipation.

Lissha placed his order and hung up.

"Place the call to the connect. Tell him we want to have a sit down tomorrow around five."

"Don't you think we should ask if he'll be available? People don't like it when you're abrasive, Kiam."

"Fuck I care what the next nigga like? And just so you know, I never ask—denying me ain't an option. Now make that call."

"Alright," Lissha said.

Walking over to her bag she grabbed the prepaid and placed the call. Surprisingly it went well and the date was set. "Everything is a go," she informed Kiam when she hung up from Riz.

"Aiight, we 'bout to make it happen."

"I'm about to make a bath happen," Lissha quipped. "I'm going to hop in the tub before the food comes."

"Do what you do," said Kiam.

She walked over to the table and took the complimentary bottle of champagne by the neck, then headed to the bathroom grabbing her bag along the way.

Lissha looked around the bathroom, the huge glass shower was inviting but that big white shiny tub was whispering her name. Turning on the water and adjusting it to her comfort, she began filling the tub then added her David Yurman shower gel.

Quickly she undressed and sank her weary body into the hot bubbles. Lissha poured herself a glass of champagne drank it down, closed her eyes and relaxed.

Lissha was soaking for only ten minutes when she heard Kiam entering the bathroom. When she opened her eyes he was passing the tub on the way to the shower butt naked.

"Ummm, excuse me," Lissha said, face wrinkled up.

"What's up?" Kiam asked as he turned on the shower.

"You don't see me over here?"

"Yeah, I see you," he responded.

"What are you doing?"

"What do it look like?" he asked, stepping into the shower.

"It looks like your standing in here butt ass naked."

"You seen a dick before right?" he asked sarcastically, closing the door and positioning himself under the water.

"Not like that," she mumbled.

Kiam acted as if she wasn't there. He lathered his body and let the water rinse the suds away.

Lissha watched every second of it.

When he was done, he dried off and headed out the bathroom the same way he walked in, dick swinging. As he passed by the tub Lissha crossed her legs.

"You need more bubbles," he said, looking down at her then pushing on without further comment.

"Close the door," Lissha yelled out.

She dipped her washcloth in the tub and put it on her face. She needed to cool off. Kiam had just given her fever. She spent another twenty minutes becoming one with the porcelin and putting to bed the thoughts that seeing Kiam's naked body had awakened.

As Lissha lotioned her skin she heard a knock on the door. She threw on her robe and joined Kiam in the dining area.

"Damn this looks good," she said as he uncovered each dish.

"I'm about to be on some real fat boy shit," announced Kiam as he took a seat.

Lissha sat across from him and they dug in.

Once their meal was done they retired to the living room. Lissha put her iPod on the docking station and sat by Kiam.

"So you ready for tomorrow?"

"I'm always ready. Business is business."

"Riz can be a real asshole."

"Don't worry I got it. Real recognize real," Kiam assured her.

Lissha sat looking at Kiam's oiled chest. She allowed her eyes to wander down to that print that sat up in his sweat pants.

Kiam picked up on her gaze and decided to defuse the situation, "So, when is the next time you going to visit Pop?"

"When we get back, I know he is going to want to know what is going on and how you are adjusting."

"Probably so. But Pop knows I'm about this life. That's why he entrusted me to come out here and oversee everything."

"Is that right?" A provocative look flashed in her eyes.

"Stop being fast," Kiam admonished like Lissha was a little hot tail girl.

"Shut up," she teased, giving him a little shove.

"On the real, your father is proud of you. You're out here standing stronger than most niggas. I respect that. Now I see firsthand why Big Zo speaks so highly of you," he said looking in her direction.

Lissha lowered her gaze. "I'm all he has."

"What about your mother? Pop never talked about her. Were they still together when he got locked up?"

"No. She's dead. She died when I was sixteen?"

"How? Was she sick or something?" he asked, hoping to get inside of her.

"No. She was gunned down."

Kiam noticed that her responses had become clipped. He saw no emotion on her face so he didn't feel that he was opening a wound that hadn't healed. "Was your mother as pretty as you? You must look like her because you don't look like Big Zo," he said.

"If you don't mind, I would rather not talk about my mother. She wasn't down for Daddy and she and I didn't get along. She's dead, that's all you need to know, and I'm all that he has."

"Well don't ever think he doesn't recognize your loyalty. Trust me, he knows," he confirmed.

Lissha smiled because Kiam was looking at her like he wanted to hug her. She stared at his lips and she became compelled to taste them.

Drifting into each other's gaze and feeling the heat that resonated between them, they both knew what was inevitable. Lissha was so ready to act on her feelings, but Kiam couldn't just throw his promise to Big Zo to the curb. At the last second he pulled back, leaving Lissha's eyes closed and her lips pursed to be kissed.

"Nah, ma."

She looked at him like, *you gotta be kidding!*

Kiam was as serious as the method of takeover he was primed to implement. He slid down to the other end of the couch, putting much needed space between them. "It's not safe over there," he quipped.

"Whatever, Kiam," she replied.

Before he could respond his cellphone rang. He answered it with relief in his voice.

"Hello."

"Hey baby," Faydrah's voice serenaded his senses.

"What's up with you?" he asked, getting up from the couch, heading to his bed.

He lay sideways across the bed, engrossed in what Faydrah was saying. When he burst out laughing, Lissha cut her eyes at him.

"Send me a picture, baby," Kiam said into the phone.

Overhearing him, Lissha's stomach turned. She stood up and tightened her robe, walked over to the mini bar and mixed herself a drink.

The more Kiam talked and laughed the more Lissha drank. By the time he hung up she was good and fucked up.

Walking to her bed adjacent to his, she looked on in disgust as Kiam smiled while flipping through the pictures Faydrah had just sent.

Lissha dropped her robe and let him get an eye full of what she knew he wanted. "I don't even see you standing there," he said, fighting the war between duty and desire.

"If you didn't notice your mouth wouldn't be moving." Lissha climbed in bed, pulled the cover over her head and went to sleep.

Kiam knew she was pissed but he needed her to be. They had almost crossed the line, and he would not be able to forgive himself if he did. He turned off the light, turned over and fell into his slumber.

Chapter 13
Back To Business

The next day Kiam and Lissha had a late lunch. Neither of them spoke a single word as they ate. Lissha felt a little awkward after last night, but Kiam wasn't even thinking about that, he was in full business mode. After lunch, they got dressed and prepared to go see Riz.

Kiam barricaded Lissha at the door. "Leave the money here," he said, noticing a satchel in her hand and correctly guessing what it contained.

She looked at him curiously.

"This is just a meeting, were not copping anything. Matter of fact, after this get-together he'll meet us halfway with the delivery."

Lissha was skeptical. Riz didn't travel.

"Don't doubt me," Kiam said, reading her mind. "I'm very persuasive."

Lissha didn't debate, she hurried back and stashed the satchel, then caught up with Kiam at the elevators.

When they reached the lobby, she stopped at the front desk and left explicit orders for their room not to be disturbed. She looked up and saw that Kiam was scanning the premises, eyeing everyone and everything. Kiam was in that zone.

They exited the hotel side by side. Lissha was wrapped in a leather jacket, stepping briskly to keep up with Kiam's pace. The wind whistled between the buildings as they headed to the car. Kiam had one thing on his mind and Riz was gonna respect it or get *disrespected.*

Pulling up to Riz's Brooklyn apartment building, Kiam and Lissha checked their guns and exited the vehicle. As they approached the steps a hot surge filled Kiam's body—he was ready.

When they reached the entrance, loud music blared through the door and the scent of weed funneled out into the hallway.

A barrage of bangs eventually summoned someone from inside. A tall, slender man with a nappy afro swung the door open, giving passage to Lissha and Kiam. "LiLi. How you been, ma?" He greeted her warmly.

"Hey Bean. I'm good," Lissha said, giving him a big hug.

"This your boy you told us about?" he inquired instantly, reaching out to shake Kiam's hand.

"What's good?" Kiam responded.

"I can't call it, come in." Bean moved to the side allowing Lissha and Kiam to pass.

"Riz, it's LiLi," Bean yelled out as he came up behind her and Kiam. "Y'all wanna burn something?" He sat down on the couch and pulled out a Dutch.

"Nah, we not here for that," Kiam answered for the both of them.

Bean looked at Lissha. "You sure?" he asked.

"Yeah, she sure," Kiam restated. He wanted it known that his decisions were not to be challenged.

Bean could already sense he was going to be a problem. He picked up the remote and turned the music off.

Riz walked in from out of the back sporting a black t-shirt, a pair of green army fatigue pants, and black Goretex boots. His short dreads were sticking up all over his head and his clothes were wrinkled like he had just rolled out of bed. Two massive Rottweilers were at his sides.

"Sit," he commanded. Each dog went to an opposite side of the couch and posted up.

"What's up LiLi?" he spoke, leaning in and hugging her neck.

"Tired as hell, you know that drive be kicking a bitch ass."

"Yeah, but the money we make together makes it worth it." Riz reminded.

He turned his attention to Kiam and flashed his iced up grill. "So you're the man that's running the show now?"

"With an iron fist," Kiam spat, looking on with a stony stare. Riz sat next to Bean and propped his feet up on an ottoman. He looked up at Kiam trying to assess him.

Kiam stood firm with his arms folded across his chest.

Riz grabbed a blunt from the ashtray and lit it up. Kiam watched his pallid mouth as he puffed and blew out smoke.

"So, what can I do for you?" Riz asked.

"I'm here to talk bricks and prices."

"I thought we already had an understanding on that?" He looked from Kiam to Lissha. Her expression told him that she was not calling shots.

Riz nodded his understanding and looked back at Kiam. "I'm not prepared to deliver any less than what Gator gets and I'm not excepting any less than he pays," he stated as he continued to inhale and exhale smoke.

"Fuck what you and Gator agreed to, that was then, this is now?" Kiam laid down his stake.

Riz looked at Bean, as if to ask if he was hearing Kiam right. Bean silently communicated that he was on point if Riz wanted him to lay Kiam's ass down.

Riz shook his head no and returned his full attention back to Kiam. "I see Big Zo has finally found a man in the mode of himself to take charge of his operation. But even Big Zo didn't come up in here and talk to me as hostile as you do."

"I'm not hostile, Bleed. But don't try to hold me to what another man agreed to. Gator has been demoted, therefore, anything he agreed to has to be renegotiated," Kiam made it clear, as he looked Riz dead in the eye without blinking.

Riz nodded his head in acknowledgement of Kiam's stance and decided to hear him out. "Talk numbers. Let me hear your proposal."

Kiam unfolded his arms and cupped his fist in the palm of his hand. "I ain't paying no more than fifteen. But I'm prepared to double the amount we usually get, and before long our order will quadruple," he predicted.

"In the meantime, you want to pay fifteen?" Riz laughed.

"Bleed, you see something comical about what I proposed?"

Lissha heard a slight chuckle behind Kiam's words and immediately tensed up; she hoped he wasn't about to air the room out. But Riz didn't respond to Kiam's unspoken challenge, and she was glad for that.

"Let's roll, Lissha," Kiam said.

Riz shot up off the couch waving his arms. "Hold the fuck up. Lissha we been doing business with you for years. You're one of my most loyal customers. Then you let this nigga come in here standing between good business?" he questioned harshly.

"She ain't got shit to say, you're talking to me. Lissha wait for me in the car," Kiam ordered.

"Lissha, is this how you're doing business now?"

"You heard him, Riz. Whatever he says, I back it." Lissha got up and headed to the door. When she touched the door knob the dogs began to growl.

"Stand down," Riz spoke out, calming the killer canines.

Lissha posted herself outside of the door gun drawn. If she heard ruckus she was going in blazing.

Inside the apartment Kiam remained poised and ready for whatever. He held Riz's stare with one just as confident. Fuck the odds, he had a full clip.

"I see you got big gorilla nuts," said Riz, coughing on the blunt he was blowin'.

"Nah, gorillas got big Kiam nuts," Kiam clarified.

"This man right here is the truth," Riz said to Bean, his longtime bodyguard. "I think I like this muthafucka. If he has the balls to come up in here by himself and challenge me on anything, I can just imagine how he crushes niggas back home."

Bean co-signed with a nod of his head. Real recognized real as Kiam had predicted to Lissha it would.

"Now I see why you're in, and Gator is out. I believe we'll do great business together."

"At fifteen a piece," Kiam maintained.

"No, I can't do fifteen. I can do fifteen-five if you get twenty. That's a ticket that reflects my confidence in your ability to tremendously increase your purchase in the near future."

Kiam pretended to think the offer over, but inside the deal was already sealed. He had been willing to pay up to seventeen a block so fifteen-five was gravy. Now he pushed for Riz to have the work delivered to him at a location that would be halfway between their two states.

Riz wrestled with him over it for a while before partially giving in to Kiam's proposition. "Ok, I'll have the product brought to Williamsport, PA. But you have to purchase thirty—for that amount I'll make it happen."

Kiam conceded the battle because he had won the war. He reached out and shook Riz's hand. "We can continue doing business," he said. "I'll have someone get at you in a few days."

"I look forward to it," replied Riz. "You need to smoke some of this heat wit' me." He held the blunt out to Kiam.

"Nah, I don't indulge," Kiam declined.

Riz could respect that. He nodded his head and sat the blunt back in the ashtray.

Kiam took a seat on the couch across from him. They talked over a few other particulars, then Kiam bid Riz goodbye. As he walked Kiam to the door, Riz threw an arm around his shoulder and whispered something in his ear. Kiam's expression revealed nothing and he said even less.

Lissha eased her hand out of her jacket and relaxed when Kiam came out looking like everything was good with him and Riz.

"You okay?" she asked as they strolled back to the car.

"You didn't hear any gunshots did you?"

"Is that a yes or a no, Kiam?" she sighed. *This muthafucka gets on my nerves. Just like a pair of panties that keeps crawling up my ass.*

"Do I frustrate you?" he asked, waiting for her to pop the locks.

"Yes, you do." Lissha slid behind the wheel. She pulled off and left him standing there looking stupid.

Kiam gritted his teeth and tapped his foot, counting the seconds in his head.

Lissha circled the block then pulled up to where he stood. The passenger window eased down and she leaned over in the seat.

"You need a ride?" she asked playfully.

He slid into the passenger seat and turned up the music to tune her out.

"Eww! Why you always so uptight? Don't you know how to relax and have a little fun?" She wrinkled her nose. "What, that bitch you were booed up with at the hotel the other day didn't fuck you good enough? I can always find you one of these BK hos to break you off."

"Why your mind always on my dick?"

She stuck her middle finger up at him and pulled off, determined not to say anything else to him unless it was absolutely necessary.

Through his peripheral, Kiam noticed Lissha's expression but he didn't have time to assuage her aggravation. His thoughts were occupied by what Riz had put in his ear.

Chapter 14
Hidden Alliances

Back in Ohio, Gator literally had his tongue in shorty's ear. She moaned and wrapped her legs tighter around his back as he thrust deeper inside her honey pot.

"Umm, baby, you know that's my weak spot. Please, I'm not ready to come yet."

"Nah, don't hold back. Come all over this black ass dick. It's yours, get it all," urged Gator, carrying her throughout the house, fucking her well.

"Is it mine?" she asked, feeling him all up in her stomach. His length and girth filled a bitch up.

"Hell yeah," he said, pressing her back against the wall. He gripped her ass with both hands and long stroked in and out.

Her nails dug deep into his back and she bit into his shoulder to keep from screaming. "Ooh, shit!" she cried as her love began to come down.

Gator felt her body tense as her walls re-gripped his thick wand. He slammed in and out of her with powerful gyrations, pulling all the way out to the tip, then ramming in balls deep. She yelled out his name. He grunted out hers, and they both exploded simultaneously.

A short while later they were back in bed. Gator was smoking a blunt; she was stroking his dick lovingly. "It gets better every time," she told him. "I want it to be mine for real."

"It can be, if you do what you gotta do," he said. He didn't have to expound, they had talked about it before. Now that Kiam was on the scene and had replaced him as boss, it was time to really press her to slump Lissha.

"I told you, we don't have to do it like that. We can just strike out on our own," she said, releasing his meat and sitting up.

He passed her the blunt. "You know it's blood in and blood out with that bitch. And now that she has that nigga Kiam rolling with her, she would really be on some vengeance shit," Gator predicted.

"We could talk to Big Zo."

"What the fuck for? You think he's gonna go against his own flesh and blood?"

She thought about that for a minute. "You're right," she had to agree. "But getting rid of LiLi now won't set us free. We would have to do Kiam too because from what I'm hearing he ain't nothing nice."

"Don't you hop on that nigga's dick too," he chastised.

"No, baby. You don't have to worry about that. I'm your bitch even though we have to keep it hid. I believe in you." She looked down into his eyes convincingly.

Gator pulled her head down and covered her mouth with his. He kissed her deep then stared up into her eyes. "That's why I'ma wife you, boo. Because you ride hard for a nigga. I know you and Lissha and 'em go back further than you and I do, but it's time for us to make our own moves."

"I agree," she said, contemplating his insistence that she kill one of her Blood Money Crew members for the sake of being with him.

"I'ma have that nigga Kiam smashed," he vowed before blowing her a gun.

Shit was about to get hectic.

112

Chapter 15
A City Under Siege

Now that Kiam had the connect firmly in his corner it was time to turn up. He had Lissha and Gator to take him around to each one of their dope houses and introduce him personally to the people that ran them. If a spot wasn't pumping hard enough, he replaced the person running it with a younger, hungrier trap boy under their employ. A couple niggas protested their demotion and got something real hot put in their domes.

"Niggas get a little rank and grow content. The problem is that y'all have them on salary. So they get paid the same whether the trap makes five bands or fifty. What incentive do they have to trap harder? Muthafuckas probably been laying up in some pussy when they were supposed to be serving," he said as he sat in Lissha's study looking over the numbers that each spot produced.

The cryptic figures were stored in a program on Lissha's laptop. She stood over Kiam's shoulder decoding the numbers for him.

Gator scowled from across the room where he sat in an over-stuffed lounge chair with his feet resting on a mauve and grey ottoman that matched the chair. *This nigga has something to say about everything, he said to himself.*

Kiam pushed away from the desk. He steepled his hands under his chin, closed his eyes, and thought everything over. The numbers were pitiful for an operation the size of theirs. When he opened his eyes he had a clear plan.

"From now on the workers were going to get paid off of commission. The more A.C. they sold, the more they'd make." A.C. is what they called crack in Cleveland.

"We're gonna give them 60/40 packs."

"What the fuck is that?" questioned Gator.

Kiam explained that 60/40 packs meant that they would give the trap boys bundles of pre-packaged rocks and they would split the proceeds 60/40.

"We'll get the bigger slice of the pie, and it'll still be gravy because we get sixty percent from all of the houses. On the flip side, this allows the workers to make much more than they had been making on salary."

"That sounds good," Lissha co-signed, processing the math in her head.

"I don't like it. They'll be eating as good as we are," voiced Gator.

"I didn't ask you if you liked it or not. Some niggas didn't like being demoted," Kiam reminded him. He didn't have to elaborate, it was still fresh in Gator's mind what happened to those that bucked the changes that Kiam was initiating.

Gator fought hard to keep his feelings from showing on his face. He got up and went to the kitchen to get a Heineken out of the refrigerator.

"I don't see how y'all made it this far following that clown nigga's lead," Kiam said to Lissha.

"He wasn't always like this. When he first came aboard he was on point. But now I think the money and the bitches has made him soft. He's not trying to elevate higher because he saw what happened to Daddy and others when they reached the top in their game."

"Did he work for Pop before he fell?" asked Kiam, wondering how Gator had wagged an indictment.

"No, Gator saved my life, that's how we met him. As appreciation Daddy plugged him in and he rose from there. Like I said, he was hungry back then, now he's not. Daddy must've recognized that," Lissha shared.

Kiam didn't press her for details on how Gator saved her life, he knew the story would come out sooner than later. It didn't matter though, that was then. He had the nigga figured out.

"Niggas like Gator are afraid to reach for the top because they believe that once you get to the pinnacle, there's nowhere to go but down," he said.

"Is he wrong?"

"If we're talking about the average nigga, he's not. For a nigga like myself, it don't apply. Once I reach the top, I'ma just ascend to another stratosphere," Kiam said.

"You're so fucking humble," Lissha remarked sarcastically.

Kiam looked at her and shrugged his shoulders. His arrogance made her secret treasure throb.

Gator returned with a beer and a sandwich in hand. The three of them talked business strategy for the next hour. After hearing Gator's input, Kiam was better able to comprehend how he had at least helped rebuild Big Zo's operation to its present status.

Gator received a text and announced that he had to leave and handle a personal matter. As soon as he left, Kiam stared at Lissha silently.

"What?" she asked, gathering up the empty Heineken bottle and the plate that Gator had left on the floor. Kiam continued to stare. *"What?"* she asked again with more emphasis.

"You're fuckin' that lame," He said, coming from left field. "I can tell because that muthafucka is very comfortable in your house. That nigga 'round here moving like he paying the mortgage on this bitch. All up in your refrigerator and shit."

"I didn't snatch your dick outta Mrs. Corporate America's mouth. So don't be all in my shit," Lissha said, never breaking eye contact until she sashayed past him and into the kitchen.

A minute later Kiam came and sat on the padded stool at the kitchen's island.

Lissha had already made up her mind that she was not having it out with him about something that wasn't his concern. His directions from Big Zo was to take over the organization and elevate it to a new height, not sniff her fucking thongs.

She busied herself at the sink apprehensively waiting for Kiam to try to go there.

"So what's up, LiLi? You in your feelings now?" he asked.

"Not hardly."

"Good. Because we have a whole lot of work to do. You're slipping, shorty."

"And how is that?"

"Storing numbers in your computer is straight reckless. It don't matter that they are coded, the feds got big head geniuses that can decode that shit in the blink of an eye."

"I'll uninstall the whole program and delete that from my hard drive," said Lissha, turning off the faucet and drying her hands on a towel.

"No. Get rid of the whole computer," ordered Kiam.

Lissha didn't argue about it, she agreed to burn the computer ASAP.

"In the meantime, go strap up. I think I know why our trap on Avon is pumping small numbers."

"Strap up? Wait a minute. I'm not defying you, but I put my life on those boys that run that house. They're on the square, Kiam. We don't have to kill them," said Lissha in the defense of three of their most loyal trap boys.

Kiam smiled at her incorrect conclusion. He had already collected his Intel. "Nah, I'm not gonna crush JuJu and 'em, we're gonna crush the niggas that are in their way," he revealed.

"Greg and Fat?" She had done her homework too. Long before Kiam came home.

Kiam nodded.

"You don't even have to get your hands dirty with their blood. I have some killahs on it already," she revealed.

"Oh yeah? Who are you talking about, ya boy?" Cynicism rang loudly.

"I'm not going to dignify that with a response," she tossed back.

"Who are these so-called killahs you're talking about?" he probed with an eyebrow raised.

Lissha came and sat on a stool next to Kiam. She smiled at him reassuringly. "You don't have to worry about these killahs, I put my life on them. They're tested and proven, and it's about time you meet them."

"I bet they're as soft as ya boy," he wise-cracked.

"Softer." She smiled. "But much more deadly."

It was time for her to introduce him to three gangsters in high heels and Maybelline.

Chapter 16
Distracted

Lissha pulled into her driveway blasting her radio, feeling like a beautiful black goddess. She had just gotten her hair, nails, and feet done, everything waxed, and did a little shopping. She popped her trunk, jumped out and grabbed her bags and headed inside.

Placing the bags in her bedroom she ran a tub of water and hit her satellite radio to set the mood. She had been running hard all day but the girls were set to come over later. *Damn.* She still had to cook and get the house ready. But she still needed to grab a few hours for herself.

She put all of her clothes away, then stripped down to her birthday suit and stepped into her bubble filled hot tub. Laying her head back against the cushion, she settled in and dozed off.

She awoke an hour later still feeling tired. She stood up in the tub, turned the shower on and quickly washed and rinsed off. The water put some pep in her step. She oiled and scented her skin and slipped into a pair of tight white boy shorts and a tank top.

Walking into her living room she picked up the remote and turned the radio all the way up. Frank Ocean's *Thinkin' Bout You* blared from the system. Singing along Lissha poured herself a tall glass of white wine, rolled a blunt and plopped down on her soft loveseat and went into chill mode.

After a few sips of wine and a half of a blunt, Lissha was feeling relaxed. In between songs she heard her cell phone ringing in the other room. "Dang, can't a bitch chill," she sighed, jumping up and hurrying to reach her phone.

By the time she reached the bedroom they had hung up. She checked the Caller ID and saw three missed calls from Kiam. They hadn't spoken in a couple days so she called him right back to find out what was up. Strolling back into the living room she held the phone to her ear with her shoulder and waited for him to pick up.

"Hello?" he answered.

"What's up?" she plopped back down on the loveseat.

"Come outside,"

"For what?" she asked, reaching for her glass of wine.

"I need to talk to you for a minute."

"Well, come in," she said, throwing her hand to the side.

"Shorty, just come outside real quick."

Lissha sat the phone down next to her then put her head back. This negro must think I'm his puppet. She sat forward, looked at the window, and blew her breath out real hard. Kiam could really work a nerve when he wanted to and it seemed like he took pleasure in doing so.

Rising to her feet she walked over to the door, slipped into her flip flops and headed outside. As she walked down the walkway Kiam's eye's settled on her 2 carat diamond belly ring that sparkled in the sunlight. She walked up to the car and got in with her attitude on max.

"What's up?" she asked, looking at him with her eyebrows raised.

"Why you outside naked?"

"I'm not naked, Kiam. Anyway what's up, man?"

"Why you giving me all this attitude? You missed me?" he asked, locking eyes with her

"Yeah, I missed you like a thorn in my ass," she turned her head to the side.

He started to say something else slick but decided to get back to business. "I need to have a sit down with your girls tonight."

"Why tonight? What if I have something else planned?"

"Cancel it. I rearranged everybody else, now I need to get with the girls to see where their heads are at before I put them on this mission."

"I told you, I got them." She huffed.

"So you trust them bitches with your life?"

"I certainly do."

"Well, you may know them like that, but I don't. And I'm not taking a fucking gamble on my shit. Oh yeah, and let's not forget that you sent one of them 'trust them with my life' bitches to suck my dick."

"Fuck you," Lissha spat then turned and grabbed the handle to get out the car. Kiam clutched her thigh and gripped it tightly, preventing her from exiting the vehicle. Lissha turned toward him with her whole face bald up, her eyes low, and her breathing quick.

"Get your hand off my leg," she said through clenched teeth, as if each word was a warning all by itself.

Seeing his smug expression made her want to punch him in the face. She balled up her fist, but his words were quicker than her hands.

"No disrespect, ma. I know those are your girls. My bad," he apologized.

Lissha just looked at him. The apology was half ass but it was a start. More than he had given before.

"Look, on the real, I need to feel them out," he explained. "Don't take it personal, Lissha, I'm just the type of man that don't like to leave anything to chance. I gotta make sure that every aspect, and everybody, is on point."

"I'm not new to this Kiam. If you're such a boss nigga, recognize that I'm that chick who'll be the eyes in the back of your head," she spat as she opened the door.

"You mad at me?" Kiam teased, giving her that disarming smile that he could turn on and off in the blink of an eye.

"Your ass is bipolar." Lissha looked down. "You gonna move your hand or what?"

"Stop frontin', you know you want my hands all over you."

Lissha shook her head. She had never met anyone like him; he was the kind of nigga a bitch loved to hate. She grappled his wrist and moved his hand. "You wouldn't know what to do with me," she replied tersely.

Kiam's eyes settled on her ass as she rose from the seat. "I bet you're itching to find out," he said as she walked away.

Lissha hurried up the walkway; she needed to get as far away from him as possible. The way he made her feel she wanted to invite him in so they could just fuck out all that aggression and get it over with.

"LiLi?" Kiam called out.

She kept her stride, ignoring his arrogant butt. When she reached the door she turned around with an exaggerated flourish, "What?"

"Be good."

Lissha flipped him the bird. Kiam just laughed and pulled off.

When Lissha got inside she sparked up her blunt. She took a few deep pulls and sat it down. Kiam always caused her emotions to do summersaults. She was trying to follow Daddy's orders but every time she got around Kiam it got harder and harder.

She sat for a few more minutes then headed into the kitchen to start cooking. As she went through the refrigerator gathering everything she needed for the meal, Kiam's question played in her head: *You trust them bitches?*

Hell yeah, without reservation she trusted her girls. When they ran up in someone's house to take that blood money or had to push somebody's scalp back, they had never let her down. She placed the food on the counter and thought back to the countless missions they had been on and how each one of them held their own. *Damn what Kiam thinks about them.*

Lissha went out in the backyard and put the beef ribs on the grill, marinating them in her homemade sauce. Her taste buds salivated in anticipation as she headed back inside to prepare the potato salad, baked beans and corn on the cob. In a short time she had everything prepped. She placed the beans in the oven and the potato salad in the refrigerator then made a toss salad to go with the meal.

While the meat simmered she hopped in the shower, threw on some jeggings and a t-shirt and got ready for the girls. Quickly she rolled a few blunts and made sure that the wine and the 1800 was on deck. It was about to go down.

A few hours later...

Lissha walked over to her iPod station and programed some music, turning the volume up loud. Just as she headed to the kitchen the doorbell rang. On the way to the door she grabbed a blunt off the glass cocktail table and put some fire to it.

She checked the peephole, and then opened the door singing, "Alriiight...." Lissha was happy to see her ladies. She smiled and blew cloud smoke in Treebie's face.

"That's what the fuck I'm talking about," Treebie said, taking the blunt from Lissha's hand.

Lissha moved back allowing the girls to pass. Bayonna was wearing a pair of red, tight-fitting skinny Jeans. She snapped her fingers and did a two-step to the music that boomed throughout the house. Donella followed suit doing her signature move, dropping to the floor and bringing it back up.

"Let's get this shit going," she said, throwing her purse on the floor next to the couch and going for the wine bottle and a glass.

Lissha went into the kitchen and grabbed the 1800 out the freezer along with the shot glasses. Bayonna lit another blunt and started it into rotation. "Damn, LiLi, it smells good as hell up in here," she complimented.

"Yeah, you know I put my ass in it this time," Lissha joked.

"I hope the fuck not," coughed Treebie, choking on that good ass loud.

"You know you love my sexy Apple Bottom," Lissha said, making her cheeks jump.

"Bitch you nasty," Treebie laughed.

They all sat down and immediately began taking shots to the head and passing blunts. Lissha puff puff passed, then began her tutelage.

"Alright, we got another hit to do this Friday. Everything is lined up and we stand to make a grip. After we do this one, we get two of our own." Hearing that, the girl's ears perked up.

Lissha took another shot of 1800 before continuing. It went down smoothly. "Also, we got this new deal with our connect," she sat her glass down and folded her hands. "From now on, y'all will have to pick up in Pennsylvania."

"Riz agreed to that?" interrupted Treebie.

"Yeah, him and Kiam worked it out. Actually, Kiam just demanded that shit and stood his ground," Lissha replayed.

Bayonna and Donella nodded their heads respectfully because they both knew that it took a man with a strong will to get Riz to bend. Treebie didn't say or do anything; she wasn't ready to jump on Kiam's jock.

"Now, just because the pickup spot and the route have changed, we still need to make sure that shit arrives safely and in a timely fashion," Lissha strongly emphasized.

"You know how we do," Treebie said, pulling her gun from her waist sitting it on the table.

"You know I hold's my own," Donella chimed in.

"Enough said." Bay sealed the deal.

Lissha nodded her head. "That's what I like to hear. And don't forget about Fat and Greg, they're in the way of business."

"We're on it like yesterday." Donella assured her.

"That's what's up." She poured each of them a shot.

They grabbed their glasses and brought them together. "Let's get this money." Lissha toasted. The women clinked glasses then threw back their shots.

Setting her glass on the table Lissha announced. "Ladies, Kiam will be here in a little while. He wants to bring us up to speed on this next move. Now, I'm warning everyone beforehand that he can be a little forceful, but Daddy put him in charge so it is what it is."

Donella didn't see a problem with it, she just hoped for some of that prime beef Kiam selfishly walked around with. Bayonna had yet to meet him, but from all that was being said she knew that he would be impressive.

Treebie grabbed a blunt and sat back. She hadn't seen Kiam since they put Finch and them on their backs.

"Let's eat," suggested Donella. Her munchies had kicked in and the smell of those ribs caused her mouth to water.

"Bay, come help me fix the plates," said Lissha, rising to her feet and looking at Treebie puffing away, lost in thought. Lissha silently prayed that her right-hand didn't bump heads with Kiam.

Lissha and Bayonna went into the kitchen and fixed the plates, then headed back to the living room. "I'm about to hurt this," Bayonna said as she sat down and began to dig in.

Just as Lissha brought her fork to her mouth the bell rang and a sinking feeling rose in her gut. She used the remote to turn the music down on her way to the door. Bayonna and Donella looked over at Treebie whose mood had gotten very serious.

Lissha pulled the door open and her eyes unconsciously roamed up and down Kiam's frame; he stood tall with his white t-shirt clinging to his form and giving a slight hint of his well-developed chest. His black Seven jeans fitted just right resting on top of his boots. He looked as scrumptious as the ribs, like his beef would melt in a bitch's mouth just as fast as the barbeque.

"Can I come in?" he asked, breaking Lissha's stare. When he wasn't fussing and bossing her around he had a nice smooth baritone.

"You gonna let me in or what?" he repeated, flashing his sexy smile.

"Whatever," she replied nervously, like a school girl with a crush.

Kiam stepped pass her and the trace of his Gucci Guilty Black cologne caressed her nostrils. Lissha closed her eyes for a second and inhaled deep. Damn. She was going to have to control of herself.

Back in the living room, she made the introductions. "You met Treebie and Donella," she gestured to the two. "This is Bayonna." She nodded toward Bay.

Bayonna wiped her hands and stood to shake his. "Nice to meet you," she extended, looking no more than sixteen to Kiam.

"No doubt," he replied then spoke to the others. "Ladies."

"Good to see you again," Donella smirked.

"What's up?" said Treebie, nodding her head slightly.

Kiam took Lissha's seat. Leaning slightly forward, he was ready to jump right in to the business.

"Um, excuse you, I'm sitting there," Lissha said, coming over to him.

He looked up at her. "Well, you can't sit on my lap so you might wanna sit somewhere else."

Lissha frowned. And with a theatrical huff she picked up her plate and sat across from him by Treebie. The girls watched their little back and forth exchange.

"Ladies, I know this is your girls night, so I'll make this quick," began Kiam condescendingly, but his tone still carried command. Everyone stopped eating and sat up.

"I've been moving shit around a lot, and quite a few things have changed in a very short time. If you're wondering where you fit in, and what your new roles are gonna be in this organization, I'm about to break it all down."

Kiam rested his arms on the back of the sofa and looked from one face to the other. It was clear to him that he held their attention. "I want y'all to slide further into the background, no more hand-to-hand sales or dealing with the workers.

"What I do want is for y'all to make the pickups. This first pickup is scheduled for next week. We gonna meet them in Williamsport, Pennsylvania. I need everyone to be on their A game. No slip ups."

Kiam detected a slight wrinkle in Treebie's forehead that hadn't been there a second ago. He would deal with that. In the meantime he went on. "I don't know these niggas we're dealing with, just like I don't know y'all. But Big Zo said y'all official and Lissha confirmed that, so my trust is in their assessment only. Y'all might not want to make them look bad."

"Let me get this shit straight." Treebie cut in. "You want us to ride out to PA and meet these niggas. Make the transfer and bring you the shit, then what?"

"What you mean then what?"

"Just what I said," Treebie shot back.

Kiam smiled at her audacity, recalling her get-down from the first ecounter. *Just like I figured, a pit bull in a skirt,* he assessed, and then got serious. "There ain't no then what. I got it from there," he declared.

"Nah. That sounds like you'll eventually cut us out. We in this shit all the way with you or you can take the fucking ride," Treebie countered. She sat back, crossed her legs and lit up.

Kiam looked at her sideways and his coal black eyes turned even darker. Lissha noticed the change and pounced in. "Look, we're not doing this," she said, directing her words more to Treebie than to Kiam. "This is the way Daddy wants this shit handled. We need all hands on deck." She looked over at Treebie who had her eyes fixed on Kiam.

Treebie took another deep pull on her blunt and blew the smoke out in Kiam's direction. "You right Li, it's business. You got my full cooperation." She looked Kiam up and down and smiled, then picked her gun up off the table and headed to the bathroom. Her intended disrespect rung loud and clear.

Kiam chuckled.

Lissha, who had already figured out what that meant, stood up. "Kiam, can I please talk to you in the other room?" she asked.

"Hold up!" He brushed past her and headed to the bathroom.

When Treebie opened the door she was startled by Kiam standing in the doorway. He pushed her back in the bathroom and closed the door. "Let me explain some shit to you. I don't have time for petty bullshit. I know you official but don't test that shit on me. I don't fold like them other pussy ass niggas. You here because Big Zo and Lissha say you cool. But if you make me feel differently, I know how to make my problems disappear." His eyes bored into hers.

"You ain't talking 'bout nothin', I feel the same way," she said.

"You can feel however you want to, just respect my position so I don't have to reinforce it on you,"

Treebie stared him in the eye and her lashes didn't blink. "I know what your position is, Kiam. The problem is I don't know what you did to earn it,"

Kiam moved dangerously close grabbing her by the jaw applying a little pressure. "Some shit ain't for you to know, just play ya fucking position. Or did you fuck your way into it?" Kiam slapped her with words.

Pulling her face back she gritted. "You don't know shit about me." Her breathing rapidly increased.

"I know more than you think I do. But I'll let you worry about that." His wry smile unnerved her but Treebie remained cool.

"There's nothing for me to worry about," she calmly asserted.

Kiam chuckled as he stepped back out of her space. "Enjoy the rest of your evening," he stated politely. Like he really did know something.

When he swung the door open. Lissha was standing in the hall with a look of nervousness all over her face. She looked past him at Treebie. "What happened?"

"Nothing I can't handle," Kiam said moving past her.

She turned her attention to Treebie who looked like she was ready to kill somebody. "Tree, what the fuck is going on?"

"Just leave me alone for a minute." She pushed Lissha back slamming the bathroom door in her face.

Resting her hands on the counter she stared in the mirror replaying Kiam's words in her mind and wondering what all Big Zo had told him.

When Lissha walked back in the living room her wheels were turning. She looked over at Kiam engrossed in a conversation with Donella and Bay and cut in. "I need to speak to you Kiam," she said in a demanding tone.

Just as Kiam was about to answer her request his cell rang. He looked at the screen and smiled. "Another time," he said to Lissha as he stood up and headed for the door.

"Hello," Kiam said into the phone.

"Hey baby." It was Faydrah. The happiness of her tone let him know that she was smiling. Kiam loved that.

"Hey you," he spoke back, using an affectionate greeting from their past.

"*Hey you,*" she echoed with sweet familiarity. "What you doin'?"

"Thinking about my girl," he answered reaching for the door knob.

"I have something special for you. Can I see you tonight?"

"Of course."

"Hit me when you get close,"

"I can't wait to hit you." He turned to look at Lissha coming his way.

Faydrah giggled as the thoughts of their last time together filled her mind and moistened her panties. "You so bad," she cooed.

"I work hard at it," he boasted jokingly, and then added, "I'll see you in a minute." He disconnected the call and returned his attention to Lissha. She was eyeing him with a face of stone.

"Anything else?" he asked

"No, I'm good," she said with a little attitude in her voice.

Kiam smiled "I'll catch up with you in a couple days. Make sure the girls are on point." He opened the door and started down the short walkway.

"They're on it, just chill and go lay up with Mrs. Fax and Copy," Lissha hurled, resting one hand on her hip and the other on the door preparing to slam it.

Kiam didn't dignify her smart comment with a response, he got in his truck and drove off.

As soon as she reached the living room the girls went in. "That nigga there. Whew!" Donella shouted out. "Fo' real, did you tell Big Zo how he is?"

"Trust me, daddy knows how Kiam is, he schooled him for three or four years. True, he can come off a little too hard but he's the butt-naked truth."

"That nigga ain't shit just like the rest," Treebie gritted looking at Lissha with homicide in her eyes.

"What the fuck did he say to you?" Lissha asked with a deep crease in her forehead.

"I just don't like that muthafucka. Call it my in-tui-fuckin'-tion."

"Sheeeiittt, what's not to like about him?" Donella disagreed. She tossed a shot back and shook her head in regret of a lost opportunity. "I still can't believe I let that sexy muthafucka leave the room without coming up off some dick?"

"What can you say, he knows what he wants," Bayonna surmised.

"Girrrlll, that nigga ain't nothing nice. Maybe we can pass that nigga around like this blunt," laughed Donella as she lit up.

Treebie turned her lip up. "Fuck that nigga. His ass on borrowed time, and I hope I'm the one that gets to punch his clock," she intoned bitterly, reaching for the blunt.

"You need to calm the fuck down," Lissha said grabbing a couple plates from the table and walking to the kitchen.

Bay took the blunt from Treebie, inhaled deep then served them up with some jewels. "Kiam is just carrying out Big Zo's instructions," she reminded her. "Ain't no telling how many nights they stayed up planning all of this. We do have to be on point.

"None of us has ever been on this level. Gator always handled the pickup and we just played our roles once it made it to Cleveland. We in the big league now, ladies. Let's woman up and do what he needs us to do," she encouraged the crew. She looked at Treebie to see if she comprehended, then she sat up and poured her and Donella a glass of wine.

Lissha stood in the kitchen door looking at the girls. Kiam had just shaken everything up, his presence changed the whole dynamic of everything they were doing. She knew that it was only a matter of time before this whole situation would come to a head. She was just praying shit didn't get bloody.

Chapter 17
Something Special

Kiam pulled into Faydrah's driveway and deaded his engine. He picked up his cell and called inside.

"Come open the door," he said, and then hung up.

He hopped out the car and strode to the door; with each step a little bit of excitement crept into his usually cool demeanor. Faydrah was the peace in the middle of his storm.

He approached the door and knocked a few times. Within seconds the door came open and his eyes were treated to her standing in the doorway with a light blue, silk lace bra and a matching G-string peeking out from under an open sheer robe.

"Hey babe," she said, moving into his arms.

Kiam received her tenderly. He squeezed her tightly as he walked her backwards and closed the door. Her baby soft skin was a comfort to his hands as he ran them down her back and over her butt.

"This is what a man needs after a long day," he whispered in her ear.

Faydrah melted in his strong arms, inhaled the masculine fragrance of his cologne, and began placing tender kisses on his neck and face. "I missed you," she confessed as her lips found his.

Kiam gave in to her kisses. He happily closed his eyes and enjoyed her soft lips and tongue as her hands gripped his back. He pulled back and sank his teeth into one of her breast then ran his tongue up her neck and kissed her again. Faydrah's entire body caught on fire.

"Baby wait," she whispered. His touch was taking over the moment and she did not want that.

"I thought you had something for me," he cooed in her ear as he fumbled with the back of her bra.

Faydrah reached up and grabbed his hands. "I do, but you need to let me be in control for a little while," she panted, pulling back to look into his eyes.

She could see the unbridled passion, and the fire from his soul pierced hers.

"You gonna come to the door wearing an outfit that says 'fuck me', then say hold up. Where they do that at?" Kiam said, stepping out of his boots.

"Don't worry, I got you. Just relax and let me do me," she said, taking his hand and leading him to the backyard.

Kiam's eyes settled on the string that lay perfectly between her ass cheeks.

As Faydrah slid open the patio door Kiam rested the rock up against her softness. "My boy wanna holla at you.,"

"Tell him I'ma have a long deep conversation with him if he'll just be patient." She moved forward and walked onto the deck.

Kiam was pleasantly surprised. Her yard was like a resort. She had a huge deck with a Jacuzzi on it surrounded by sheer white curtains. There was an in-ground pool and a huge gazebo surrounded by netting with a white cushioned lounge chair swing in the middle. There were flowers in an array of bright colors strategically placed throughout the yard and tall, potted palm trees. Flickering lanterns lit the area, setting the mood just right. Kiam gazed up into the pitch black sky; there were a few stars which flickered dimly in the far distance.

"You hungry," Faydrah asked as she opened the lids on the platters.

"You know I like to eat," he responded with a sexy smirk on his face.

"Come sit down." Faydrah smiled. She had prepared his favorite foods and couldn't wait to see his reaction.

Kiam took a seat at the table. His eyes lit up when he looked down at his plate and saw deep fried catfish nuggets, baked macaroni and cheese with five cheeses, collard greens and a bowl of banana pudding. She had remembered that these were the dishes that Miss Charlene used to make for him every Sunday.

"Thank you, baby," he said, standing up and kissing her lightly.

"I told you I got you," she replied affectionately.

They shared a few sweet kisses before they began to eat.

The food was delicious, and the ambience was perfect. They talked and laughed about the old days and how bad Kiam was. It felt good to him to have someone that he could just be himself around, someone who shared his past and was a perfect addition to his present.

When their plates were empty, Faydrah began clearing the table.

Kiam stood up. "Where's the bathroom, baby?"

"It's down the hall on the left." She pointed through the curtain in the doorway.

After Kiam disappeared into the house, Faydrah prepared the next stage of her plan.

She turned on her Pandora, hit the remote to dim the yard lights, lit a few candles then started up the Jacuzzi.

After washing his hands and rinsing his mouth with the Listerine he found in the medicine cabinet, Kiam grabbed a wash cloth and towel and hopped in the shower. It had been a hot, muggy, day and he wanted to get refreshed.

While Kiam showered, Faydrah poured them both a drink and placed them in the cup holder on the side of the Jucuzzi. Looking up at a full moon, she slipped out of her robe and bra then stepped into the warm water.

The music was playing and the candles were flickering. Against this romantic backdrop Kiam emerged from inside wrapped in a black fluffy towel.

Faydrah enjoyed looking at him, he was sexy without effort, and he was all hers again.

Kiam stood in front of the tub gazing down at her with hunger in his eyes. He licked his lips slowly and let the towel that was wrapped around his thirty-four inch waist fall to the ground. His iron rod stood straight up, ready to do damage.

When he stepped in the Jacuzzi, Faydrah leaned up and kissed the head of his dick, sending chills up his spin.

Pulling back, Kiam said, "Tonight let me please *you*." He went to his knees and lifted her out the water. Placing her on the edge of the tub, he slipped off her G-string.

Faydrah's center throbbed as he gripped her firm in his arms, threw her legs over his shoulders, and placed tender kisses on the insides of her thighs. His tongue slid to the crease of her leg causing her breath to quicken as he came closer to the furnace that burned at her center.

Kiam continued his tease until he felt she couldn't take anymore. He delicately ran his tongue up and down her pulsating kitty, then he zoned in on her bud of pleasure and alternated between sucking it gently, and firm.

Faydrah moaned and gripped the back of his head, prodding him to suck harder and take her to the point of no return.

Kiam knew what she wanted, but he wasn't ready for her volcano to erupt. He continued to tease and please at the same time.

Faydrah threw her head back as Avant and KeKe Wyatt crooned through her speakers My First Love.

Long as I live/ You will be my/My first love/My first love/ and my only love ...

Faydrah gyrated and quivered as Kiam ran his tongue up and down her wet lips.

Showing no mercy, he held her firm in place, sucking and circling her clit with the tip of his tongue until she rained h.er sticky sweetness inside his mouth.

Releasing her legs he came up and looked in her eyes. "Thank you, baby" he whispered softly.

"For—what?" she asked breathlessly.

"For just being you."

"Kiam, I love you," she rasped, wrapping her arms around his neck and tracing his lips with her sweet tongue.

"I love you too, baby. Now come ride this dick," he commanded.

He definitely didn't have to ask twice. Faydrah stood up and looked down at his mammoth erection with desire. Kiam leaned back, positioning himself for her to straddle him. He put his arms out along the edge of the Jacuzzi and prepared to get the royal treatment like the king he was.

Straddling his lap Faydrah wrapped as much of her hand as she could around his throbbing thicknesses and guided him inside of her. She took her time sliding down on his pole, inch by wonderful inch, until she had all of him inside her.

"Ooh, yesssssss," she moaned, rocking her hips and sliding up and down his length.

Kiam stared into her eyes taking each breath as she released it. She was riding his dick like she owned it. Kiam placed one hand on the small of her back pulling her into him. She leaned back angling his dick just right to hit that special spot deep inside of her.

Faydrah closed her eyes and gripped his shoulders as her pussy began to contract. "I'm about to cum," she moaned.

"Get that shit baby,."

"Kiam," she cried as she rode faster, teasing her spot until she came long and hard. She bit into his neck while continuing to ride.

Rain drops began to drizzle down on them as he held her in place.

"Kiam, baby, it's starting to rain," she whispered feeling another orgasm coming on.

"Mmmmm, fuck the rain, ride this dick."

Her soft breast rested against his chest and he held her in his arms, never wanting to let her go.

Faydrah felt so connected to him she could read his thoughts. "Kiam, you're all I need," she moaned. It came out as a cry of pleasure, from a place no other man had ever touched.

Her eyes became misty as she felt his thrusts pleasuring those tight walls that caressed his steel.

"All this dick is yours, ma," he said, pulling her all the way down on him.

The rain came down harder, but Kiam paid it no mind, he was caught up in the enjoyment of her muscle play. Faydrah was the only woman that could get him wrapped up in every emotion of sex and make him let go when he wanted to hold back.

He pressed his lips lightly against hers and probed into her mouth with his tongue. Faydrah shuddered to his every touch, he was the air she needed to breath and she inhaled him deeply.

She felt as if she had stepped outside of her body. Becoming overwhelmed by the love they shared, she broke down. Tears slid down her face as they both exploded.

"Kiam, I never want to lose you," Faydrah cried.

"You won't." He held her tighter.

Wrapped in each other's arms they both breathed heavily while the rain poured over them.

"What else you got for daddy?" he whispered into her ear.

Faydrah looked into his eyes. "I think I need you to make me touch my toes," she purred.

Kiam was about that. "Stand up and grab the edge of the tub," he directed.

Faydrah wasted no time getting into position. She braced herself while looking over her shoulder. He looked sexy coming up behind her stroking his dick as rain water rushed over his smooth chocolate skin.

He grabbed her ass and spread her round cheeks. Looking down at her flower opening up for him turned Kiam on. He wrapped his hand around his stiff muscle and guided it inside her wet, hot walls.

Faydrah held in her breath and bit down on her lip. With each deep stroke she tossed that ass back at him.

"All of this belongs to me," he proclaimed, gripping her hips and forcing deep grunts to escape her lips.

"Yes Kiam," she mumbled.

"Make this pussy suck my dick," he growled.

Faydrah pushed back and rotated her hips and squeezed her muscles. "Like this?" She slow grind as he filled her up with every inch.

"Sssss. Just like that," he said, enjoying her every move. "Put your foot up on the edge of the Jacuzzi. Open that pussy up for me." He took control.

Faydrah gave him whatever he wanted.

Positioned perfectly, he made a few more power strokes and hit the spot that gave them both intense pleasure.

Faydrah's moans became louder and her breathing increased as a soul rocking orgasm came over her. "Oh my god," she cried out, gripping the edge of the tub.

"Oh shit," he quaked. "Hold it right there, ma."

Faydrah wanted to beg him to flood her until it ran down her thighs in rivulets, but she was out of breath and couldn't speak.

Kiam sounded like he was howling at the moon when he released his hot cum inside of welcoming tightness. Faydrah cried out in ecstasy then babbled his name.

After they recuperated, Kiam pulled her up into his arms and kissed her deeply. "Your neighbors gonna be looking at you funny tomorrow," he joked.

"So," she said not caring. "If they ain't having good sex and cumming then they should kill themselves."

"Let's go inside and dry off," he chuckled.

"Only if you let me wet you up afterwards."

"You know what I like."

They stepped out of the Jacuzzi, still touching and kissing. Faydrah gathered up the towel and her underwear and they headed inside.

When Faydrah woke up the next morning with Kiam lying next to her, her heart fluttered. Kiam was her everything. Just having him near was all she needed to cope. But a cloud of uncertainty always followed the warm feeling he gave her; he was in that life and the reality that at any minute she could get a call telling her that he was gone was more real than the warm body lying next to her.

Faydrah sighed deeply and snuggled closer to him. She needed to become full with his presence to last her when he wasn't there.

Chapter 18
Unfinished Business

The good loving Faydrah gave him did not keep Kiam from getting up and handling his business the next day. A man with huge ambitions couldn't afford to lay up in pussy 24/7 regardless to how good it was or how he felt about the woman. The streets were his wife, everything else was a mistress.

After leaving Faydrah mumbling in her sleep and dreaming of a house full of little Kiams, he hit flip mode and took to the streets checking traps and making sure that his workers were on their grind.

Just when the sun was about to go down and most cats were thinking about what club or which female they were gonna hit that Saturday night, Kiam decided it was time for him to deal with a situation that had been heavily on his mind. He rode through and picked Czar up.

"Where we headed, fam?" Czar asked as they drove off from his house.

"To get some answers," Kiam said.

Czar rubbed his hands up and down his legs as he settled in his seat. Kiam's tone made him nervous.

They rode in silence from out Indian Hills with the sounds of the streets growing louder as they drove down Euclid Avenue, through EC, toward Lee Road.

"Where's DeMarcus's car lot?" asked Kiam, coming to a stop at the traffic light.

"Bust a left, it's not too far down," said Czar, feeling a bit more relaxed. It was gonna be fun watching Kiam confront DeMarcus. *Man, I wish I had some popcorn.* Czar smiled in anticipation of the drama.

An icy cold glance from Kiam wiped the grin off his face.

Kiam made the left and drove down Lee Road until Czar pointed out DeMarcus's car lot. Kiam pulled into the lot and parked at the front door.

He saw that DeMarcus sold some real nice new and previously owned cars and trucks. It was near closing time so only a few customers were around. *Perfect*, Kiam thought as they got out the car and went inside.

An attractive mocha complexioned woman greeted them at the entrance. She was wearing a dark blue business suit with a skirt that stopped just above her thighs and showed off smooth, well-toned legs. She had a long, beautiful and expensive Asian-hair weave that flowed down to her generous ass. She wore small black, square-framed glasses that showcased an undercover freak type of look.

"May I help you gentlemen?" she asked, averting her eyes away from Czar's.

"Is DeMarcus around?" he replied, looking at her with a hard gaze of unfriendly familiarity.

"No, but he's on his way over from the other lot. Maybe one of our sales representatives can help you. Are you looking to buy an automobile?" This question was directed to Kiam, she knew that Czar already had a small fleet.

Kiam didn't respond at first, he was busy looking around the office. There were two high-end seating areas with 60 inch flat screen televisions. There was also a coffee/cappuccino station with all the fixings and two small refrigerators with several name brand drinks and snacks, all free to accommodate the customers. On the walls were plaques and awards of excellence that the sales people had earned. This wasn't any half-operation, from the looks of things the lot was doing well.

"How long before DeMarcus gets here?" he asked, ignoring the question that passed through her sexy red lips.

"DeMarcus should be here any moment. You can wait for him here in the lobby," she said, grabbing the remote and turning on the television. "We'll be closing in fifteen minutes but he should be back by then. Please enjoy some refreshments while you wait." She extended her hand toward the snack area.

Kiam disregarded her hospitality. "Where's DeMarcus office?" he asked Czar.

Czar pointed to a room on their left and Kiam walked in that direction. The female was dead on his heels.

"Oh no, you can't go in there," she protested and jumped in his way when he reached the office.

"Chill, ma, it's all good. Just send him in to see me when he gets here." Kiam swept her aside.

She looked back at Czar questioningly.

"Daphne, it's cool, he's DeMarcus's people," he explained.

Kiam walked in the office and closed the door. Looking around the plush, brightly colored room he began to take inventory. He stood looking at the photos on the wall; there was dozens of pictures of DeMarcus and different guys who had purchased vehicles.

Kiam slowly walked to the other side of the office with his hands clasped behind his back. His eyes settled on a framed picture of Miss Charlene that sat on a shelf. He picked it up and stared at it; a small pain pinched his heart. He silently vowed to find and destroy the man responsible for her death.

He sat the picture back in its place and took a seat behind the mahogany desk.

Ten minutes later he heard DeMarcus' voice outside the door; he was assuring Daphne that she was not in any trouble. When he came into the office and saw Kiam leaned back in the chair with his feet propped up on the desk, he frowned but quickly changed his expression.

"What's up, nigga? I heard you were home, what took you so long to come holla at me?" He flashed a phony smile and closed the door.

Kiam's expression was blank. "If you wanted me to holla, you would've let me know where to find you and I wouldn't have had to come looking for you. But it's all good," he responded, taking his feet down and folding his hands on the desk.

"I see it *is* all good. You don't look like you're hurting for anything. But you know if you need something, I got you." DeMarcus propped himself up on the edge of the desk.

"You ain't got shit I need, but you do have something I'm demanding—just on general principle." Kiam chuckled.

"Demand?" DeMarcus nervously fidgeted.

Reflexively Kiam's hand went to his waist; it was just a habit. A little chuckle then he would put a nigga on his ass. But this wasn't that, at least not yet. So he brought his hand up and placed it on top of the desk. "You're a funny nigga," he said.

"What you mean?" DeMarcus asked.

"We grew up in the same house so you know better than most that I'm the wrong person to piss off, yet you sit there and insult me."

"How am I insulting you, Bruh?" DeMarcus gestured with his hands.

"Cancel that *bruh* shit," spat Kiam. "A brother don't leave you dead in the water for eight years. So don't even come at me like we're family, nigga. I shouldn't have had to ask you for a damn thing, you should've laid the red carpet out for me as soon as I touched down. But fuck all that, I just wanna know if you've heard anything about who killed Miss Charlene."

"Nah, I haven't heard nothing." He looked over at her picture as sweat began to form on his forehead.

"I went by the old house and my stash was still there, but I'm willing to bet whoever killed her was looking for it. Now, who the

144

fuck else besides yourself would've known that I had money there?"

"Ain't no telling, but if I were you I'd start with that snake muthafucka that's out in the lobby," said DeMarcus.

It was funny because Czar had said the same thing about him.

"If you felt that way, why haven't you handled the situation by now? You mean to tell me that you're letting—"

A knock on the door stopped him in mid-sentence.

"Come in," said DeMarcus.

Daphne stuck her head in. "Everyone else is gone. Do you want me to hang around?" she asked.

"No, you can go on home I'll be there later on," he said. "Lock everything up before you go."

"Okay, see you later on."

Czar came into the office as Daphne was leaving. Lust danced in his eyes as he watched her switch off.

He grabbed a chair and straddled it backwards. Kiam noticed that Czar and DeMarcus looked at each other with unbridled contempt.

Kiam wasn't the type to say anything behind a man's back that he couldn't say to his face thus he continued the conversation. "Like I was saying, if you suspect that this nigga right here had something to do with Miss Charlene getting killed, why is he still breathing?" he questioned DeMarcus, point

Czar's eyes went from Kiam to DeMarcus then back to Kiam. He shot up off of the chair and grabbed DeMarcus by the collar. "What type of bullshit are you trying to put in the game?" he snarled, pushing DeMarcus against the desk knocking shit over in the process.

DeMarcus slapped Czar's hands off of him. "Nigga, you know what I'm talking about," he spat. He regulated his breathing and straightened up his tie.

"Nah, I don't know shit besides you seemed to come up good in the hood after your grandmother got killed. The way I see it, you're pointing the finger at me to keep the light off of your punk ass. What I'ma rob and kill Miss Charlene for? My money been grown up for years."

"So you say," DeMarcus disputed. "But don't nobody know what you got but yourself. I hear all of that boss hustla shit coming out ya mouth but I know for a fact your pockets were leaking back then."

"What?" Czar laughed dismissively, backing up a little. "Boy, you'll catch a rabbit fucking a grizzly bear before you'll catch me broke."

"That's what ya mouth say," DeMarcus shot back.

Kiam sat back, crossed his legs, and watched them hurl accusations back and forth.

"You a bitch nigga trying to disguise your jealousy with anger. But don't worry, I fuck her real good," DeMarcus chided him, causing Czar's his smile to retreat.

Finally part of the truth came out. DeMarcus turned to Kiam. "Bruh, this clown is still mad because I snatched Daphne off his arm. See, he tricked a lot of money on her but the bitch wanted me. That nigga's beef is about a ho."

Czar's face balled up and the thick vein by his temple almost bulged out the side of his head. DeMarcus had struck a nerve.

"Fool, I don't beef with no nigga over pussy. I'm just putting it out there; I think you killed your grandmother because she wouldn't tell you where Kiam's stash was."

"You sound stupid!" He turned to Kiam. "Bruh, I know you don't believe that shit. Me, kill Mama over some money? Hell, over anything! Nigga, I would take dick in my ass before I would do some foul shit like that. For real, Bruh. Fuck what this jealous-hearted nigga trying to put in your head, it's all love, and that's how I felt about Mama."

Kiam didn't need to hear anymore to know that the DeMarcus's vow was insincere. Ever since they were small DeMarcus had been a cruddy muthafucka, and Czar wasn't much better. Either one of them could have been lying. One thing for sure, he wasn't about to sit there all night trying to figure it out.

The two men shouted back and forth like cackling hens. When Kiam couldn't take anymore he put an abrupt end to it. "Shut the fuck up!" he barked, sending an eerie vibration throughout the room.

Both men abruptly stopped talking and sat down glaring at each other. Kiam reached in his pocket and pulled out a coin. Looking at DeMarcus, he said, "Heads or tails?"

"Huh?" DeMarcus was slow to catch on.

Kiam cut his eyes at Czar and held his stare.

Czar swallowed hard.

"Heads or tails?" said Kiam.

Czar understood what was at stake; this was a cold-hearted form of Russian Roulette. He threw his hand in the air. "Hold up, my nigga. I don't understand why you're putting me in this." His voice quivered.

Kiam pulled his tool from his waist and sat it down in front of him on the desk. "One of you niggas better choose or I'm deading both of you. Best to decide your own fate."

Czar swallowed again.

DeMarcus finally got a clue, but fear held ahold of his throat and wouldn't allow him to call the coin toss. The only sound that came out of his mouth resembled a whine.

Kiam reached for the forty-cal that he had sat on the desk.

"Heads," called Czar.

Kiam flipped the coin. It turned over in the air several times, almost in slow motion, before gravity brought it back down from the ceiling. Kiam caught it in the palm of his right hand. *Whop!* He slammed it down on the desk with his hand covering it.

Czar and DeMarcus rocked nervously in their seats. Kiam lifted his hand just a bit and peeked up under it to see how the coin had landed. When he saw it he chuckled, and one of their fates was sealed.

The banger came up off the desk in Kiam's hand in one smooth motion. In that fraction of a second before he aimed at the loser and squeezed off a perfect shot, Czar's ass hole tightened and DeMarcus pissed his pants.

Boom!

Czar's head snapped back and his brains sprayed against the wall behind him as he toppled over in the chair, crashing to the floor onto his back with one leg grotesquely twisted under his body.

DeMarcus's mouth was agape.

Kiam's expression had not changed, it was just another kill. He flipped the quarter to DeMarcus. "That's your lucky coin. Put that shit on a chain and wear it around your neck for good luck. Trust, you're gonna need it if I find out it should've landed on tails."

He stood up, walked around the desk, and put another slug in Czar's cranium as casually as if he was looking at his watch.

He looked back up at DeMarcus and now his eyes were squinted. He said in a real low tone, "You been out here eating good the whole time I was on the inside and you didn't do shit for a nigga."

"All you had to do was call or write and let me know what you needed, Bruh," stuttered DeMarcus.

Kiam raised the gun and pointed at his head. "Call me that shit again and I'ma change the color of the walls up in this bitch."

"Okay, man, what do you want? Just tell me how I can square things up."

"I want half of everything you own. Your drug spots, your businesses, your stash. Everything! Even your bitch." He fired a shot mere inches over DeMarcus's head.

DeMarcus damn near jumped out of his skin.

"Test me if you want to," gritted Kiam, and then he strolled out the door as nonchalantly as he had walked in.

Ca$h & NeNe Capri

Chapter 19
The Chase and the Catch

The week flew by as Donella and Bay looked forward to Saturday night with excitement and morbid anticipation. Bayonna moved around her apartment rushing from one room to another trying to get ready before Donella arrived to pick her up.

It was Ladies Night at the Tequila Ranch and the place would be overflowing with d-boys, athletes and other made men. After dealing with all of Kiam's demands lately the girls were in need of some loud music, drinks and male attention.

Bayonna stood looking in her wall length bathroom mirror. She was definitely feeling the reflection that stared back at her. She looked too cute in her black skinny leg jeans and silver sparkling bra. She was styling her hair when she heard her door bell ring. Placing the flat irons on the sink she hurried to the door to let Donella in.

As soon as she opened the door Donella looked at her over her Chanel shades and shook her head with slight disappointment. "Why your ass ain't never ready?" she asked.

"Just come in." Bayonna grabbed her by the hand and pulled her into the living room.

"Damn, Bay. What the fuck happened in here?" Donella asked, looking at the piles of clothes, shopping bags, shoe boxes and cleaner's plastic all over the floor and couches.

"You know I have a hard time finding shit to put on," replied Bayonna, rushing back into the bathroom to finish her hair.

"This shit is ridiculous. Bitch, you gotta do better than this," said Donella, stepping over the debris. She shook her head again and reached in her bag and pulled out two small bottles of Ciroc.

"Whatever, open that shit so I can get the night started."

"Here, and hurry up its 10:30. I wanted to get there before eleven." She passed her the open bottle.

"Bitch don't start. You can't rush perfection," Bayonna chirped, taking the bottle to the head. "Wow," she crowed as the coconut flavored liquid ran down her throat.

Donella laughed then began downing hers. Just before she finished it she held her bottle up so they could toast. "To the chase."

"And the catch," Bayonna added as they clinked bottles.

They downed the rest of their drinks and threw the bottles in the trash. Bayonna completed her look by putting on a little eye liner and glossing her lips. After she put on her black see-through shirt and silver Red Bottom stilettoes she was ready to go.

The ladies left out the house looking delectable and hot. Donella sashayed down the street in her dark blue Seven jeans, leopard Red Bottom open toe six inch heels and brown halter top that rested at the top of her jeans exposing her toned shoulders and arms. They jumped in Donella's silver metallic 2012 BMW 335i sports car and threw on a club CD to set the mood, with their mission in full focus.

They popped their fingers to the music and zoomed toward their destination. The Beemer rode so smooth Bayonna thought about buying her one just like it even though she already owned a Jag' and a Infiniti truck.

When they reached the club, Donella pulled onto the street and drove at a crawl, scanning the area for a parking space. As luck would have it some chicks were pulling out. She drummed her fingers on her thigh, impatiently waited while they fumbled around their little Honda Accord.

"These silly bitches," Bayonna said as she watched the drunken females laugh and play instead of getting the hell out of the parking space. She reached over and beeped the horn.

Donella looked over at her, surprised. "Bay, chill. Why you all hyped?"

"Fuck them; they need to hurry the fuck up,"

One of the females flipped her wrist and yelled out. "Wait your turn!"

Without hesitation Bayonna grabbed the door handle and was out the car. "Wait my what?" she said, walking over to the car, hips swaying, heels clicking.

"Oh shit, my bad, Bay," the driver said as she realized who her friend had gotten slick out the mouth with.

Bayonna squinted her eyes trying to remember the girl's face. "Gail?" she said. It was one of Gator's groupie ho's.

"Yeah, girl how you been?"

"I'm good now, but for a second it was about to get ugly out here," she said, looking over at the bitch with the mouth.

"Oh, she cool Bay." She looked to her girl. "Kaleese, this is Gator's people." She tried to calm the situation.

"Yeah, well if she cool tell her to watch her fucking mouth," Bayonna said.

She peered at Kaleese, holding eye contact until the woman wilted. Kaleese didn't dare open her mouth again. As soon as Gail mentioned Gator she already knew she had better keep her mouth closed.

"It ain't nothing Bay, I got it. Let me pull out so you can get in. I just left your brother inside; it's turned up in there. Y'all have fun," Gail said, getting in the car. She didn't want any problems, she had heard about Bayonna and her crew and she was not built for a war with them.

When Kaleese got in the car Bayonna headed back to Donella's vehicle and hopped in.

"What was all that about?"

"Nothing, that was that bitch that Gator fucks with."

"Bitch, you off the chain lately." Donella shook her head, Bay was bursting out of her shell.

Once they were parked they walked past the long line of people waiting to get in. Being that they were VIP, they went to a side entrance and knocked three times. The door came open and they were hit with weed smoke and loud music.

"What's up Bay?" The 6'5", 300 pound muscular bouncer took her hand, pulling her toward him.

"Hey Bones," Bay said giggling.

"Hey Nella," he said as she followed Bay into the basement of the club.

"Don't call me that," muttered Donella, crunching up her face.

"Why you so damn mean?" Bones remarked.

"Whatever." She brushed him off, moving past him and Bay.

Bones stood there scratching his head for a second. He looked at Bay, showing all thirty-two teeth. He had the biggest crush on her but she just played with his mind and pockets. Donella couldn't stand his black ass; it was something about him she didn't trust.

"Come on, Bay," she yelled over the music.

Bayonna threw up her hand for her to wait a minute. She was trying to get in this nigga's pocket and Donella's bad attitude was about to fuck that up.

Donella twisted her lips up and turned to scan the room for Gator and the crew. There was money all over the place. The owner of the club had the basement set up for all the ballers and celebrities that wanted to party without having to deal with a gang of groupies.

The VIP room was jumping, strobe lights bounced off of the walls and the music thumped. The stools at both bars were occupied and there weren't many empty tables or booths. Both small dance floors were crowded and the ratio of women to men was at least seven to one, which meant it was cutthroat as usual.

Donella's eyes roamed the room, watching the chickens that had made it to the basement. They were damn near naked, working hard trying to come up on some paid dick.

She shook her head. "Thirsty bitches," she mumbled.

When her eyes settled on Gator sitting at one of the bars, she started in his direction. "Come on," she hurried Bayonna.

Spotting Gator, too, Bayonna walked around Donella mumbling, "You'll fuck up a wet dream."

"If ugly ass Bones is in it, it's a nightmare," Donella shot back following her over to Gator.

Their boy was in his element. He was rocking a button down shirt with gray Armani pants that lay smoothly on top of his suede Ferragamo 'Giostra' loafers. His dreads were twisted down tight in the front and pulled back into a pony-tail, allowing the diamond earrings in his ears to sparkle as brightly as the strobe lights. Two thickly built females clung to his sides, getting high off his swag.

Bay and Donella walked right up to where he was seated; ignoring the hungry ho's he was entertaining.

"What's up, nigga, you buying?" Bay asked as she rested her hand on his back.

"What's up sis?" Gator leaned in and kissed her cheek. The icy piece on his platinum chain brushed against her chest.

"Hey Dee," he said to Donella as she reached in and hugged his neck.

"Hey you," Donella responded.

The two women that he had been entertaining looked at Bay and Donella with hard faces.

"Don't worry honey; we're not the competition," said Donella.

Gator smiled, he loved the attention. He stroked his newly grown goatee, showing of the shine on his wrist. The boy was a stunna at heart. He pulled out a bankroll and peeled three bills off for each of the women. "Order some drinks at the other bar while I holla at my fam," he said.

They took the money and sauntered off to do exactly that. Donella shot him the evil eye. Bay caught it but didn't think anything of it. Gator shrugged his shoulders and smiled arrogantly. *This is the muthafuckin' life.*

"Where's the rest of the crew?" he asked, looking around for Lissha and Treebie.

"Lissha about to go see Big Zo, and Treebie probably somewhere terrorizing, you know how she do," Donella brought his drink to her nose. "What's this?"

"Gimme my shit," he said, snatching it from her hand.

"You ain't gotta snatch it, nigga," Donella said, hitting his arm.

"I hate that shit, Treebie ass love to stick her nose in people's shit. That bitch rubbing of on you. Yo, give them whatever they want," he yelled over to the bartender then got up. "Get y'all drinks and meet me in the back room." He placed a hundred dollar bill on the counter and walked off.

Bayonna and Donella got their drinks then headed to a private room in the back of the basement.

When they stepped inside Gator was seated comfortably in a tall leather chair sipping his drink.

"What's up?" Bayonna asked as she took a seat across from him

Gator laughed, looking at her with a drink in each hand, "Damn, Bay, you trying to get fucked up."

"Hell yeah, I'm out trying to have a good time," she said, taking a sip of her Hennessey and Coke.

"So what's good? Y'all happy with new management?" Gator asked, searching for any discord in the ranks.

Donella looked over at Bay then back at Gator, she knew that she needed to keep her mouth closed and let her handle it.

"You know me, as long as my money right I don't give a fuck who in charge," Bay replied, taking another sip.

"So I guess you done jumped on the nigga's dick too?" He turned his question to Donella.

"I ain't on nobody's dick. Big Zo put this shit in motion. If you got a problem with Kiam then speak to Big Zo. You got his number," Donella stated, holding a firm gaze.

"Don't get smart with me. I'm just taking a pulse beat."

"Well, don't ask dumb ass questions if you don't want smart ass answers," Donella shot back.

"Just as I thought, that nigga got all of y'all on his nut sac," he spat, taking down more of his drink.

"Look, Gator, we came out to have a good time. If you want to shake things up, do it. But what you ain't gonna do is have us in on some conspiracy type shit, I don't get down like that." Bayonna said, rising to her feet.

Donella stood also. "I guess we'll catch you later," she said, heading to the door.

"We bigger than this," Gator called out as he watched her leave.

"I'm out too," said Bay.

"You ain't taking your drinks?" he asked, looking at her two drinks on the table.

"Nah, I'm good. This whole little meeting left a bad taste in my mouth."

"I'ma remember you said that when all this shit turns upside down."

"You do that," she said as she went to catch up with Donella.

"We gotta watch that nigga."

"Already on it," Donella responded as they headed up to the main club.

The catch…

As Bayonna and Donella moved through the crowd their eyes scanned the room for Fat and Greg.

"There they go," Bayonna said, giving Donella a light elbow to the ribs.

"Where?" she asked, looking in the direction of Bayonna's finger.

"Over there in VIP, come on," she said excitedly.

157

They marched over to the VIP section and tapped on the glass door. The bouncer cracked the door like he was the police. "You got an invite?" he grumbled.

"Tell Fat and Greg, Bay is out here."

The man looked them up and down then shut the door.

"This nigga," Donella spat.

"I know, every week he act like he secret service in this bitch," Bay added, looking through the glass and seeing Money Bags Carter and his King Kennedy Projects' crew balling a couple of booths down from Fat and Greg.

A minute later the door opened, "Come on," said the bouncer with an attitude.

Bayonna just shot him a dirty look.

Donella sucked her teeth as she walked through the small space he provided.

When they were in the room Bay looked over at Greg and Fat, they had strippers popping pussy all over them. They were throwing hands full of money at them ho's as if they were caked up.

Bay's stomach started to turn as she studied them from across the room. *These are the little niggas causing all the problems?* They didn't look over twenty-one. They were skinny, their jeans were skinny and from the looks of it so was their money because it looked like they were throwing ones.

"Come on girl, let's get this shit over with," Donella whispered in Bay's ear.

Bayonna shook her head and went into character. She threw her hips wide as they walked over to Fat and Greg's booth. "Damn, nigga, can I get some?" she yelled out over the boom of Trey Songz hit *Bottoms Up.*

As she continued walking toward them she wiggled her hips and snapped her fingers to the music.

"Oh shit, look at you," Greg hollered as Bayonna teased him with the rotation of her hips and ass.

Donella walked over to Fat and sat right on his lap, fingering the piece that hung down on his platinum chain. The letters MBK shined across the fist-sized piece in diamonds.

"I heard this was a baller's party, can we join?" she asked, grabbing a bottle of Patron off the table and popping it open.

"Hell yeah," Fat cheesed, and his lil' dude became alert as soon as Donella's fat ass began grinding on his dick. He had been trying to get at her for months and hadn't gotten pass hello, but tonight seemed to be his lucky night. He knew all along that he was gonna tap that ass sooner or later.

Bayonna pushed through the thirsty tricks and took a seat on Greg's lap, causing him to rock up immediately.

"Oh, so you trying to give a nigga some play?" he asked, looking at her nipples through her shirt.

"You know we don't fuck with no bum ass niggas, we trying to chill with the best tonight." She gassed him up further by stroking the sides of his face.

Greg looked over at Fat who was all in Donella's ear putting his mack down. He looked back at Bayonna and started to do the same.

Bayonna leaned in and whispered in his ear. "Uh, don't you think you should get rid of these trick bitches? I sure don't want them popping their nasty pussies in my face."

Greg waved the bouncer over.

"What's up G?" he asked, standing there with his chest about to burst out of the tight shirt he had on.

"You can get the rest of these bitches outta here, we good," boomed Greg.

The burly bouncer began grabbing strippers by the arm and escorting them to the door.

For the next two hours the foursome popped several bottles, danced, and laughed. As the empty bottles stacked up, Donella and Bay got them real comfortable.

"So what else y'all got planned?" Greg asked.

"We trying to chill with y'all," responded Bayonna. Looking into his eyes she mouthed, "I'm ready to fuck."

Greg shot up out of his seat with his tongue hanging out of his mouth. "You ready to roll out?"

"I'm ready to do more than that," she answered, straightening her clothes and placing a single kiss on his lips.

He looked over at Fat and Donella, she had his platinum and diamond chain twisted around her finger pulling him close and whispering in his ear.

"Let's roll nigga." Greg interrupted their moment with his urgency.

"Chill, Bleed," Fat responded, looking up barely able to see through the slits in his glassy eyes.

"Let's go," Donella said as she ran her hand between Fat's legs sealing the deal as she rose to her feet.

Greg and Fat followed the ladies out of the club. They happened to be parked only a short distance from Donella's car.

"Ya'll following us?" Donella asked as she popped the locks.

"Nah, let me ride with you. Bay can ride in my car with Greg," Fat responded.

Bayonna walked to the parking lot and jumped in Greg's Audi S5 Cabriolet. She leaned back in the cool leather seat and they followed Donella and Fat.

When they reached their destination in Shaker Heights the streets were quiet. Donella drove slowly toward the house, turning down her radio as they pulled into the driveway of the ranch style dwelling.

Greg pulled behind Donella and turned off his engine.

They all filed out of the vehicles and headed to the door. Bayonna turned her key in the lock, opened the door, and hit the lights.

Greg and Fat were filled with excitement from the mere thought that they had come up on some untouchable pussy. Every hustler who was getting money in the city wanted to bag those boss ho's.

"Have a seat. Let me roll up some loud and get us something to drink," Bayonna said as she walked to the kitchen.

Fat and Greg took a seat on the couch and Donella walked over to the window, closed the blinds, then turned some music on.

"We about to get fucked up," she said, walking over to the fireplace and lighting the candles to enhance the mood.

Greg and Fat looked at each other and smiled. Their crew wasn't gonna believe that they had smashed those two top-notch broads.

When Bayonna emerged from the kitchen she had a drink in one hand and a baby Luger in the other. Treebie was on her heels with a pump.

"What the fuck!" cried Fat.

"Relax," Bayonna said, taking a swig of her drink. "You wanted to get fucked, didn't you? Be patient and you will,"

"Y'all bitches for real? Y'all about to try us like dat?" Greg erupted. "Y'all must be muthafuckin' crazy!"

"No, y'all the muthafuckas that's crazy," Treebie corrected, pulling one in the barrel.

Sweat beads popped up on Fat's forehead. "Look, you can have whatever we got," he hurriedly offered, digging down in his pockets and tossing his bands on the table.

"Bitch nigga, do we look like we take small change?" Treebie groveled then blasted him in the knee.

Fat howled.

"Oh shit," Greg jumped, putting his hands in the air. Now he realized it was not a game. "You ain't gotta do this." He had lost all the bass in his voice.

Fat rocked back and forth in pain, holding his right knee and watching the blood ooze between his fingers. Breathing heavily and beginning to panic he did the only thing that came natural. He begged. "Please, Treebie. Please, I got kids."

"Good, then I'm saving them the embarrassment of being raised by two bitches," she growled then shot him in the other knee.

"Owww! Come on, please don't do this shit," he cried out. Tears ran down his chubby face as her attempted to stand up on legs that could no longer support his right.

Screaming out in pain he collapsed to the floor and began crawling in a desperate and painful attempt to reach the door. Treebie aimed the pump at him stopping him in his tracks.

Behind them, Greg tried to negotiate their freedom. "Look, whoever put y'all on us, we'll pay you double."

"You still think you going home? Awww," Donella knuckled her hand under her eye in a half circular motion. "Poor baby," she taunted.

"Please, we'll give y'all anything. just don't kill us," he begged.

"You ain't got shit we want but real estate, nigga," said Donella. Her face showed no compromise as she pulled on a pair of driving gloves then grabbed a piece of rope from under the back of the couch.

Greg shifted nervously on the couch. "Go ahead and make this bitch roar," warned Treebie, raising the pump to his chest. Greg looked down both barrels and shuddered. Behind him Donella tightened each end of the rope around her hands. In a nanosecond it was around his neck.

Greg fought to keep her from cutting off his breath. As he struggled to get his fingers underneath the rope his eyes bulged with plea. The restricted blood flow in his neck capsulized into his pulsating veins, threatening to explode. "Please, I'm begging you," he cried.

"Nigga, shut the fuck up," Treebie barked.

"Please!"

"Alright," said Donella, releasing her grip and stepping to the side. For just a second Greg thought he had gotten a reprieve. He looked over at his man who was lying on the floor going in and out of consciousness. The pump sounded off with a boom that echoed throughout the room. Greg felt an excruciating pain shoot through his shoulder. "Bitch you shot me." He grabbed his arm and winced.

"No shit," Treebie responded then shot him in the other arm.

"What the fuck is wrong with you?" he grimaced in pain as blood poured from his wounds. "It's enough for all of us to eat."

"Is that what you were thinking when you came at our young boys talking about fuck Kiam and them bitches?" Bayonna asked, sitting her drink down and walking over to her bag.

She grabbed a needle and a small bottle and shook it up. Sticking the needle into the bottle she drew the acid into the syringe until it was full. Donella wrapped the rope back around his neck. His arms were useless now and he couldn't fight, so he pled.

"Fuck them bitches, huh?" Treebie repeated his words to him again.

"It wasn't like that. Look, you can have whatever you want. We will give you any one of our corners. Y'all want Avon? LA— Lenacrave and Angelous? I'll give y'all all that." Greg grunted as his arms began to burn.

"*Give?* Muthafucka you ain't no position to give, this is a straight up jack move." Treebie said then chuckled as she moved a little closer.

Donella kept pulling on the rope causing him to gag and his eyes to water.

Next to him Bayonna bent down and smacked Fat in the face. "Wake up, nigga." Her voice was dispassionate and hard, nothing like the purrs she had whispered just a while ago.

Blinking back the pain, he opened his eyes slowly as tears ran from the corners. He could hear his boy being prepped for death a few feet away.

"See, Greg, you probably made some good choices in life, but you made three very costly ones. Rule number one, never go anywhere without your strap. Rule number two. . . *Trust No Bitch?"* said Treebie.

Greg looked at her like no one had ever taught him that.

Treebie shook her head, those lames weren't about that life. *How the fuck did they blow up?* she wondered.

"Besides going somewhere without your *whistles* and trusting the wrong bitches, y'all made the biggest mistake of all, and that was fucking with Blood Money," Treebie said through gritted teeth.

Greg's eyes got wide when he heard her utter the words that haunted the streets. His mind started running the countless stories he heard about the niggas who were jacking muthafuckas and killing wholesale, leaving behind their signature of blood money. Now, at the door of death, to find out that they were really women fucked his head up.

"Surprised?" she asked, holding her barrel firm in his face. "See, now that you know our little secret, you gotta die. But don't worry, playboy, you're about to become part of our urban legend," she snickered, then nodded at Bay and Donella.

Donella pulled harder on the rope around Greg's neck, tightening both ends. Greg clawed, trying to get his fingers up under the rope to release the pressure but the gunshot wounds to his shoulders made him weak. He kicked and struggled but it was all in vain—his life was almost over.

Bayonna took the needle and stuck it in the side of Fat's neck releasing the toxic fluid. His body began to jerk and convulse.

Donella turned Greg's head toward Fat so he would spend his last minutes watching his boy suffer.

"Fuck those bitches?" she gritted. "That's what y'all said? Maybe in the next life, but never in this one!" She pulled harder.

Greg tightened his eyes when he saw Fat's face swell up from the acid that coursed through his veins.

Fat began to gurgle and spit up blood as gapping wounds formed around his eyes and mouth.

Bayonna grabbed a five dollar bill from her pocket and rubbed it in Fat's mouth then began to force it into Greg's. He squirmed and tried to clamp his mouth tight in a last show of bravery.

Bayonna grabbed her gun and smacked him in the mouth causing it to open wide enough for her to stuff the bloody bill.

Greg choked and gagged as it settled to the back of his throat.

Donella pulled harder and harder as the excitement of the kill turned her on.

Greg's legs began to lash out violently as he fought for his life. Bayonna came up behind Donella and pulled tightly on the rope with her. The force of both of their grips pulled at Greg's neck causing it to snap.

Treebie stood over the two men and smiled at their condition. "Punk ass niggas, hope it was good for you," she spat.

Bayonna and Donella released the rope and stepped back to look over their work.

"Damn that felt good," Bay said, breathing quickly.

"Hell, yeah. I think I came," Donella said and they all bursted out in laugher.

"Bitch, you need to see somebody about that shit," said Treebie.

"Let's get these niggas wrapped up. Bay bring their car around back," Donella directed.

"Alright roll some shit up, I need some motivation," Bay said, grabbing the car keys from the coffee table.

Treebie rolled up, while Donella opened the bags and spread them out. When Bay came back inside they smoked two blunts, took a couple shots of Patron, then went to work.

When the bodies were secure in the bags, Treebie reached down and removed Fat and Greg's worshipped chains from around their necks. She dropped the icy pieces in a small black velvet pouch and pulled it closed.

Together the girls drug the bodies outside and hoisted them up in the trunk of Greg's car.

"Dang, I didn't know dead muthafuckas were so goddamn heavy," said Bay, exhausted. It was her first time dragging a body, usually she just turned someone's lights out and breezed in the wind.

"You have to eat your Wheaties," quipped Treebie, wiping sweat from her forehead with the sleeve of her shirt. They all laughed, then went back inside to clean up.

Pulling their hair back they got strapped up in their blood money uniforms.They drove the car down to 123rd and Lenacrave where they knew it would be found and left it parked at the curb.

The next afternoon Treebie put a call into Kiam to meet her at the Red Lobster on Warrensville Road. When she pulled up he was sitting in his car leaned back listening to Meek Mill *Dreams and Nightmares.*

Kiam watched as she walked over to his vehicle; he had to admit Lissha's crew was sexy as hell, each with a different attribute of beauty.

Treebie leaned in his window. She didn't smile or say hello. She simply said, "Don't ever question our get-down."

She tossed proof in his lap that they were official, then walked off.

Kiam picked up the bag and looked inside. He pulled out the shine that Fat and Greg wore religiously and saw sparkles of blood on both chains. A large splotch of dried blood was caked up between the letters on one of the MBK pieces.

A smile hit the corner of his mouth, he had already heard how they were found and now he beamed with pride to know it was someone from his camp that did it.

As Treebie pulled off she looked at him and winked. Kiam nodded his head as her tires screeched on the way out the lot. It was official, Kiam was more than comfortable with sending the girls for the pickup.

"A bitch that loves to kill," he said aloud as he pulled off. "Every nigga needs one."

Ca$h & NeNe Capri

Chapter 20
Debriefing

Lissha pulled into the parking lot of the prison and tried to steady her mind to sit through eight hours of visitation. She looked over the grounds and saw the same heart-wrenching sight, concrete and barbed wire. Even though the sun was shining bright there was a cloud of hopelessness and despair that seemed to hover over the penitentiary.

Lissha inhaled and began to transfer her driver's license and money from her purse to a small clear clutch. She combed her hair then flipped the visor up and got out the car.

As she walked toward the gates a few regulars waved and struck a conversation. She was almost to the doors when she heard, "Hey, Lissha."

She looked back to see the wife of one of Big Zo's old cell mates. Though the woman was only a few feet behind her she yelled out like she was a block away.

I can't stand her loud ass.

"Hey, sweetie," Lissha half-heatedly spoke.

"I haven't seen you in a while," the woman continued then tried to hug her.

Lissha rolled her eyes as she patted the woman on the back. "I know, I been running girl. You know how it is," Lissha said, pulling back.

"Yeah, girl, we been coming here for a long time," she blabbered as Lissha tried to walk away.

Lissha moved to the doors hoping that she would get the hint, but she didn't. She followed Lissha inside the jail, talking her to death.

When they entered the drab visitation room, Lissha got depressed. Going through this process year after year could break the strongest person. But unlike others she would not give up on her loved one.

Lissha waited until her talkative stalker found a seat, then she bolted to the vending machines and purchased all the items that Big Zo usually wanted. She bought him hot wings, burgers, a salad, chips, soda, and two fish sandwiches. He never ate everything that she bought, but it didn't matter, she just wanted to have it there for him.

After she was settled in her seat, she looked at her watch and counted the minutes. Time ticked at the pace of drying paint. After a forty minute wait, Big Zo emerged from the back fixing his shirt and looking over the room for Lissha. When his eyes settled on her, he smiled. She was seated with her head resting on her hand with her eyes closed.

Big Zo walked toward her nodding and waving at a few guys and their families along the way. He walked up and stood right in front of Lissha then tapped her leg. Lissha slowly opened her eyes and a smile spread over her face.

"Hey, baby girl." Big Zo smiled back at her.

"Hey, Daddy," Lissha responded and got up to give him a hug.

Big Zo held her tighly in his grip, it had been over a month since he saw her and her presence was comforting to his soul. His baby girl was indeed a rider. Time would never make her stop visiting.

When Lissha pulled back, Big Zo rubbed her face and gave her another smile "So how have you been?" he asked, sitting down and folding his hands in his lap.

Lissha sat down, too. "I'm just trying to maintain, Daddy," she casually replied, opening a soda.

"How are the girls?"

Lissha shook her head. "Well, Donella and Bayonna are never a problem. Treebie, that bitch be on some other rebel type shit." Big Zo looked at her with the side-eye, he always had to remind her about her mouth. "My bad for the language," she quickly apologized. "Like I was saying, Treebie is way too extra sometimes. She continues to test me."

Big Zo squinted his eyes. "Does she handle business?"

"Always. But…"

"But what?"

"Nothing." Her words recoiled back into her throat.

"Speak your mind, baby girl."

With little convincing she continued. "Treebie just needs to calm her ass down. We got into it a few times over Kiam. On the real, she doesn't trust him. That's it in a nutshell."

"Look, the bitches are your business. If she's outta line, that shit is your fault." Big Zo got serious. "I don't have time for rebellion in my camp. I sent you someone who will handle business and put me in a better position. Don't let anyone stand in the way of that. Family. Friend. Or foe." He gave Lissha look that made her want to crawl under her chair. She never wanted to disappoint him.

She looked down rubbing the side of the soda bottle and wondering if she was built for this mission after all.

"Look at me," he said calmly.

Lissha lifted her eyes.

"Everything that I have—everything that I'm willing to sacrifice is for us. You gotta stick to the plan, if we got one weak link, then the whole fucking chain will break. You understand?"

"Yes," Lissha said a little above a whisper.

"Okay. Now tell me about Kiam."

Lissha took a deep breath. "He reorganized everyone. He put all the strength in the right places, and he had us fall back with the exception of pickup."

"So, Gator doesn't handle that part anymore either?"

"That's the way Kiam wants it. Should I tell him to put Gator back in charge of the pickups?"

"No, I was just asking," he said.

"Okay. Kiam also negotiated to have our squad meet Riz's team half way instead of us having to go all the way to New York to pick it up."

"I don't want you trafficking the shit period. I don't care if it's just from one end of the street to the other, because if you get cased up everything falls apart."

"I know. Treebie and 'em are picking it up. The first pick up is this week." She paused and separated her thoughts, so she would say the right thing. "I know you put Kiam in charge and he is handling business, but he is very arrogant. I always worry that he will say the wrong thing to the right person then we're back to step one."

Big Zo rubbed the bottom of his chin as he processed his thoughts. He could see that her judgment was coming from more than business, there was also some emotion attached. "You got feelings for Kiam, don't you?"

"No," she quickly denied.

Big Zo steepled his fingers under his chin and chose his words effectively. "Look, I know Kiam is very charismatic and has a powerful aura, but I need you to stay focused. I can't afford for you to mix the relationship."

"I haven't," she protested.

"I hope not. Remember, this is serious. It's the only shot I have to ever get out of here so don't fuck it up by thinking with your butt."

"I won't, Daddy. You taught me better than that," she reassured him.

"Good. Under no circumstances are you to allow that man into your bed." Big Zo formed a small frown on his face. "We clear?"

"Yes Sir," she pouted. They sat in silence thinking about what he forbade her to do.

Lissha brightened up first. "Are you ready to eat?" she asked, smiling to let him know that his baby girl was always on his side.

Big Zo nodded yes and she went to the microwave to heat up his food.

While Lissha was away Big Zo was in deep thought. So many had failed him, would she be next? He couldn't see that ever happening; not his baby girl.

Lissha returned with his food piping hot. She sat it down on the table and handed him some napkins, then unscrewed the top off his fruit drink. "Thanks, baby," he said, picking up the burger and chomping off a big bite.

Lissha sat back down and waited for him to look up. Big Zo's eyes wandered around the visitation room as he ate. Lissha leaned over and wiped the corners of his mouth with a napkin. "Daddy," she said. "I spoke with the lawyer that I told you about months ago. He says he sees some things in your trial transcript that he may be able to use to get your conviction overturned."

"Yeah? What he want, fifteen million?" he asked sarcastically.

"No. He'll do the appeal for one hundred and fifty thousand. That's nothing."

"We might as well flush that hundred fifty down the toilet. I don't believe shit any attorney says."

"He's supposed to be one of the best. He worked on BMF case down in Atlanta years ago."

"Is that supposed to make me feel good? Did he get Big Meech off?" The question was rhetorical because they both knew the answer was no.

Lissha fought to keep the look of fatigue out of her eyes, she wanted very badly for something positive to happen in his appeal process, otherwise he would die in prison. She would do anything to prevent that from happening.

Big Zo knew her better than she knew herself sometimes, so he understood the look in her eyes. He reached across the table and pinched her cheek like she was a little girl. "Lissha, has Daddy ever led you wrong?" he asked directly.

"Never," she confirmed without hesitation.

"And I never will," he promised. "Forget about attorneys, those muthafuckas are nothing but leeches." Lissha nodded, she would not bring the topic up again. "Now what's up with Blood Money?" he quickly changed the subject.

She moved a little closer and began telling him what they had on the table. Big Zo listened attentively, downloading each piece of information and plotting on how he could use it to enhance the plans he already had in motion. His astute mind put each piece into place. The time flew by and the next thing they knew it was time for her to go.

Big Zo took one last sip of his soda then rose to his feet. Lissha stood up and gave him a big hug. "I'll be back in a few weeks," she said with sadness in her voice.

"Don't worry, baby girl, when this is all over we'll be set. Just do like I tell you and it will all work out."

"Yes sir."

"Tell Kiam I said I'm proud of him. Remind him that he is to do everything in his power to keep you safe. Nothing else comes before that."

"I will. Love you, Daddy."

"Love you, too." Big Zo turned her a loose and watched as she joined the long line of visitors waiting their turn to exit the facility. At the door she turned back around and waved.

"Talk to you soon," he mouthed.

"Okay." She motioned with her thumb and index finger.

Big Zo turned to look at Lissha one last time before she left, he noticed that the sadness had washed over her face. He knew it wasn't just because she missed him. He strongly suspected that she was torn between his orders and feelings that she had developed for Kiam. He had to make sure that if he didn't get through to

Lissha, he'd surely get through to Kiam. Under no circumstances could they cross that line, and he would defend that order with his life.

Lissha filed out the prison door and moved swiftly to her car, choking back tears. The thought that Big Zo might never get out of prison, and the weight of his demand, was overwhelming. As soon as she shut the door and started her engine tears began to roll down her face. She had begun to want the very thing that he would not permit her to have.

As she headed to the airport, she knew that she had to make a decision. Everything depended on that.

Chapter 21
Putting It Down

While Lissha was away visiting Big Zo, the shipment arrived without incident or delay. Kiam had Gator disperse it to those he had put in position to handle it from there, then he sat back and counted the evidence of other niggas' broke pockets. They had the whole Eastside turned up with their product which Kiam had renamed *Schizophrenic*. He learned years ago that one must do what others won't, in order to have what others don't.

Most dealers were selling whip to increase their profits, but Kiam's team had that real fish scale still in the casket, meaning the kilos were unopened and uncut. Low prices and fat weight had fiends twerking to the rock houses. Niggas were checking their calendars because it felt like it was '87 all over again when crack first hit the scene.

True to his word, Kiam had strong-armed half of DeMarcus's Miles Road territory. From 93rd all the way up to 131st every nickel sack, gram, ounce or brick sold was that Schizo'. And their other territories were pumping just as hard.

Besides the dope money, Kiam had stiff armed his way into ownership of a few profitable gambling houses on the Eastside. The city was bowing to his power. *All hail to the king.*

Since Kiam didn't trust Gator to walk and chew gum at the same damn time, he only allowed him to make small drops and oversee part of the daily operations. Gator could barely handle that because pussy had his mind on the type of shit that brought entire empires down.

Kiam felt there was something funny about a man who always wanted to be pretty. *That muthafucka might as well put on some lashes and pumps,* he thought. With that in mind he chose the young boy JuJu to handle the brick sales and to oversee a gambling house on 117th and St. Clair that he had took from an old head.

177

There was something Kiam saw in little man that reminded him of himself. JuJu was about his paper and he took no shorts.

The three of them were riding in Gator's white Expedition. They pulled into DeMarcus's car lot and Kiam got out as soon as the truck came to a stop. "Come on youngin', let's go upgrade your status, you ain't gonna get no good pussy with that bus pass," he said, closing the front passenger door.

"I'm cautious but I damn sure ain't slow, I need some pussy that will make a little nigga feel tall than a muhfucka," he shot back, sliding on his Aviators.

Kiam chuckled as he headed for the front door.

JuJu climbed out the back rocking a pair of crisp black jeans, a grey T, and brand new J's. He stood only 5'6" but size didn't mean shit, he packed two fo-fo's resting against his waist, and they damn sure weren't there to hold his belt up.

Youngin' wasn't afraid to act a fool. When the opposition didn't bend, he folded 'em, and today Kiam was rewarding him for his loyalty and obedience. He had Faydrah looking for a condo for little man, if JuJu stayed down his blessings would be plentiful.

"Y'all good, right?" asked Gator, looking down at his cell phone at a text that had just come through.

"Yeah, we straight, you can bounce. Don't forget to go over on Star and make sure that *that* money is right. When you scoop it up take it to Lissha," said Kiam as he swung the door open and stepped inside.

Gator nodded while struggling not to show that he didn't like taking orders from Kiam. He sat with his poker face until both men were inside. When he drove off the frown that he had held back forced its way on his face.

He quickly glanced at his phone and read the text message. It was *her* asking him to call. They hadn't really talked since they'd seen each other at the club. He knew she would be a little salty but he didn't care, baby girl was Team Gator all day. Pulling up to a stop light he hit her back right away. "Yeah, what's up?"

"What you doing?" she asked accusingly.

"Damn, why you make it sound like you think I'm up in some pussy?" Gator laughed

"Ain't no telling with you, if a bitch blink too long yo' ass be right up the next bitch's ass," she flat out charged.

"Go 'head with all that bullshit, I'm on my way over to the trap then I'm coming your way. What's up?"

"What the fuck do you think is up? A bitch needs something stiff and cooperative."

"Well, you know what I'ma need?"

"What you gonna need?" She folded her arms and waited for his answer.

"I'ma need to hold on to the back of your head while you give me a knee bending experience."

"How come every time I ask you for some dick you wanna put it in a bitch mouth?" she asked with her lips twisted to the side.

"You know this nigga don't act right unless he gets to have a conversation with some tonsils," he stated with a slight smile on his face. His dick jumped as the last word left his lips.

"Well, you keep a bitch eyes rolling so you know I'ma do whatever you want me to," she promised.

Gator's foot got heavy on the gas with that thought. "I know you got me. But on the real, you know what I really want you to do."

"Don't even go there." She stopped him before he could get started. Ever since they had switched up the pickup, he had been pressing her to let him know when and where it went down.

"What, that bitch got you shook?" Gator asked as he eased his window down, honked his horn, and blew a kiss at a lady that was driving beside him.

The lady smiled at him, but then a big headed dude that had been reclined back in the passenger seat sat up and grilled him. Gator reached in his waist and flashed his steel. "This ain't what you want," he yelled out the window and the guy swallowed whatever slick words he had started to say.

"Who are you talking to?" she angrily asked.

"Nobody, just some clown that almost got his face splattered. Anyway, what's up? You gonna do that or what?"

"You gotta give me time, Gator. Damn. We've only done one pickup. Let me peep everything out and get Riz's people more comfortable with bringing the shit halfway so they'll relax a little."

"Fuck dat. They don't have to relax. I got something that will relax 'em for eternity," he said, patting the banger that he had put back on his waist.

She smiled, envisioning him doing something demonstrative with his hands. "I know you will, boo." She chuckled. "But, baby, they had a small army riding with them to protect their product. They had everybody but Jesus and his Disciples."

"Okay, but I'm gonna stay on you. It's time for me to make some moves of my own. The way I'm feeling, fuck Lissha, Big Zo, and Kiam."

She didn't respond. Gator was on a suicide mission, allowing his hatred of Kiam to get the best of him.

"I'ma call you when I'm through handling business and I'm on my way," he said.

"Okay, I'm waiting. Hurry up, you know a bitch will start without you," she purred.

"Get it wet for me baby, I'll be right there." He disconnected the call.

"Pick out any whip you like, I'll be right back," Kiam instructed his young boy.

While JuJu browsed the cars Kiam walked inside. This was not the first time since smashing Czar that he had seen DeMarcus, but it was the first time that he had been back to the lot.

Daphne perked right up when she saw Kiam coming. She had family that lived on Miles Road and they had all told her how he was putting it down.

"Hi, Kiam." she spoke, coming up to him with a wide smile on her face and a look in her eyes that said more than any words could ever convey.

Kiam looked at her with a sneer and nodded almost imperceptibly. *Bitch don't know me.*

Daphne had on a cream-colored Michael Kors pants suit. Huge diamonds sparkled on her fingers and two carats dripped from her ears. A diamond heart-shaped pendant hung around her neck on an invisible chain.

It don't matter how you dress them up, Kiam wanted to tell DeMarcus, *a ho was still a ho.*

Kiam didn't give her a second thought as he proceeded back to DeMarcus's office.

Daphne rushed up behind. "Um, I'm sorry but DeMarcus is in a meeting with his banker," she said hurriedly as he reached for the door knob.

Kiam stopped, pulled his hand back, and turned to look at her. "When he's through let him know that I'm outside," he said in a gruff voice.

"You can wait for him in my office if you'd like," she quickly offered. "It has air conditioning. I know you don't want to wait out in the hot sun."

Kiam caught her flirtatious tone. *I'd rather burn the fuck up than sit in her little air conditioned office.*

"Be happy with what you got before you run into something you can't handle," he warned, then turned and walked outside.

Daphne stared at Kiam's back. *Whew! That muthafucka turned me the fuck on.* She liked her men the same way she liked a dick— hard.

As Kiam walked out the door onto the lot Daphne promised herself that she was going to get that, one way or another.

JuJu was with a salesman looking over a brand new white 2012 Land Rover Evogue. It was sitting on 22 inch rims whispering his name. The sticker price on the front window read $55,000. Kiam had told him to pick out whatever he liked but he didn't want to seem greedy.

"What's up, Ju? You like this or what?" asked Kiam, coming up behind them.

"Yeah, this bitch is real nice but I'm not trying to make you spend a grip. Really, I'm good with my Tahoe until I can cop this myself," said JuJu.

"Never mind all of that, you want this right here, it's yours." He opened the driver's door and checked out the interior of the SUV.

"You want to test drive it?" the sales guy asked Kiam, sensing that he carried the wallet.

Kiam looked at JuJu, who nodded yeah. He could already picture himself profiling through the hoods in that sexy muthafucka. He knew that girls were gonna be trying to fuck the grille, but he wasn't going to allow pussy to cause him to lose focus like Gator had.

While JuJu and the salesman took the Land Rover for a cruise, Kiam walked over to a black murdered out 2012 Cadillac Escalade that he had noticed. The sun bounced off the pearl paint, glistening up into his face. He used a hand to shield his eyes from the glare as he walked around the vehicle, checking it out.

Satisfied that the truck was built to represent a man like himself, Kiam patted the hood. "This me right here," he said, not concerned with the sticker price.

DeMarcus emerge from inside. He was wearing a blue suit and canary yellow tie, walking alongside of an older man. They shook hands and the man walked to his car. When DeMarcus noticed Kiam standing there a look of apprehension shadowed his face.

DeMarcus retreated to his office with Kiam right behind him. The first thing Kiam noticed was that DeMarcus had replaced the blood soaked carpet.

The door banged when Kiam closed it causing DeMarcus to slightly jump.

"What's up, *bruh?*" Kiam said. "I must make you nervous?"

DeMarcus didn't respond.

Kiam walked around the desk and took a seat behind it, leaning back in the chair and propped his feet up on the desk.

"Really, is all of that necessary?" asked DeMarcus.

"Is breathing necessary?"

DeMarcus took in a mouth full of air in an attempt to remain as calm as possible.

"This is how this shit is going down. I'ma talk, you're gonna listen," Kiam made it known. "First, you have a white Land Rover Evoque and a black Escalade out on the lot. I want both of them, draw the paperwork up."

"How you paying for them?" asked DeMarcus suspiciously.

"I'm not. Those two are on the house."

"Man, that's over a hundred grand!" protested DeMarcus as he slouched down on a couch.

Kiam stared at him with a coldness that sent a chill up his body. "Nigga, shut the fuck up and get to working on the titles."

"Man, you're killing me," complained DeMarcus.

"Be careful what you ask for. Fuck around and speak your own death into existence." Kiam smiled sinisterly.

DeMarcus sighed with resignation as he got off the couch and walked behind the desk and stood waiting for Kiam to relinquish his chair.

Kiam saw the defeat in DeMarcus' eyes. He didn't pity him, he felt the muthafucka owed him more than that. He rose from the chair and propped himself up on the edge of the desk while DeMarcus got on the computer.

"What else besides the trucks?" he asked in a clipped tone.

"Nothing else from the lot, but like I told you the other day, I'm your connect now. I expect you to start buying your work from my young boy JuJu. You'll meet him in a minute." Kiam looked down at him. His press game left DeMarcus little room to breathe.

DeMarcus looked up from the computer. "Man, I already gave you half of my corners and I didn't even trip it. You felt I owed you that and I respected how you felt."

Kiam shot up off the desk and leaned down into DeMarcus' face. "Nigga, you didn't respect nothin'. You feared this shit, that's what made you surrender those corners. And you were wise to do so because I'm not fucking around."

Kiam grabbed ahold of DeMarcus's collar and held it with a firm hand. "You're buying ten whole ones a week at nineteen-five apiece. If that steps on your connect's toes, *fuck him*, tell him to come see me. My blood pump boss not bitch." He released DeMarcus' collar then moved back to his seated position.

DeMarcus shook his head but said nothing. This was going to be a huge loss he'd have to eat, but he saw no other way to continue living. The vision of how Kiam had done Czar was still fresh in his mind. He knew Kiam's tool didn't discriminate. The question was, what was his connect going to say when he told him that he had found another supplier?

Chapter 22
Playing Both Sides

Daphne pulled her ear away from the door just in time. She heard the door open, then the sound of footsteps behind her as she made her escape. She hurried back to her office and used her cell phone to place a call

"Yeah? What you want? I'm busy," he said in a deep bear-like voice that always seemed to make her nervous.

"Um, I need to see you," she whispered, fidgeting with the ring on her thumb.

"For what?"

"It's about DeMarcus, and it's very important," she said, peeking out her office door to make sure he wasn't walking up on her.

"Okay, meet me at the house on Lakeview. Be there in a half hour, I don't have time to waste so be on time. I got a lot of shit going on today." He hung up.

Daphne took the phone from her ear and stared at the blank screen. "Damn, can a bitch get a goodbye?" she said under her breath. "Heartless ass black bastard."

She couldn't wait for the day she reshuffled the cards and dealt herself the better hand. Then, that muthafucka was gonna pay for all the shit that he had ever done to her.

She went to DeMarcus' office and told him that she had a doctor's appointment. He was seated behind his desk looking like somebody had just violated his asshole and he was trying to decide whether or not he was still a man. *We might as well switch genitals*, she said to herself, leaning down to kiss him goodbye.

Forty-five minutes later, she was getting carpet burns. Wolf-man grabbed the back of her head and made her gag. He looked over at his man, who was sitting in a chair on the other side of the living smoking a blunt and playing a video game.

"Nitti, you see how this bitch swallows the whole dick? Nigga, you ain't never had a ho with head like hers," he bragged.

"The bitch tight with her shit, huh?" replied Frank Nitti, never taking his eyes off the Xbox. He didn't wanna look at no other man's wood.

"Fuck yeah. Nigga, I done had my dick sucked in all fifty states. Nah, make that fifty-two, cause an Eskimo bitch sucked it in Alaska and a Hawaiian ho brained me in Maui. I'm telling you, ain't nan sucked it better than this bitch right here."

Frank Nitti laughed.

"You want her to bless you after she gets done with me?" offered Wolfman, closing his eyes as Daphne began working her throat muscles on his long, thick pole.

"Nah, I'm good," Nitti declined.

Wolfman's ass rose up off the couch, Daphne was doing her thing. "Yeah, make me bust all down your muthafuckin' throat," he growled.

"Come on, then. Gimme that nut," she said, as she sucked and stroked him simultaneously.

Wolfman forced himself deeper down her throat and howled as he erupted inside of her mouth. He pulled out before he emptied his nut and shot the rest on her face. "Bitch, you the best," he said, slapping his dick against her forehead.

"Umm," she smiled, licking her lips.

While Wolfman fixed his clothes she went upstairs to the bathroom and brushed her teeth and gargled. Inside the bathroom Daphne looked in the mirror and fought back the tears. He always made her feel like a two dollar ho and she hated him for that. At one time she had loved him with all her heart, and he had seemed to love her just as much until she made the biggest mistake of her life. After that she was nothing to him.

Daphne didn't want to think about that right now. She blinked back her tears, took a deep breath, and thought with a coldheartedness that matched his. *Get your game plan together first,* she reminded herself. *Let him laugh now and make him cry later.*

When she returned a few minutes later Wolfman was seated on the couch stroking his thick and unkempt full beard. Now he was all business.

"What's up with your boy?" he got straight to the point.

He listened as she recounted everything that she had heard. When she was done, he looked at Frank Nitti and asked, "You ever heard of this nigga Kiam?"

Nitti smiled. "Yeah, I know him well. We almost bumped heads years ago before he went to the feds. He used to be a ski mask kid back then, and he was ferocious with that hammer."

"You sound like you ready to bend over and let him fuck you," snorted Wolfman.

Frank Nitti wasn't soft. Even though Wolfman fed him, he didn't hesitate to shoot him a cold stare. "I'm just saying, nigga," replied Wolfman softening his tone.

Nitti let it ride. He thought for a moment before adding, "I been hearing Kiam's name a lot lately, but I thought it was a different nigga because I had never known him to fuck with the work like that. Plus I thought he was still on lock."

"Well, now you know he's not. And he's out here fucking with my mula." Wolfman cracked his knuckles.

"They say he fucks with that bitch Lissha and 'em. They're dropping work called Schizophrenic all over the city. I think that's why our profits have slowed down."

"What happened to Gator? I thought he ran that crew?" asked Wolfman.

"I don't know. I guess they're under new management. Kiam has that whole clique turned the fuck up. Damn, I should have known it was him. We might have to shut them down before they get too big. You want me to send some goons at him?"

Wolfman didn't answer right away. When he did, he said, "Nah, let's see what's really up with him first."

Frank Nitti set the game control down and looked at his boss man. "I already know what's up with him, that nigga a killah. He probably soaked up game in the pen and now his hustle match his gangsta. Let's hit him before he gets too big."

Wolfman shook his head no, he was thinking of a way to bring Kiam into the fold and make his team stronger. He looked at Daphne. "You met the nigga, can you put the pussy on him and reel him in?"

"I doubt it. The nigga is a boss," she replied. "But I can try."

"I don't need you to *try*, I need you to make it happen." Wolfman pulled out a wrinkled hundred dollar bill and tossed it at Daphne's feet. "Step your game up. I want Kiam."

Letting the money remain where it lay, Daphne stepped toward the door with a purpose, but it wasn't exactly the one Wolfman had set for her.

As soon as she was out the door, Wolfman said to Nitti, "We're gonna have to cancel that bitch after this, I can see the double-cross in her eyes."

Chapter 23
Let Me Go

Lissha was emotionally worn out after her visit with Big Zo. She had gone home and locked herself up in the house for days as a result. As she moved from one room to the next she tried to talk herself into a good mood. She stood in her kitchen door staring at the sink full of dishes and felt defeated.

"This don't make no fucking sense. Bitch, you live alone and got dishes pilling up," she chastised herself as she walked over to the sink, put on her pink rubber gloves, and turned on the hot water.

Once she got started, it was on. She cleaned her kitchen, pulled open her curtains and blinds and went to work sweeping, mopping, dusting and changing her linen. The bathroom was her last task, she cleaned it from front to back and put up a fresh shower curtain then she hopped into the shower.

When she emerged from the bathroom, she oiled up, threw on some sweat pants and a t-shirt and checked her messages. There were several calls from Kiam which she wasn't planning on returning. She knew if anything went wrong he knew what to do and, if not, he would surely bring his inconveniencing ass right to her door. She had come to the conclusion that she was going to back way up off him.

She flipped through her contacts and hit Bay. "Hey momma what's good?" Lissha said into the phone.

"Ain't shit. I'm getting my nails done. What's up with you?"

"Nothing really. I need to get out of this house. Where's Donella and Treebie?"

"Donella is on her way to pick me up. I don't know where Treebie ass at. But we about to go out for lunch."

"A'ight, come scoop me up on the way."

"Okay. See you in a minute. And bitch be ready."

"Whatever. Bye."

Lissha disconnected the call and hit Treebie's phone twice, back to back, but got no answer. "Where this bitch at?" she said aloud, placing her phone on the dresser. Treebie never missed calls so that shit had Lissha wondering.

She pondered for a minute then headed to her closet to change clothes.

Treebie sat on the plane playing back in her head the conversation that she had with Wa'leek.

"You need to come see me." He was straight to the point.

"I got too much going on right now."

"We ain't having a conversation about this shit. Get on the flight, see you when you get here," Wa'leek said into the phone then hung up.

It had been two months since she'd seen him and she knew if she didn't make the trip that nigga would find her and act a fucking fool. When she landed at Newark International airport her stomach began to ache.

She walked briskly through the airport to baggage claim, grabbed her small Gucci duffle then headed for the exit. As soon as she stepped out the door she saw him standing there looking fine as hell, clean from head to toe. He was mobbing in jeans, a pair of icy white sneakers, bright white V-neck t-shirt, and he was clean cut with a mean look on his high yellow face.

"That's all you got?" he asked, reaching in and taking her bag.

"No, I got some more shit, they gonna bring it to the car," said Treebie sarcastically as she headed for the passenger side of the car.

"Watch your mouth, before you get fucked up." Wa'leek smacked her ass on the way past.

"That shit feel good don't it?" She said as she ducked her head and slid inside the car.

Wa'leek shot her a quick smile, popped the trunk and tossed the bag in the back.

When he got in the driver's seat, Treebie's eyes roamed all over his body, he had added several more designs and color to his sleeve tattoo. He rested his hands on the steering wheel and shot her that hard stare.

"Why you eyeing me like that?" he asked, looking at her through his low gray eyes.

"Ain't nobody looking at you," she said, rolling her eyes.

"Stop shooting a nigga all that heat and let me taste them lips."

Treebie took a deep breath then turned and leaned toward him. She pulled him to her by the back of the head and kissed him deep.

His soft, juicy lips pulled her in. She turned her head allowing him to slip his tongue damn near down her throat. Their lips remained locked until a car horn blared behind them.

"Damn," Wa'leek said, ignoring the car behind them, as he stared at her breast sitting up in her shirt. "You done fucked around and made my soldier salute. You know what that mean?"

"No, I do not," she responded, sitting back in her seat.

"Don't worry, you will," he said as he pulled off.

When they got to his West Orange home Treebie was pleasantly surprised. He had redecorated with a very tasteful array of reds, blacks and whites. The brown throw rug that she hated had been replaced with a thick, black wall to wall carpet that felt like fur. She eyed the 84' Plasma mounted to the wall and the high-tech stereo equipment in a glass case in the corner.

"Why you acting like you never been here before," he asked, coming up behind her.

"I'm just admiring your decorating skills. This must be an upgrade for your little ho's you bring home," she stated accusingly.

"Let me explain something to you. You're my wife but you ain't here. I ain't no fucking homo so you know I get pussy. But them bitches know they fuck me, they suck me, but after that, I call they ass a green or yellow. Because they gotta get the fuck up outta here." He rested his hands on her waist and pressed his lips to her ear.

Treebie turned her head.

"Your legs are the only ones I slide in between with my heart involved. And any bitch I fuck with know that." He put his arms around her.

Treebie leaned back into his embrace and wrapped her mind around what he had just said. At the very least she had to respect his honesty and she knew that no secondhand bitch could take her place.

Wa'leek bent his head down and nibbled on her neck."Now go hit that shower and get sexy so we can hit the streets. I'll be right back, I gotta take care of something real quick," he said, removing his arms from around her waist.

She quickly spun in his direction. "I did not come all the way out here to sit around the house while you run the streets." She frowned.

"You better save all that tough shit for them bitch ass niggas in Ohio. Do what I told you." He kissed her lips and walked off.

Treebie was staring at his back when he turned around. "I want you to wear that dress I laid out. And hurry up, I'll be right back." He opened the door and walked out slightly slamming it behind him.

"That nigga get on my nerves," she said with a sigh as she walked to the bedroom.

When she opened the door what she saw confirmed his claims. A large picture of her hung on the wall over the head of his bed. Several small framed pictures of them on vacation in the Caribbeans sat on his dresser and nightstand.

"A bitch know her pussy good when a nigga got a shrine," she joked aloud as she pulled her shirt over her head, walked into the bathroom and hopped in the shower.

Two hours later Wa'leek returned with several bags in his hands. Treebie was sitting on the couch in her bra and panties, flipping through channels.

"Why you ain't dressed?" His eyebrows drew inward.

"Because I knew your ass would take forever, I didn't want to wrinkle my shit up.,"

"Yeah a'ight," he said, walking past the couch and down the hall into the bedroom.

Treebie turned off the television and followed him. When she walked in the room he was dumping clothes out of one bag and money out the other. She watched him stack and organize the neatly wrapped bills and head to his closet.

Out the corner of her eye,

Ca$h & NeNe Capri

194

she saw him put the money in a stash door in the wall.

"You ain't gotta peek, what's mine is yours, all you have to do is ask. Never give me a reason not to trust you," he said over his shoulder.

"What?" She felt like she had been caught with her hand in the collection plate.

He turned back around to face her. "I don't repeat shit when I know people heard it." He hit the light and shut the closet door.

Treebie sat on the bed with her hands folded and her mouth turned down. "Get dressed," he ordered, pulling his shirt over his head moving toward the bathroom. "When I come out the shower I wanna bounce."

As soon as Treebie heard the shower come on she got up, scented her skin then slipped into her clothes. Wa'leek had chosen for her a tight red, off the shoulder, knee length body dress and Red Bottom stilettos. Wa'leek came out the bathroom butt ass naked. Treebie's mouth watered when her eyes settled on all that dick. She watched every muscle in his body flex as he moved around the room.

"Dick look good don't it?" he asked then took it in his hand stroking it slow, bringing it to attention. "Why don't you talk to him real quick?"

Treebie sashayed over to him and took position. "Don't mess up my dress." She looked up at him as she took him in her hand.

"Make sure you swallow like a good girl and you won't have no problems," he instructed while watching his dick disappear into her mouth. Looking down at her, he tried to control his breathing as she spat all over his rod and slurped it right back up then took him to the back of her throat and gave him an oral massage.

"Ssss . . ." he hissed. "Work that shit," he moaned. After a few more jaw breaking movements he released long and hard to the back of her throat. Treebie pulled back, careful not to spill one drop.

Rising from her squatting position, she ran her tongue over her lips then kissed his. With a dramatic flair she turned and switched off to the bathroom. She stopped at the door and looked back at him over her shoulder. "A bitch bad ain't she?"

"Fucking trooper," he agreed, walking up to smack her shapely ass before she closed the bathroom door.

They arrived at Bella Italia for dinner. Not long after they were seated the waitress appeared with drink menus. "You know I don't like you drinking. Bring her some water with lemon," he told the waitress before she scribbled down the order.

Treebie looked up at the girl reproachfully. "Sweetie, please bring me a tall glass of Chianti, and you can bring *him* some water. Thank you." She handed the waitress the menu and the girl sauntered off.

Wa'leek shook his head. "You so hardheaded."

"You are not my father," she said, rolling her head to the side

"Why when I hit that spot you call me daddy?"

"Shut up," Treebie said then laughed.

When the drinks arrived the waitress cautiously placed the wine in front of Treebie and the water in front of Wa'leek. Treebie smirked. "Don't be scared. He is way more bark than he is bite."

The waitress smiled. "Are you ready to order?"

"Not yet, give us a minute," Wa'leek answered, giving Treebie an intense stare.

After the waitress left, Treebie began sipping her drink. Wa'leek drank his water then they caught each other up on what was going on. The conversation was going good until Wa'leek started his shit. "So when you coming home?" he questioned, touching on a subject that always ignited a fight.

"I don't know." Treebie braced herself for the battle.

"Fuck you mean you don't know?" Wa'leek sat forward placing his elbows on the table.

She looked into his eyes and saw that his mood had changed just that quickly. She tried to choose her words wisely before answering but no matter what she said, or how she said it, there was going to be a problem. "You know I got things I have to do. When I'm done, I'll be home," she said.

"What the fuck is that supposed to mean? You done left some dick to follow behind some pussy."

"Don't do that, I never come between you and your team."

"I didn't leave my fucking family to go bust a gun for the next bitch," Wa'leek replied bitterly.

"You fucking left me out here by myself. If it wasn't for Big Zo I don't know what I would have done—I owe him," Treebie countered.

"You don't owe that muthafucka shit. I did four years for our loyalty to Big Zo, all debts are paid. So fuck him," he gritted.

Treebie's blood was boiling. The more he talked the angrier she became. "You made your choices. And I made mine. You know where my loyalty lies but right now I gotta hold Lissha down."

"Man, fuck that bitch." The boom of his voice caused the couple at the next table to look in their direction.

"No, fuck you," returned Treebie. "I'm not doing this shit with you, you must be outta your mind."

"Why you so loyal to that bitch?"

"Big Zo is my people. I am loyal to him, plain and simple. Lissha is his daughter and I do what I gotta do with her to keep the peace and make my money."

"I don't give a fuck about none of them muthafuckas, and that new nigga you working for, he ain't shit either. I'll fuck around and come out there and rob and kill all them niggas."

Treebie had heard enough. She got up, knocking into the table so hard that her glass tipped over. Red wine spilled onto the white table cloth. "Take me home!"

Wa'leek grabbed her arm. "Sit the fuck down," he ordered, looking up into her eyes. Treebie stood there ready to defy him.

The manager rushed over to their table. "Is everything okay?" he asked.

"We're fine," said Wa'leek holding on to Treebie's arm firmly. With his other hand he reached into his pocket and sat a hundred dollar bill on the table. "Sorry for the inconvenience. He released Treebie's arm and stood up.

Treebie brushed past them and stormed to the car. When Wa'leek got outside she was breathing fire. He let her go off for a minute then explained his position. "My bad," he offered in apology. "But I'm fresh outta loyalty to that nigga. I want to put my family back together and I can't do that with you outta state risking your life for them. You feel me?" He put his hand under her chin and tilted her head up so that she could see the sincerity in his eyes.

Treebie didn't respond. She stood there burning up. As soon as she heard the locks click, she slid into seat and stared out the window with her elbow resting on the door. Wa'leek climbed behind the wheel and turned on the music. Not a word was uttered between them as they drove back to his house.

Chapter 24
Mind Fuck

Treebie jumped out the car and double timed it to the front door. The sound of her heels clacking on the concrete echoed in the silence of the night.

Wa'leek walked up behind her and opened the door. Treebie stormed in the house, moved to the bedroom and began gathering up her things.

Wa'leek turned on the stereo in preparation for the yelling match that was about to ensue. When he looked up Treebie was headed his way with her bag.

"Where the fuck you think you going?" He questioned harshly.

"Take me to the airport," she demanded.

"Fuck you mean? You ain't going nowhere." He reached in and tried to snatch her bag from her hands.

"Stop, Wah. Move! I should have never came here," she yelled back, refusing to let go of her bag.

"You gonna turn on me for them niggas?" he barked.

"It's not about them. Now get off my shit and move."

Wa'leek yanked her bag out of her arms and tossed it across the room. "Yo ass ain't going nowhere," he said forcefully, grabbing her by both arms and pulling her to him. Treebie tried to snatch away but the more she tussled with him the tighter he held her.

"Get the fuck off me," she spat.

"Shut the fuck up."

"No, you shut the fuck up," she disobeyed. "Get your hands off of me, Wa'leek. Right fuckin' now!"

Wa'leek pinned her against the wall forcing her arms above her head. "Wah stop," she cried, struggling against his body.

Wa'leek put both of her hands together and grabbed her by the throat. "Gimme a kiss."

"No, get off me."

He released her throat and reached in his pants, releasing that steel. Treebie squirmed between him and the wall as he reached under her dress and yanked her panties down around her ankles. "Wa'leek no, stop it!" Treebie fought as his fingers slid effortlessly between her thighs.

"You know this what you need," he said, staring at her with those hypnotic eyes.

"Wah, don't!" She continued to resist as she felt his finger push deep inside her.

"Don't what?" he whispered, picking up speed.

"Don't—do—this."

"Why not?" His voice dropped to a deep bass as his fingers delicately stroked her.

Treebie's cries of protest slowly turned into moans of pleasure. Wa'leek continued to reach for that spot as her breathing confirmed that she was ready to submit.

"Get it wet for me, baby," he whispered in her ear placing light kisses on her neck.

"Wah," she panted and her body began to tremble. He released her hands and wrapped her legs around his waist. Slowly, he slid all the way in. Treebie closed her eyes and sucked in her breath. Wa'leek went in deeper and stroked with command.

Treebie climbed the wall in an effort to escape his thickness. "Ain't nowhere to go," he rasped, holding her in place and thrusting harder. Treebie wrapped her arms around his neck and gave in to his command. She rolled her hips in harmony with his.

Wa'leek held her as he walked to the bedroom bouncing her up and down on all that dick. Each time she rose and descended Treebie's moans grew louder.

The next morning, Treebie awoke wrapped in Wa'leek's arms. When she opened her eyes he was staring into them with a tenderness that was foreign to his character. He kissed her good morning and said, "I need you, baby. I don't wanna fight with you."

"I don't want to fight with you either, Wah. I love you," she replied with sincerity.

"Come home, baby," he said stroking her cheek.

She didn't reply because she refused to lie to him. Wa'leek understood what her silence meant but he could not accept it. "You gotta let them go, ma," he said softly.

"I will when the time is right," she promised.

"Fuck that, the time is now."

"I thought you didn't want to fight?" she reminded him as she stared into those gray eyes.

"A'ight ma," he relented, but he knew how to get her to bring her ass home.

Over the next two days, Wa'leek worked on Treebie's mind and body. When the weekend was over and it was time for her to return to Cleveland, he was confident that he had her back under his control.

On Monday afternoon, he drove her to the airport confident with the seed of dissention he had sewn deep in her heart.

"When you bringing that wet back?" Wa'leek calmly asked, looking over to Treebie from the driver's side of his Ranger Rover.

"Soon," she answered, leaning over to taste those sweet lips.

"Hurry up, don't make me come for you."

"I won't. Just have a little more patience, baby," she said.

"I can't promise you that."

Treebie knew that time was running out. When she got out of the car she grabbed her bag and switched to the entrance for flight departures. Wa'leek beeped the horn and she slowly turned around. "You walking like something happened to you." He grinned.

Treebie just smiled big, flagged her hand, and disappeared inside.

Dropping his smile, Wa'leek pulled off and hit his Bluetooth. "What's up, my nigga?"

"Long time no hear," Riz slurred into the phone "What's good?"

"What you know about this new nigga Big Zo got working for him?"

Riz got quiet. "Maybe we need to sit down."

"I'm on my way." Wa'leek hung up and headed for the Holland tunnel.

202

Chapter 25
Heated Exchanges

Kiam hopped out of the truck with a black and burgundy backpack in his hand and strolled up to Lissha's door and rung the bell. He only had to wait about thirty seconds before she swung the door open.

"Hey." She stood there in a wife beater and a pair of yellow boy shorts.

"What's up?" His eyes ran from the top of her head down to her feet. She noticed him staring but made no comment. Usually she had something slick to say. Today was different.

"You're early. It's six o'clock, you said seven," Lissha complained.

"So what? You want me to come back in an hour? You must got a nigga up in here."

"No, I don't. But if I did, why should that concern you. Daddy told you to oversee the business, not me. This is grown woman shit over this way, and I'm perfectly capable of managing my own personal life."

"Grown, huh? I got something that makes big girls feel like little girls," he teased.

She shot him a look that told him not to go there, and in case he didn't get it, she reprimanded, "You better keep your mind on business before you find yourself wondering what the hell hit you and who was behind the wheel."

"I bet you been rehearsing that little comeback all day. I would clap for you but I got shit in my hands. And don't be fooled, I might tease and joke but when it comes to business, nothing gets in my way. Not even little pretty girls like you," he replied unperturbed.

"Whatever. Come in and handle your business so I can watch your best feature."

"What's that?"

"Your back." She turned and walked to the living room with him watching her booty bounce with each step. Lissha looked back just in time to see the lust in his eyes. He was looking at her like he wanted to bend her over the arm of the couch and show her that he was running more than just the business.

"I just wanna know one thing," he said.

"What?"

"Is it as good as it looks?" his eyes traveled down to that fat V between her thighs.

"Better," she shot back. "Too bad you'll never get to know for yourself."

"Don't bet on that," Kiam said arrogantly.

"Don't you bet against it," she matched his confidence.

"I never let what people say I can't do stand in the way if I wanna do it. Real niggas write their own script. If I wanna hit it, I'ma hit it. Just hope you can handle it when I do."

Lissha ignored his comment; he wasn't hitting nothing over that way. "You can have a seat, I'll be right back," she said, sauntering off into another room.

Kiam sat the backpack down at his feet and took a seat on the couch. Lavender scented candles burned in various areas around the living room. The soft sounds coming from the IPod dock relaxed his body and his mind.

When Lissha returned she had changed into a pair of baggy sweats and a loose-fitting top. Kiam looked up at her and laughed.

"What?" she asked.

"You're still sexy as a muthafucka, ma," he said. "You can't hide that no matter what you put on."

"Ain't nobody trying to hide nothing," she lied. "Anyway, don't worry about how sexy I am, you just keep up with that little goodie-goodie chick you've been seeing?" she said, sitting down across from him with her legs folded underneath her.

"Eyez? Goodie-goodie? Nah, you got her all wrong. You should know better than to judge a book by its cover. Baby girl used to hug the block with the big dogs. She's corporate now, but she's still gangsta with her shit."

"You said all that to say what? All bitches bleed."

"I ain't come over here to tongue wrestle with you." He stopped her. "I guess Gator ain't taming that pussy right so you giving me all that attitude. But it's all good, that's what happens when you give a little boy a job that was meant for a grown ass man," He rested his hands on each leg only inches away from his dick and stared at her trying to figure her out.

Lissha felt his eyes all over her and her body began to heat up. Her nipples tingled and her kitty purred. She hated that she couldn't stop herself from wanting him. Her mind told her to follow the script that Big Zo had written, but the epicenter of her womanhood had a mind of its own. She unconsciously squeezed her thighs together and tore her eyes off of him.

Kiam seemed to sense her dilemma. He smiled knowingly and patted a spot on the sofa right next to him. "C'mere, shorty," he said, his voice thick with primal seduction.

"Nah, I'm good." Lissha shook her head. She knew that if she went over and sat beside him and he didn't push her down and get all up in that pussy she would end up throwing his ass down and taking her some dick.

"You sure?" he asked.

"Yeah. I'm not going to let Daddy down. One of us gotta be trustworthy." She was determined to stand firm.

She turned her head away from Kiam before his mouth watering gaze made her change her mind. The moment of weakness passed. She was good now.

Her words were like a punch in the chest. The warning was clear. She had just set things on the right track with that statement. Kiam knew exactly what he needed to do.

"Okay. Well, I wanted to drop this off to you." He reached down and picked up the backpack and handed it to her. Lissha opened the flap and looked inside at the bands of dead faces. "Take care of the girls and make sure Pop is straight," Kiam instructed.

"You don't have to remind me to take care of Daddy, that's what I do. I been doing it long before you showed up, so what makes you think I would stop now?"

Kiam cocked his head to the side. "Fuck is your problem?"

"Fuck is yours?" she asked right back.

"You know what, I think you want me to do to you what Gator can't."

"And I think you want Daddy to do to you what you know he *will*."

Kiam was up off the couch as soon as the comment left her lips. He grabbed her by the face and gritted, "You trying to disrespect me?" His voice was low but lethal.

Lissha said nothing.

"See, when you be around pussy ass niggas too long you forget how you should never talk to a man." He tightened his grip on her face and forced her to look in his eyes. "You see any bitch in me?"

"No, I don't. Now get your fucking hands off my face." She dug her nails into his arms.

Kiam accepted her half-hearted submission. He released her and allowed himself a minute to cool off. When his chest stopped heaving up and down, he said, "You almost got fucked up, shorty. Don't ever try to pit me against your father again. I love and respect Big Zo to the utmost but I fear no man." He turned his back to her and walked to the door.

"Kiam," Lissha called out.

"Fuck you want?"

"I apologize," she said. "I would never pit you against Daddy."

He shot her the deuces and kept on pushing. He didn't know what the fuck he was doing playing with her anyway. His loyalty

206

to Big Zo had to trump lust, and his love for Faydrah should have extinguished any flame that sparked between him and any other woman. It was time for him to dead the bullshit and stand firm on principle.

Chapter 26
New Beginnings

Faydrah moved around Kiam's new condo opening appliances and carefully putting them in their place. Uncovering the couch and love seat, she smiled at the idea of her finally being able to see Kiam enjoy life.

He watched her joyfully move about the rooms hanging curtains and arranging the furniture that she had helped him pick out. While he walked off to answer a call from Lissha, Faydrah opened several boxes looking for the lamp that she had bought to go with the living room furniture.

Her eyes popped out of her head when she saw that she had opened the wrong boxes. Two of them were full of money and a count machine. The third box that she opened contained guns, a silencer, vests, black clothing and boots. She snapped the boxes shut like she had seen somebody's dark family secrets.

Faydrah wished like hell that she hadn't mistakenly opened the wrong boxes, because now her mind was racing and her joy was gone. When Kiam returned to the living room she was still bending over the box which contained the weapons. His eyes roamed over her body admiring her curves in her tight leggings and tank top.

Coming up behind her he wrapped his arms around her waist and whispered in her ear. "Let's go break that new king-size in." He pressed himself against her butt and began walking her up the stairs.

"I have work to do, Mister," she giggled.

"Me, too, I gotta see how these springs work," he shot back, steering her into the bedroom. Playfully, he tossed her up on the bed then crawled between her legs.

"Stop Kiam," she screamed with laughter as he bit and tickled her stomach. In spite of what she had seen, she could not stop herself from enjoying his rare playfulness.

He pressed his body down onto hers and planted soft kisses on her lips. She parted her lips, demanding his tongue, while her hands went on an expedition. The surge of testosterone that shot through his body had him ready to put that ass to sleep.

"Kiam wait," she pleaded as his hands slid under her shirt and gently caressed her breast. Kiam ignored her plea as he traced her lips with his tongue. "Baby, we need to talk."

"About what?" he asked, grinding his steel against her clit while planting soft kisses on her neck and collar bone.

"No, seriously." She pushed him up slightly to look into his eyes.

"What's on your mind, shorty?" he asked, still in full fuck mode.

"What's going on, Kiam?"

"We about to fuck real hard for a little over an hour then fall asleep and start all over again," he rasped, leaning in and kissing her again.

"Kiam, wait. I need to talk to you for a minute." She gently pushed him up.

"What's up?" He paused to hear her out.

"What are you doing? I saw some things that let me know you're back in the streets."

"What you talking about, Eyez?" he asked.

"I don't have to explain. You know what I saw." Kiam sat all the way up and rubbed his hand over his face.

Faydrah sat up next to him. "I wasn't being nosey, I was looking for that lamp I bought you," she explained, then her expression turned somber. "I guess I knew before I saw those things, because I know you. You're right back in that life," she accused.

Kiam laid on his back resting his hands behind his head. "I gotta do, what I gotta do," he said.

"What you gotta do? What does that mean?"

"You know what this is Eyez."

"No, I don't. I know that you just gave up eight years of your life over some bullshit." She glared down into his face.

Kiam sat up. "I'm not doing this with you right now." He shook his head.

"Why not, Kiam? Because I'm touching on some truth?" she challenged.

Kiam stood up and headed out of the bedroom. Faydrah hopped up and caught up with him at the door. She grabbed his arm and planted herself in front of him. "Where are you going? Really, you're going to just walk away in the middle of a conversation?"

"For real, shorty, I'm not trying to talk about it. Move out the way." His words hurt, because they confirmed her suspicions, but she choked back the pain and continued trying to reach him.

"Baby, I love you," she said. "I always have. Many days I thought about moving on. But I couldn't because I knew I couldn't let go of you. It didn't matter that we didn't keep in touch, you owned my heart. I kept dreaming that you would come home and leave these damn streets alone so we wouldn't ever have to be apart again."

Kiam stood quiet as she took him by the face and continued her plea. "You are a brilliant man, the same effort you put into hustling and killing, you can put into something positive and become just as successful."

Removing her hands from his face Kiam affirmed his position. "I hear you. But I'm not in that place right now. I got things I have to do. I got mad love for you, but it's you who has to decide what you're gonna do. I already know what I gotta do. Now you can either ride with a nigga or hop off," he said as he walked away.

"What kinda statement is that?" she railed. "I guess that's some bullshit those jailhouse niggas put in your head."

Kiam turned on his heels moving back in her direction. "I'm my own fuckin' man. I don't need no nigga to validate who I am." He raised his voice, peering down at her.

Faydrah gritted her teeth and stood up in his face. "Who you trying to convince, me or yourself?" Unlike the niggas on the street she had no fear of his reputation. With her he was just Kiam.

"I don't have to convince you of shit. I'm a loyal nigga, you know that. I made promises to a man that I love and respect like a father, so I'm going to keep my word. That's my get down, you already know that. I would never disrespect you, but if you can't roll with what I gotta do, then you know what you gotta do."

She rested her hand on his chest. "Yeah, you're right," Faydrah agreed. "You are loyal. But the person you need to learn to be loyal to is yourself."

Kiam looked away as her words threatened to shatter his illusions of what being official meant. As mad as it made him for her to challenge the code that he lived by, he knew deep inside her words came from a caring place. But the ego that lay within him would not let him submit.

Faydrah saw that in the stubborn set of his jaw. *Why in the hell am I wasting my breath?* she asked herself. She removed her hand from his chest and set her own jaw. "You're right. I am going to get off," she stated as she walked downstairs to gather her things.

Kiam rubbed his fist in his hand. He wanted to stop her but a false sense of pride took the wheel and was driving a wedge between him and the only woman he ever really loved.

As Faydrah hit the door, struggling with her shoes, her purse fell to the floor. Snatching it up, she flung it over her shoulder then franticly searched for her car keys.

Kiam walked into the living room, plopped down on the couch, and silently watched her. He was too stubborn to utter what his heart demanded that he say.

Faydrah said, "I was just going to walk outta here and not say anything else to you, but I'm not built like that. All this shit you got going on up in here." She waved her arms around. "It's all going to crumble around you. And the very muthafuckas you vow loyalty to are gonna be the ones to stab you in the back." Her voice cracked and her eyes filled with tears.

Kiam's heart ached over the pain he was causing her, but his response didn't show what he felt inside. "You done?" he asked bluntly.

Faydrah held back her tears and forced a smile. "I damn sure am," she replied with strength. She grabbed the door knob and snatched the door open, slamming it as she stormed out.

When she got outside the door all of her emotions spilled over. She leaned up against the wall, held her purse tight in her arms and let the tears fall. She slid to the ground as the pain in her spirit no longer allowed her legs to support her weight.

Placing her face in her hands, she wept. She cried for who Kiam could be and who he was determined to remain. She never wanted to upset their bond but she knew that she could not live with herself if she didn't tell him how she felt.

On the other side of the door Kiam was dealing with the same feelings. His heart told him she was right, but the beast in him had made commitments he was not going to ignore. Conflicted and angry, he got up and headed to the door to return to the streets. He looked down and saw her sitting on the floor with her back against the wall, sobbing.

"Baby, what you doin'?" he asked softly.

Faydrah looked up with pain and sadness in her eyes. "I don't want to live without you Kiam," she said from the heart.

"Come here ma." He reached down and gently lifted her to her feet. Faydrah went into his arms and leaned her forehead against his chest.

"Baby, please get outta the streets. Do that for me," she asked in a desperate tone.

"I'm not going to lie to you. I can't get out right now. But I promise, nothing I'm doing will hurt you. I need you to chill and let me do what I do," he maintained.

Faydrah had to allow that, because letting go was no better option than trying to live without air. "Okay, Kiam," she agreed, "but you have to promise me that when shit is piled against you, you'll get out."

"I promise, shorty." He held her closer to his chest. "Now let's go back inside. You out here embarrassing me in front of my neighbors." He pulled her inside and closed the door with his foot.

"Shut up." She hit his arm. "You should be glad somebody cares about your black ass." Faydrah sat her bag down and pouted her lips.

"What?" Kiam smiled. "Does this mean I can't see them legs on my shoulders?" He licked his lips enticingly.

"You think your ass is cute."

"Girl, you see all this." Kiam put his arm up displaying his bicep. "Nigga on point."

"Whatever. You just better be careful. And that chick I saw at your hotel room. You watch her. I don't trust that bitch."

"I got it. Now come make up with me. You got my little nigga all upset." He walked over and picked her up.

Faydrah wrapped her arms and legs around him as he carried her to the bedroom and laid her on the bed. He took his time undressing her, then he slowly undressed himself.

Naked and wrapped in passion Faydrah laid tenderly under his precise push. Each stroke affirmed their love but she could tell that he was no longer the Kiam she fell in love with, he had morphed into something else.

With each pleasure-filled release she wondered what had changed him. Was it the time in prison or the feeling of abandonment each time he lost someone he loved or trusted?

Either way she knew it was only a matter of time before she would be lying with a stranger. She wondered how much of herself was she willing to lose while trying to save the broken pieces within him.

Chapter 27
Treacherous

Lissha moved around her house trying to get her mind right to deal with Kiam. She had not seen him since their little altercation the other day. It was pick up time and he insisted that she go with him. She both dreaded and looked forward to seeing him.

A moment after she grabbed her gun, her phone rang. Checking the screen revealed that it was Big Zo. "Hello," she answered.

"Baby girl." His voice boomed into the phone.

"Hey, Daddy." She forced her voice to sound chipper.

"You alright?" he asked

"Yeah, I'm good. How are you?" she replied, trying to shift the weight in the other direction.

"I'm good now. I'm just checking on you. I had a feeling that you might be going through something because you haven't called in a few days." He gently probed.

"Everything is fine. I'm about to go to the store with Kiam."

"Yeah?"

"Mm hmm, they just got some fresh watermelon in and I know it's on sale." She shot him some code real quick.

"Alright handle your business. Hit me when you get back."

"I will," she assured him, reaching for the button to disconnect.

"Lissha?"

"Huh?" She put the phone back to her ear.

"Get your shit together. We got too much on the line," he reiterated, pacing back and forth in his cell.

"What you mean, Daddy?"

"You know what I mean. I know you, I can hear the wavering in your voice. But I taught you better than that. Don't make me regret my decision. Talk to you later." He hung before she could respond.

Lissha wanted to throw her phone against the wall, run to her room and jump back under her covers and pretend that none of this was happening. As soon as she started into her feelings she heard a car horn outside her door.

"Oh, boy, here we go," she sighed, heading for the door. And as if the day couldn't get any worse she looked up and saw the bitch from the hotel propped up in the front passenger seat of Kiam's truck like the fucking Queen of England.

Lissha took a deep breath, closed the door, and strutted down the walkway. She climbed into the backseat and closed the door, staring at the back of Kiam's head with disgust in her eyes.

Sensing she was shooting him prisms he reached up and adjusted the rearview mirror and gave her a smile. "Good afternoon, Miss Lissha," he said all formally, like he was driving Miss Daisy.

"Ain't shit good about it. I thought we had business to handle, I didn't know it was bring your friends to work day."

Faydrah looked over at Kiam and smiled. She was not frazzled by the heat that was coming from the back seat.

Kiam looked over his shoulder at Lissha. "This ain't no friend," he clarified. "This is the result of what happens the next morning after you make that pussy purr." He leaned over and kissed Faydrah's lips.

Lissha wrinkled up her nose.

"I take it your man didn't come home last night," Kiam jeered, then turned the music up, put the car in gear and pulled off.

"Fuck you, Kiam."

Faydrah gave him a look telling him not to even entertain the bullshit. Kiam nodded his understanding. He looked up in the mirror watching Lissha put on her shades and turn toward the window.

As Kiam drove downtown to drop Faydrah off at work he periodically looked at Lissha who was becoming angrier by the minute. Being that Faydrah was a true team player, she fed right into Kiam's little games and giggled and rubbed all over him as he drove.

Lissha sat fantasizing about pulling out her heat and blowing both of their minds all over the front window.

When Kiam pulled up in front of Faydrah's job he turned down the music, reached in his pocket and pulled a nice stack out and handed it to her. "Get that shit that makes a nigga act the fuck up," he said.

"And bring you home to me?" she added.

"No doubt."

"Okay, baby." She leaned over and kissed him passionately while sliding her hand over his print.

"Don't be sleep," he said.

"You know how to wake me, don't you?" she cooed, giving him her sexy gaze. Stepping from the vehicle, she grabbed her purse and looked back at Lissha. "Have a good day."

Lissha threw her an evil smirk. "You have a *safe* one."

"Oh, trust me I intend to, because anything that could prevent that from happening, I know how to remove it." She held a short eye lock with Lissha before flashing Kiam a smile. "Bye, baby," she said as she walked away.

"Eyez, behave," Kiam yelled out.

Faydrah waved her hand over her shoulder and kept it moving.

Lissha was not amused. "Your bitch ain't house trained, you better make sure she know who is running this shit before she gets fucked up," she said to Kiam.

"The only thing you running is ya mouth," he laughed.

Lissha mumbled something slick under her breath that Kiam didn't quite catch, but he recognized her attitude for what it was. "You jelly?" he smiled.

"Of what? A bitch that gets good dick because her man's mind is filled with how good *my* pussy feels? Fuck outta here. I'm a product of Big Zo, that bitch ain't got shit for me. And neither do you." Her mouth tightened as the words left her pretty glossed lips. Kiam smiled. "You're so cute when you're trying to be mean." Lissha shot her middle finger straight in the air.

"Get in the front, I ain't no fucking chauffeur." Kiam hurled back at Lissha.

"Kiam, please don't fuck with me right now. Because if I come up there I might do something we both will regret."

"You ain't talking about shit, you wanted distance between us, so you got it. Deal with it." He threw that killer glare her way then pulled off.

Lissha quickly picked up on the fact that his words said one thing but meant another. A smile came across her face as she realized she had succeeded in getting in his head just like he was in hers.

"Take me by Treebie's before we start picking up. I need to get at her real quick," she said as he turned up Prospect Avenue.

Kiam didn't respond, he drove in silence with only the music as a buffer between the discomforts they both were feeling.

When they pulled up to Treebie's townhouse, Lissha jumped out the back seat, walked up on the steps and rang the bell. She waited a half minute then knocked on the door a few times.

Treebie opened the door in her robe looking as if Lissha was a Jehovah Witness. "Why the fuck you on my shit like that?" Treebie asked with a mean mug.

"Why the fuck you ain't answered your phone in three days?"

"I was taking care of some business. What's up?"

"Taking care of business?" Lissha threw her head to the side. "We got shit pending and you just disappear? What the fuck is going on with you?" Lissha asked, as her eyes settled on a few light hickies on Treebie's collar bone.

"I'm a very grown woman. I don't question your actions, so don't question mine."

"Have you bumped your muthafuckin' head?"

Treebie smiled looking over at Kiam whose eyeballs were focused out the front window. His body language read aggravation. "What happened, you and your little boyfriend get into it?"

"First of all, don't do that. Second, you need to get your ass on point. We ride on these niggas in two days. Its's blood money, bitch, you know I don't play with my shit."

"And I don't play at all. I'll be ready, snatch your thong out ya ass and try to have a good day. I'll be over tomorrow."

"You get on my nerves," Lissha clacked as she turned to walk back to the car.

"LiLi, you need to go ahead and give that nigga some pussy so you can get your mind right," Treebie said and began cracking up.

"Fuck you, Tree."

"Not me bitch, fuck the nigga that has your ass on fire. A good nut might calm you the fuck down," she laughed then shut the door.

Treebie's laughter echoed in Lissha's mind as she jumped in the back seat. She was pissed and feeling like she was back at square one in her feelings. Kiam shook his head. *She gon' hop her hard headed ass right back in the back seat, huh?* He turned the music back up and pulled off.

They encountered Gator at their first stop in East Cleveland. He came out of the trap house on Hayden and passed a shoe bag full of mula through the window to Kiam. He cut his eyes at Lissha and held his stare. She knew what he was thinking but she didn't give a damn. Just because she wasn't dealing with him anymore, didn't mean she was fucking Kiam. She mean mugged Gator right back.

"That's what happens when you fuck with the help," shot Kiam as he bent a corner and hopped back on Euclid Avenue.

Lissha ignored the trite remark and Kiam let the subject die. He hit JuJu up real quick to let him know that he was coming by his place to pick up the money he had for him.

"That's cool, I got it on deck," replied JuJu. The weekend dice games at the St. Clair joint was beginning to do big numbers. Kiam was glad that he had decided to get down with that hustle.

Lissha welcomed the brief reprieve because as long as Kiam was on the phone he wasn't talking to her. She stared out the window tuning out his conversation.

After collecting from JuJu they hit a few of their other houses around the city. Within two hours they had successfully made every stop. They had the money tucked tight in the trunk, now they just needed to drop it off at the safe house and then they would be out of each other's hair.

"Why did I have to ride with you to do this?" she questioned him as they drove down East 116th toward Kinsman.

"You need to know where our new spots are in case something happens to me," he explained.

"I'm not that lucky."

Kiam ignored her sarcasm. Reaching 116th and Union, he pulled into the Sunoco station. "I need to get some gas real quick," he said.

"Do you, boo boo," she shot back, keeping her face to the window as if that would make her invisible.

Kiam pulled up to the pump and jumped out. "You want something?"

"Nah, I'm good," she answered making sure not to look in his direction.

When he was inside the store, Lissha jumped out the truck and stood next to it while flipping through her cell phone. She shot Big Zo a quick text letting him know she was safe and would be transferring money into his account in the morning.

222

She looked up into the store and saw Kiam engaged in a heavy conversation. Lissha sighed loudly, she was ready to get home. Aggravated, she turned to get back in the truck.

"I guess you a big shot now, huh?" The feminine voice came from behind her.

Lissha whipped her head around and every muscle in her body seized up. "Get the fuck outta my face," she hissed. Her eyes nervously searched for Kiam.

"You ain't shit." The woman lashed out at her.

Lissha moved toward her with her lips pulled back. "That's because the pussy I dropped from wasn't shit," she said, bristling inside.

"I don't know how the fuck you can live with yourself."

"And I don't know why you're still living."

Lissha and the woman began slinging heated remarks and curse words back and forth. They both had wicked tongues and plenty of ammunition to hurl at each other.

Kiam looked up from his conversation inside the store and saw Lissha and the woman standing nose to nose, going at it.

"I'll get with you another time. Hit me up." He touched fist with Frank Nitti and hurried out the door.

Moving swiftly in Lissha's direction he heard the woman say, "Fuck Big Zo, I hope his punk ass die a slow, painful death,"

"Be careful that the grave you wish on him doesn't grab your ass first."

"Yo, what the fuck is going on?" Kiam stepped in and pushed them apart. He looked from Lissha to the woman, waiting for either of them to explain. All of a sudden Lissha's mouth was on mute.

"This dirty bitch is the worst thing that ever happened to me," said the woman. She turned back to Lissha and hocked a glob of spit in her direction. Lissha jumped back then lunged forward punching her dead in the face.

"Oh yes, bitch, I been waiting for this day," the woman snarled, bouncing on her toes as she reached up and wiped blood from her busted lip.

Kiam backed up a little as fist flew back and forth with unleashed fury. The sound of the punches bounced off their faces causing bystanders to flinch in pain.

Kiam grabbed Lissha by the waist and lifted her off her feet and moved her to the truck. "Calm yo ass down, you drawing too much attention. We dirty," he whispered tersely.

"Get the fuck off me." She kicked and pulled at Kiam's arms trying to break free.

"Let that bitch go," the woman begged.

Lissha wiggled out of Kiam's arms, snatched his whistle off his waist and pointed it at the woman, "I fucking hate you!" she yelled out.

The woman tore her shirt open and began pounding her fist over her heart. "Do it. Don't be no punk as ho. Do it. Pull the trigger!"

Lissha was shook up, she stood with her arm extended and her trigger finger frozen as tears began to run down her face.

"Do it!" The woman egged her on. But this time the woman's voice cracked. "I ain't got shit to live for. You and that man took everything I had!"

The gun shook in Lissha's hand as she re-tightened her grip to keep from dropping it. The woman stared at the weapon, inviting the end to her pain.

Lissha looked at her with no pity, but she could not bring herself to put her out of her misery. Their eyes held each others as the past ran through both of their minds. Lissha interpreted it one way. The woman interpreted it the opposite, but what had happened between them was irreversible.

Sweat and tears ran down the woman's dark brown face, trickling past her bloody mouth. Lissha's chest heaved up and down as she tried to calm the many emotions that fought for control over her. Squeezing the trigger would put an end to everything that had happened between them.

"Fuck you doing?" Kiam's voice jarred her from her thoughts. She let her arm fall down to her side.

Kiam cautiously took the gun from her hand. She relinquished it without protest, but the anger in her soul remained red hot. She casted an evil eye at the broken woman and snarled, "Stay the fuck away from me because the next time I see you, there will be no mercy."

"Likewise bitch," said the woman, about to get hyped all over again.

"Come get in the car, Lissha," urged Kiam, grabbing her by the arm. "Fuck all of this drama. This that hot shit."

"Get the fuck off me." She snatched away and walked off.

"Where the fuck are you going?" Kiam tried to move behind her.

Lissha didn't say anything she high tailed it to the corner where people were boarding the #15 bus. She pushed pass a few people in line and hopped on.

Kiam turned back to the woman, he needed answers. "Who the fuck are you?" he demanded to know.

"I'm her dirty little secret," she replied, lowering her eyes. "You better be careful. That bitch is treacherous. I wouldn't trust that heifer with her own thoughts." She pulled her shirt closed and walked away.

Kiam wanted to go after her and force her to explain, but the sirens in the background trumped all that. He jumped in his truck and pulled off, puzzled over what he had just witnessed.

After dropping the money off, he made a beeline to Lissha's house. He parked and sat outside, determined to get every question he had answered either by will or by force.

Chapter 28
A Test Of Loyalty

Two hours later Lissha, slid out of a cab and moved quickly toward her door. Kiam jumped out of his truck, walking with long stealth-like strides. They reached her door at the same time. "What the fuck was all that shit about?" he barked.

"None of your fucking business." She put her key in the door and pushed it open.

"Fuck you mean it's none of my business? We was out there with mad money and you creating fucking heat, 'bout to get our asses snatched the fuck up." The vein in his neck was like a whip cord as he followed her into the kitchen.

"Look, you were probably out there waiting to see if I made it home safe. Well, here I am, so you can be on your merry fucking way." She tossed her keys on the counter and turned to go in the living room.

Kiam snatched her little ass back around so that she was facing him again. "You think I sit out in front of bitches houses to make sure they get home safe?" he blared.

"I don't know what you do, and I don't care." She marched away from him.

Kiam was right behind her.

Lissha sat down on the sofa and reached for a half of blunt that was in an ashtray on the end table. Kiam stood over her, seething. "You must be fucking stupid." He placed with his fist in his hand while trying to regain his composure. "Now, this is the last time I'm gonna ask you what the fuck that shit was about."

Lissha sat the blunt back down and looked up at him. "It could be your last time or your third time, and my answer will be the same. None. Of. Your. Business." She dragged each word out, making sure to drive her point all the way home.

Kiam started to explode, but thought better of it. "Yeah, you right, it ain't none of my business. But if you ever put me in that type of situation again, I'll blow your fucking head off," he warned then turned to the door.

"Muthafucka I ain't scared of no nigga. You ain't saying shit." She pounced up off the couch and walked up on him.

Kiam turned around. "Don't ever walk up on me," he said.

"Or what? What?" Her arms flew out to her sides animatedly, challenging him to release his rage.

Kiam fought back the impulse to slap the shit out of her. Had she been any other nigga's daughter he would've rattled her teeth.

"Yeah, that's what the fuck I thought," she continued to mouth off. He knew what the fuck her problem was. It was time he shut her up.

In one move Kiam pulled her into his arms and put his lips to hers. Kissing her deep, he took her breath and finally shut her up. She received him as if she had been waiting all her life for that moment.

Lissha allowed his tongue to command all her attention and his hands to follow. When her pussy started to throb her thoughts boomed Big Zo. She tried to slam the doors to her mind shut and just follow the command of her body, but Zo hadn't schooled her to get down like that.

All of a sudden Lissha pulled back. "Kiam, no. We can't." She pushed him back and tried to catch her breath.

"Why not?" he asked, then pulled her back into him and took more of what he wanted. Lissha gave it willingly. She sucked on his tongue as he gripped her ass and walked her backwards toward her bedroom. Lissha was panting with an anticipation that had her pussy screaming.

As they reached the bed he pulled at her clothes.The heat between them was incinerating. "Kiam," she cried out, trying to stop what was destined to be.

228

"Let this shit happen," he responded on lust-filled breath.

"I can't betray Daddy. Please Kiam remember your promise."

Kiam's hands stopped where they were. He pulled them back, breathing hard and standing there with a dick even harder.

She looked up into his eyes as tears left hers. "We can't," she mumbled regretfully, shaking her head from side to side. They looked at each other in silence for what felt like forever but was actually only a few seconds.

Kiam spoke first. "You right. I'm sorry, get some rest." He kissed her forehead then turned to the door.

When Lissha heard the door close, she yelled out in frustration. "Why?" She sat hard on the floor, put her face in her hands and cried.

Kiam moved as if his life depended on it. When he got in the car he slammed his palms down on the steering wheel and let out a loud and frustrated sigh. He had almost crossed the line.

He was beyond conflicted, he had a woman whom he loved and another one that was his forbidden desire. And he had accepted a mission that could bring everything crumbling down.

He drove off thinking he needed to readjust his priorities because the last thing he wanted to become was a muthafucka a nigga couldn't trust.

Ca$h & NeNe Capri

Chapter 29
Retreat

Kiam felt the weight of his actions pounding in his head and heart as he inserted the key in the door and walked into his condo. He walked upstairs with the burden making his legs feel like lead.

Inside his bedroom, he hit the light and his attention settled on a picture of him and Faydrah on his nightstand. He was giving her a piggyback ride; her arms and legs were wrapped around him tightly and she wore a smile that reflected the love she had for him.

When he tallied everything up, she was the fuel that replenished his dark soul when the streets threatened to turn it into an abysmal dungeon.

He removed his gun, placed it on the nightstand, and sat down on the bed. The day played back in his mind in slow motion. The situation with Lissha and the strange woman, and the fact that he had almost done something he swore he would not do—sleep with Big Zo's daughter.

He shook his head as Lissha's words cut into his heart confirming that he needed to get on point and keep it like that. *Remember your promise,* she had pleaded. What he needed to do was get money and find a way to free the man that had given him the keys to an empire. Too many niggas forgot about loyalty once their feet touched down on the outside of the prison fences. *Death before dishonor,* he reminded himself.

He thought about the only two women he had ever loved. He had lost one while caged. Now that he was out, he wasn't going to lose the other. Eyez loved and knew the man he was when his gun wasn't blazing. Their bond was impenetrable; it had held her heart captive while he was away, and it had led him to her doorsteps the moment his feet touched back down in the grimy city streets that had first introduced them to each other as kids. It was time for him to show her that he appreciated what they shared.

He reached for his phone and Googled some resorts in the area. A list of them popped up on the screen. He scrolled down until an advertisement for Big Rock Cabins caught his eye. It was a nice little getaway spot in the Appalachian foothills of Southern Ohio, secluded far from the hustle and bustle of the city. It seemed to offer exactly what he was looking for.

Kiam secured a reservation for the weekend. He needed a few days to get his mind right, and with strong lieutenants in place this was the perfect time for him and Faydrah to get away and strengthen their love.

Satisfied with his plans, Kiam hopped in the shower and began to mentally prepare for the little getaway. The water cascaded down his body and helped eased the tension that came from the life he had chosen.

With his priorities back on track sleep came easy for Kiam that night. When morning came he packed a few things then headed to the store to pick up some essentials that would make the weekend just right. Once he had all of his bags of tricks he stopped through the spots and gave out specific orders. His last stop was to see JuJu.

"Look, make sure you keep your eyes on these niggas, and if shit go wrong put a nigga on his ass. I'm only comfortable with casualties being those of the next nigga's team," he imparted.

"I got you," JuJu assured him.

They shook hands and bumped shoulders, then Kiam jumped in his truck and headed downtown to pick up Faydrah.

Faydrah was at her desk pounding away at her keyboard and talking loud into the speaker phone to colleagues in two different states. They were trying to iron out problems with a special project that they were working on.

When she saw her door open and Kiam standing there, her pretty light brown eyes brightened a bit more and the serious expression on her face quickly turned into a wide smile. He held a large bouquet of yellow, orange and blue assorted flowers wrapped in pink shiny paper with a big bow.

Faydrah instantly lost interest in the business call. Her eyes sparkled as she waved him over to her desk. Kiam handed her the flowers, and leaned down giving her the sweetest kiss she had ever tasted.

Excitedly, she put her finger up and mouthed, "*One minute.*"

Kiam took a seat in a chair across from her desk and watched as she buried her nose in the flowers and inhaled their fragrance. She sat the bouquet on her desk and finished typing the report as she glanced up at Kiam and made funny faces.

He shook his head at her silliness, it reminded him of that time when they were twelve and his appendix burst. She came to his hospital room and blew up the rubber gloves and drew faces on them in an attempt to cheer him up.

"Okay, I believe that sums everything up. I will email the proposal to both of you by noon Monday. Enjoy your weekend," she announced to the parties on the conference call, then disconnected.

Now she didn't have to hold back. Rising from behind her desk, she squealed, "Aww, baby." She walked around the desk and climbed on Kiam's lap, hugging him around the neck and placing tender kisses on his lips.

"Thank you, baby, I love them." She reached over and fingered the bouquet.

"I love to make you smile," he said.

She laid her head on his shoulder. "I needed that," she said. The day had been a stressful one up until then.

"You need something else too," he grinned, placing his hands on her butt.

"So, what you want to do tonight?" She wriggled her behind on his dick.

Kiam kissed her on the back of the neck. "I wanna do you on your desk right now."

"Down boy." She slapped his hand and giggled. She got up off his lap, pirouetted, and walked back behind her desk to wrap up her end of the project. "So am I getting some tonight?" she asked.

"I'm leaving town."

Faydrah snapped her neck to the side and looked at Kiam like she was ready to choke him. "Leaving town? Where you going?" She couldn't keep the disappointment out of her voice.

"Not me alone, baby - *us*."

"Going where? I can't just leave town, I don't have anything to wear. Besides, I have work I need to finish up before Monday. Really baby, I can't get away this weekend," she sighed.

"Yes, you can," he said. "I picked out everything I want to see you in for the next couple of days. Get your laptop and let's go."

"Baby!" She stomped her feet like a five-year-old.

"Wrap that shit up, I want to get on the road before rush hour." He looked at his watch.

"You serious?" Kiam didn't respond he just raised one eyebrow. Faydrah thought for a minute then grabbed her thumb drive, downloaded her files and emailed herself a backup. Quickly, she left the room to give instructions to her secretary and to copy a few documents she would need.

Returning to her office where Kiam sat tapping his foot in mock impatience, Faydrah packed up her laptop and three manila envelopes. She grabbed her briefcase, her purse, and the flowers. Kiam shook his head.

"Baby, let me carry that for you," he said, relieving her of the briefcase.

He frowned at her when she tried to hand him her purse. "I'm just kidding," she laughed.

"Don't play, shorty," he feigned a mean mug.

Faydrah locked up her office and they headed out. "This better be good," she warned, looking at him flirtatiously.

"Isn't it always good?" He licked his lips and flashed that sexy smile.

"You saw a bitch throwing shit in a bag like it was a state of emergency issued, didn't you?" Faydrah said, and they both chuckled.

When they got in the truck Faydrah kicked off her shoes and surfed his satellite radio for an old school station. Marvin Gaye was singing *Let's Get It On.* Kiam and Faydrah snapped their fingers to the beat and sung along.

We're all sensitive people/With so much love to give, understand me sugar/Since we got to be/Let's say, I love you/There's nothing wrong with me/Lovin' you/And giving yourself to me can never be wrong/If the love is true /Don't you know how sweet and wonderful, life can be...

As they drove, Faydrah beamed from the inside out. This was the Kiam she fell in love with. She bottled up every moment, carefully tucking them into her memory as if they were her last.

Three and a half hours and many old school songs later they arrived at their destination. When they pulled into the wooded area Faydrah's eyes were all over the place. They settled on the sign that read Big Rock Cabins. Kiam parked the car in front of the registration office and walked inside to retrieve their keys. Faydrah continued to look in every direction enjoying the serene backdrop of trees and flowers.

Kiam jumped back in the truck, passed her the keys, and then drove along the path deeper into the woods. Pulling alongside a wooden staircase outside their cabin, he turned off the engine and hopped out. Faydrah got out as well and moved to the back seat to get her things. Walking to the trunk where Kiam stood gathering bags she enjoyed the grass below her feet.

"What's all that?" she asked, looking at the many bags in the trunk.

"Stop being nosey and take these." He handed her the bag with the sheets, pillows and comforter, then grabbed the ones with the food and drinks and cleaning supplies.

Placing his bags on the porch he went back to the car to grab a few more items.

Faydrah opened the door and fell in love. There was exposed timber framing and natural wood throughout. The only thing modern was the TV, fireplace and the stereo. The open living room had a long couch, two arm chairs and a fire place right in front of it. The medium sized kitchen and island sat off the left. Huge picture windows brought all the scenic surroundings inside.

She placed the bags on the floor next to the table and moved to the small sun porch that had a grill, a small table, two chairs and a hot tub on the elevated deck. A forested ravine view topped off the moment. It was like time stood still, but her heart raced with excitement.

Kiam walked up behind her and wrapped his arms around her waist. "We needed this," he said softly, kissing the back of her neck.

Faydrah took a deep breath and leaned back against his chest. "Thank you, baby," she gushed as they stood looking out and enjoying the sounds of life. It seemed like several birds were having a very interesting conversation.

They took it all in for a few more minutes then headed inside to get situated for the night. Faydrah walked up the quarter-turn staircase that lead to an open loft with a pillow-top queen-sized bed. She turned on the ceiling fan that hung overhead in the vaulted living room.

Stripping the bedding, she folded it up neatly and sat it on the chair across from the bed. Next she began putting on the sheets, pillow cases and comforter Kiam brought. She reached in the bag and removed the scented candles and began lighting and placing them around the cabin.

Kiam put away the food and set up their toiletries in the bathroom. They met back up in the living room where Faydrah helped him light the fireplace.

As the flames licked at the firewood, Kiam placed a black fur throw rug right in front of the fireplace then they hit the shower.

When they emerged from the bathroom Faydrah got comfortable on the couch while Kiam prepared dinner. She sat watching him move around the kitchen with a focused expression on his face.

Faydrah's stomach started growling as the aroma of the steak and onions, candy carrots and yellow rice wafted out to where she was relaxing. Kiam was throwing down in there. When he was done cooking, he prepared their plates then joined her on the couch.

"You hooked a sistah up," she beamed as she tasted the succulent T-bone.

"Damn, I did this?" he said, chewing the tender meat.

"Yes, baby you did, and it's so sweet of you. Is this what I have to look forward to the rest of my life?" she asked, looking up at him lovingly.

Kiam leaned over and kissed her softly. "This and a whole lot more," he promised. He knew she was wife material and he damn sure wasn't going to let the next man have her.

When they were done eating, Faydrah helped him clean the kitchen then he sprawled across the rug in front of the fireplace. Faydrah went upstairs and grabbed the comforter and a book out of her purse. By the time she returned Kiam was relaxing on his back with his hands behind his head, thinking about a hundred different things.

Faydrah turned the radio on, adjusting the volume to low, then she spread the comforter on one side of him and sat down on it

Indian-style. "Grab that remote, let me see what's on TV real quick," said Kiam.

"Nope, I'm about to read to you."

"Read to me?"

"Yes. Is that a problem?" she asked.

"I guess not."

"Come here." She pulled him up. Kiam positioned his head against her chest, resting his back between her legs. Faydrah smiled, looking down at him staring at the book like it was capable of robbing him.

"Relax, it's not going to hurt."

"That's what I said to you nine years ago, but I was wrong," he joked.

"Shut up, nasty." She tapped him on the forehead.

Kiam chuckled as she opened the cover of *Sweet Persuasions* by Maya Banks and began reading. He had to admit to himself that he was enjoying her animated tone as she eagerly turned the pages. Faydrah was all into it. When she got to the first sex scene Kiam began making her pages come to life.

He turned over and positioned his face between her legs. She slowed down as his hands began to glide over her lower lips. Tingling all over, she looked down as he stole her concentration. "Keep reading," he whispered as he ran his tongue slowly up and down her sweetness.

Faydrah continued to read on but with labored breathing as music played softly in the background. Her eyes rotated back and forth between the pages and Kiam as he produced a flood between her thighs.

When he began sucking on her clit the book hit the floor and her moans filled the room. Kiam was handling his business and she was rewarding him with her sweet nectar all over his lips. She rubbed his head as he kneeled before her royal throne and allowed his tongue to worship her.

238

"Yessssss," she cried out as her honey poured. Her thighs gripped the sides of his head and her body arched off the floor in an inverted C.

Kiam kept tasting her until the room began to spin. Faydrah had gone to the edge and back and now it was his turn. He rose to his knees, released the beast, grabbed her ankles pulling her under him then pushed himself deep into her wetness.

Faydrah held onto him tightly while trying to make sure to shift beneath him just right. She knew that he loved it when she moved her hips in a slow circular motion and stared up into his eyes.

"You like this, baby?" she asked softly.

Her pussy felt better than freedom. The light moans that left his mouth confirmed that she was pleasing every inch of him. Kiam rested his gangsta— something he was comfortable doing only with her— and enjoyed her every movement. Between her soft thighs there was nothing for him to prove but his love and desire.

The crackle of the flames that danced in the fireplace accompanied the heat-filled strokes he gave her. Passion surged through their bodies like electricity. No words were needed, every movement spoke volumes as they rolled on the rug from one pleasure-filled position into the next.

As if the universe heard their hearts, Silk began to sing lightly in the distance.

Baby won't you let me look inside your soul/Oh my baby, let me make you lose control/Let me be the one you need, baby just come to me...

Kiam covered her pretty face and lips with soft wet kisses as she tensed up with every powerful push.

"Baby," she moaned. Her legs trembled from the pleasure that he gave.

"You're my everything," he whispered causing tears to release from the corners of her eyes.

She squeezed him tightly while rotating her hips faster, pulling him in deeper.

Bracing himself for the release, Kiam bit softly into her neck and let his essence flow into her core. It felt like he would come forever and her natural sheath welcomed it. They both moaned each other's name as the last of his thick, warm fluid fed her womb.

"I will love you forever," she whispered, holding him gently against her breast.

"I know," he said softly.

There in the middle of the log cabin the past, present, and future came together in harmony. She was his and he was hers, and only death could break their bond. They fell asleep in each other's arms satiated by their intense love-making.

The next morning Faydrah got up and showered, threw on a short sun dress, grabbed her laptop and started working. She looked down at Kiam and shook her head. He was out like a light, snoring softly. Constantly running the streets on little rest over the last few weeks had caught up with him.

Shortly after she was done with her work Kiam got up and staggered to the shower. She giggled to herself because she could see the results of last night's heated passion.

A quick shower brought him back to life. He reappeared talking smack and denying that she had that behind weak in the knees. They traded kisses back and forth then he went off to prepare some things, but he wouldn't say what.

Faydrah prepared some chicken shish kabobs with peppers, onions, pineapple and shrimp; she marinated them in a garlic butter sauce.

Kiam's timing was impeccable, he returned just as she was taking the kabobs off the grill. "You ready," he asked, walking out on the deck.

"Ready for what?" she questioned as she placed the last of the food on a tray and covered it with foil.

"To go on a little picnic."

"Huh?" she exclaimed, wiping her hands on the dish towel and setting it on the table.

Kiam took her by the hand. "Come on." Faydrah grabbed the tray with the food as Kiam dragged her off. When she got to the other side of the cabin she saw that Kiam had set up a blanket on the soft green grass, with a little straw basket filled with fruit and chocolate and a can of whip cream. Bottles of Moet & Chandon sat chilling in an ice bucket with two glasses beside it.

"Let me find out," she said, looking over at him with surprise sparkling in her eyes.

"They only locked up my body, my mind was always free to create and this is something I always imagined us doing," he said.

Faydrah smiled at him as he assisted her to sit. She breathed in the fresh air and lavished in the warm sunlight as it danced in the open field.

Kiam opened the drinks and filled both of their glasses. He held up his. "To the rest of our lives."

"Cheers." She clinked her glass against his, confirming that she shared his vow of forever.

They sipped champagne then Kiam fed her grapes and strawberries and shook up the whip cream. Faydrah tilted her head back and allowed him to spray it in her mouth. Slowly, he leaned in and kissed it off her lips.

Faydrah savored the taste of his berries and cream flavored kisses. "You like putting white stuff in my mouth," she joked.

"Sure do."

They laughed then continued to eat the treats he had set up along with the food she had prepared. When they were done Kiam reached inside the basket for another treat. All of a sudden he snatched his hand back. "Oh shit, what the fuck was that?" he shrilled, leaning back.

"What?" Faydrah became alarmed.

Kiam peeked in the basket then slowly began to reach inside a second time. "No, Kiam, don't!" she shrieked, afraid that a snake may have gotten inside of the basket. Her eyes were filled with a little fear.

"I got it, hold up," he said bravely.

Faydrah closed her eyes and pulled her hands close to her face.

"Oh shit, I got it." He pulled his closed hand back.

Faydrah peeked through her fingers. "What was it?"

"This shit movin'." He shook his hand with a nervous look on his face.

"Kiam, throw it!" she cried.

Instead he held his hand up for her to see. "Look."

"Nooooo!" She shut her eyes again and tried to move back.

Kiam grabbed her leg and held her in place.

"Stop, let me go," she yelled out.

"You don't want to see it?"

"No, stop it."

"Look, it ain't that big."

"Kiam stop."

"Just look."

Faydrah slowly opened her eyes to see him smiling and holding a beautiful diamond ring between his forefinger and thumb. She gasped.

"Scary ass," he joked.

"You play too much," she whined, holding her chest.

"Eyez," he said, suddenly becoming serious. "I can't do this life thing without you." He dropped his smile and took her h placed five carats on her finger.

242

Faydrah lost her breath. Tears welled up in her eyes as she looked into his. "And you won't have to," she cried, wrapping her arms around his neck.

"You promise?"

"Yes, baby I promise. I've been dreaming of this day forever. I'm going to make you very happy."

"You can make me very happy right now," he replied with a look that could not be mistaken.

"You ain't saying nothin'." She reached for his zipper and pulled out her best friend. Kiam instantly stiffened to her touch.

Climbing onto his lap she eased down on his steel. "You didn't say yes," he moaned.

"I'm about to," she said as she began riding him to the rhythm of her heart.

With all of nature as their witness they consummated their vow to be together forever. The last thing on Kiam's mind was Lissha and the violation that he had almost committed with her.

Chapter 30
A Wrong Move

While Kiam was three hours away from the city with all thoughts of her eradicated from his mind, Lissha wasn't exactly sitting around regretting what hadn't happened. It was in a corner of her mind but other things demanded her attention.

Lissha, Treebie, Donella and Bayonna moved calculatedly around Treebie's basement getting into character for tonight's caper. They had already fulfilled their obligations to Spank so everything they collected from tonight's job would be one hundred percent profit.

Treebie pulled on the blunt, then sat it down. She strapped on her vest and covered it with two thick t-shirts. Then she completed the hookup with a black hoodie. She sat back down on the couch and looked over at Bay and Donella who were already completely dressed and loading their guns.

Lissha was at the counter a few feet away downing shots and getting into beast mode, but it seemed like there was something else fueling her fire. Something more than her love of the carnage.

"LiLi, you good?" asked Treebie.

"Yeah, I'm straight," she said, taking another shot of Rémy to the head.

Treebie rose to her feet, walked over to where Lissha stood, and put a hand on her shoulder. "Regardless of what may go on in our personal lives, we in this shit together."

"I know," Lissha said, making eye contact with the one who was like her left arm. She knew that no matter what, Treebie would never cross her or fold up.

Treebie had a look in her eyes that mirrored the sign on her soul that read *kill or be killed*. "We almost ready?" she asked, looking around the room.

Bay put the clip in her Nine and said, "Hell yeah, I'm ready."

"Me too," announced Donella, picking up her pump shotgun with the rubber pistol grip handle.

Treebie looked at Lissha, who gave her a look that meant she didn't even have to ask. "I was born ready," Lissha replied click-clacking one in the chamber of her ratchet.

They all met at the counter where they performed the final part of their ritual: tight ponytails, fitted nylon hats pulled to their eyebrows, voice distorter, face mask, and lastly, the blood red contacts.

Pulling thick black hoodies over their heads, they raised their shot glasses. "We go in this muthafucka four and we come out four," Lissha gritted.

A clink of their glasses emphasized the vow. They downed their drinks, slammed their glasses on the counter, and headed for the door one behind the other.

The small one bedroom dilapidated house on 117th and St. Clair was rumored to be one of the biggest paying gambling spots in the city. The girls parked a few houses down and quickly got into position. Lissha and Donella crouched down by a set of garbage cans on the right side of the door. Treebie and Bayonna were crouched behind a set of bushes on the left side.

Treebie had done all of the foot work finding out that inside there would be two guards at the front door and one at the back, and as many as ten gamblers. All the men were very familiar with the other end of a trigger. These were street niggas true and through. The girls knew they had to go in quick, loud, and deadly.

Patiently they waited for their mark to arrive. It was funny how no matter how hard a team tried to fill their circle with strong rings you could always find a weak link.

When Treebie saw Lil' Bump coming up the walkway her blood rushed through her veins. She gnashed her teeth, gripped her gun, and slowly stepped from the shadows. "Bleed, if you make one country move I'll turn your mother's sweet dreams into nightmares," she growled.

"Fuck is this?" He instinctively moved his hand to his waist. Treebie raised the gun to his chest and his arms shot above his head. "Don't kill me, Cuz," he pled. *I'ma play along, but the second you slip I'ma push ya whole forehead back.*

What he would soon find out was that slipping wasn't part of their get-down. Donella stepped out shoving her gun right in his spine. "You better cooperate then, or I'ma make you a mutha-fuckin' paraplegic," she muttered.

"I don't ha—"

"Shhh!" Treebie put her finger to her mouth, silencing him. Damn all that talking, time was valuable. They had to get in and out because *johnny* rolled by frequently in this hood.

"I need you to put your ugly ass face to that peek hole. You better not blink, yell or make the wrong move or your little sister Aniya, and your mother, Selena, will die a slow, agonizing death. Cooperate and they get released in an hour," said Treebie. She had the names right so Lil' Bump couldn't chance that it was a bluff, and the voice distorter made the threat come out very ominous.

Taking him by the back of the neck, Treebie pushed him to the door. There was fear in his heart and a big ass gun pressed to the base of his skull. Bayonna and Donella formed a line behind Treebie and Lissha took up the rear.

"Smile, muthafucka," Treebie ordered him.

Lil' Bump knocked on the door.

"Who is it?" a gruff voice asked from the other side.

"It's me, Cuz. Lil' Bump."

Treebie heard those locks click and her nipples hardened. As soon as the door opened a crack she shoved Lil' Bump forward and blasted a hole in his back, sending his insides all over the card tables.

The crew ran up in the house like body snatchers, changing the pulse of the whole operation. The two guards at the door reached for their bangers but their reaction was a second too slow. Bay and Lissha's guns popped off in sync. *Boc! Boc! Boc! Boc! Boc! Boc! Boc!* They put the two men down with a deadly burst of gunfire that let the others in the house know that they were not fucking around.

Donella dashed toward the back of the house, running into the man that had been guarding the back door. As he reached to his waist, she hit him with two shots in the head. He staggered back and his body slid down the wall leaving a streak of blood all the way to the floorboard.

Behind them Treebie slumped two at each table, then the girls positioned themselves around the room. Lissha closed the front door and put her back up against it.

"Put your muthafuckin' hands in the air," Treebie barked to the card players that still had their body parts intact. Slowly hands went up. Each man held a stone face as they searched their minds for a way to turn the tables.

"Y'all know what the fuck this is," Treebie shouted. Donella and Bayonna grabbed black cloth bags from their back pockets and threw them on the table.

"Do y'all know who you're fucking wit'? This ain't no street you walk baby nuts on. This 117th and muthafuckin' St. Clair. You gotta have big ass balls to run up in here," a young thug shouted from his seated position.

"Well, I must be in the right fucking place, because my shit grande," Treebie gritted and grabbed her crotch.

"Nigga, fuck you," yelled out a tall slender nigga. In a flash his hand went under the table. When it came up he had his whistle in his hand and he let off several shots. Two of them caught Bayonna in the chest and slammed her back against the wall. Her ratchet fell from her hands as she hit the floor, unconscious.

"Muthafucka!" screamed Treebie. She aimed her Glock at him and emptied the clip. His body jerked with each round that pierced through it and he slumped down to the floor bloody and crooked. Treebie zoned out, she was still squeezing the trigger after there was no more ammo in her gun and no more life in his body.

"You see that," screamed Lissha, using her gun to point at the dead bodies lying around the room. "Don't be the next muthafucka to get it." She held her whistle on the remaining men as Treebie snapped out of her zone and slammed a fresh, fully loaded clip in her piece.

Donella blasted a nigga on GP before bending down to check on Bayonna who was just regaining consciousness. Her bullet proof vest had saved her life but she was momentarily in shock. Her breathing was labored and her chest burned.

Bayonna gathered her wits, picked up her hammer and climbed to her feet. Methodically, she walked over to the dead man that had tried to murk her. Half of his face was blown off and his chest was opened up like a busted can of tomato paste. Bayonna stood over his corpse and showed it no respect. "Bitch ass nigga," she spat and pumped three in what remained of his head.

While this was going on the others kept their guns trained around the room in case another fool had big nuts. They eyed every one of them and were ready to place them in a church looking up at the roof if they so much as flinched.

"Everybody just chill," said a short dude with dreads. He was sitting in a chair away from the table, unshaken by the gore around him. His voice was level and his eyes were alert. Lissha looked at him and almost blew her disguise. It was gotdamn JuJu.

"Aw, fuck!" she muttered under her breath. Donella and Bayonna was thinking the same thing. Somebody had really dropped the ball. Treebie didn't give a flying fuck. JuJu could get it too.

"D-double, fill them bags up," he ordered his runner from his reclined position.

"Do that shit slow muthafucka," Donella yelled out with her pump tight in her grip and his head sharp in her sight.

D-double, JuJu's lieutenant, jumped up and went over to the stash spot and filled the bags then dragged them over to Donella and Bayonna's feet. On his way back to the table he accidently bumped into Treebie. Donella and Bayonna cut his ass down, swiftly and without mercy.

"Clumsy ass muthafucka," snorted Bayonna. She was blood thirsty now.

With their friends' bodies dropping all around them, two other dudes decided not to sit there awaiting their executions. They silently communicated with each other with their eyes, then tried to get up and reach for their guns. In the process they knocked over the card table to create a distraction, but they were fucking with stone cold killahs that were trained to go.

Lissha's trigger finger went crazy, she hit one of the men in the chest with five successive shots. Donella's pump made carnage of the other brave heart. "Y'all niggas still think it's a game?" she barked.

Silence filled the room as the remaining three men held their lips tight with contempt. Bayonna glanced at Lissha who gave her a slight nod. She grabbed the two bags and pulled them to Lissha's feet. Lissha gave a second nod and Donella hit one dude and Bayonna hit the other leaving JuJu as the one to tell the tale.

Treebie moved over to JuJu and put her gun to his mouth. "If you gonna kill me, Bleed, handle your business, but I damn sure ain't gonna bitch up," he said in a voice that didn't tremble.

"Is it worth trying to be tough over the next nigga shit?" She stood ready to air his ass out.

"It's all good because this shit right here comes with the life I signed up for. But I promise you, my nigga will find you. And when he do, he's gonna give pain a whole new meaning."

"Oh, so you're somebody's right-hand man?"

"Fuck you."

"Nigga, you a bitch. Open your mouth so you can suck my dick like you sucking his," Treebie gritted as distasteful thoughts of Kiam filled her mind.

"Bleed, you got the game fucked up. I'm not opening up shit. You gonna have to knock my fucking teeth out."

"Oh yeah?" Treebie forced her gun into his mouth almost pushing it to the back of his throat.

JuJu winced and gagged but he didn't fold. Lissha was wondering what Treebie was about to do. JuJu was on *their* team. *This bitch done lost it.* Lissha silently looked on.

"Get this muthafucka down," Treebie ordered. Bayonna walked over and grabbed him around the neck restricting his breathing. His eyes glistened as his airway tightened. Blood and fragments of teeth slid on his tongue and settled on both sides of the barrel.

"Get this nigga secure," commanded Treebie, running out of patience. If the gunshots had been heard, johnny could be on the way.

Donella moved fast. She pulled out a roll of duct tape and strapped JuJu tightly to the chair. Treebie continued to run the show. "Grab this nigga's hand," she barked.

Donella grabbed his wrist and forced him to hold his hand out. Lissha looked on as poor JuJu suffered at the hands of her crew. She felt some kind of way because he went hard for the team, but there was no pulling back now.

Treebie looked down at JuJu from up under her disguise. "I bet when you woke up this morning you never envisioned this shit, huh?" she taunted him.

JuJu said nothing, he couldn't see their faces so he studied their mannerisms, anything that would help him hunt them down later. There was something peculiar about the way they walked and moved. He filed that in his memory.

"I almost gave you a pass," Treebie went on. "But since you work for a bitch, the penalty is misery." She pulled the gun from his mouth, grabbed his right wrist and blew a hole straight through the palm of his hand.

One foot reactively slammed against the floor as he yelped out in pain, "Shit." His lips quaked as his adrenaline coursed through his veins, settling his trembling body to a slower vibration.

"Now you can be his *left hand* man," snickered Treebie.

Bayonna grabbed a bill from her pocket and shoved it in JuJu's bloody palm, closing his fist around it. Pain shot up his arm and sweat dripped from his collar. Valiantly, he did not scream out in pain or beg for mercy.

Removing the bloody bill from his hand and stuffing it in his mouth, Bayonna said, "Tell your bitch ass boss man that Blood Money said thank you."

Treebie stepped forward and toppled the chair over. Juju's head cracked against the floor.

Carefully, with their heads on a swivel watching for any sign of the police, they moved out the door and to the car.

When they walked into Treebie's basement. Lissha began snatching her clothes off. "Shit! Why the fuck didn't we know that was Kiam's spot?" she asked, resting her hands on the counter.

"I don't know, we checked everything out just as we always do," Donella responded as she pulled her hood over her head.

Bayonna pulled off her hoodie and vest and examined her chest. It was bruised and sore.

"Man, this shit is fucked up," Lissha said.

"Why? Because you got feelings for the nigga?" Treebie shot some shade in her direction.

"Bitch don't play with me. We done fucked around and robbed ourselves. You don't see a problem with that?"

"You don't see a problem with the fact that Kiam got shit going on behind your back. Big Zo supposed to know everything that nigga doing." Treebie looked at her, waiting for a comeback. When Lissha didn't retort, she smiled. "Yeah, that's what I thought." She proceeded to take her off her gear.

"It don't matter, knowing whose spots we're hitting is your fucking job. Now we gonna have Kiam's crazy ass on our heels."

"If you mention that muthafucka's name one more time," Treebie said, gnashing her teeth.

"You issuing threats, bitch?" Lissha came from behind the counter.

"Don't fucking test me." Treebie stood firm, looking into Lissha's red eyes.

"Test you?" Lissha threw back at her. "Bitch, I'll *bless* your muthafuckin' ass, that's what I'll do." She stepped in Treebie's grill.

"Bitch, don't get your shit pushed back." Treebie stuck her finger in Lissha's mug.

Lissha slapped it down.

Donella ran over and stepped between them. "I'm not letting y'all do this shit. We ride together not *against* one another." She pulled Treebie back a step.

Lissha was still spazzing. "She fucked up, plain and simple. Now I gotta fix this shit." She blew out an exasperated breath.

"Bitch, you ain't in this shit by yourself. You worrying about what that punk ass nigga got to say and Bay almost lost her fucking life," Treebie yelled as she pointed over to Bayonna. "Look at her! She over there fucked up. You holla out that 'go in

253

four' shit, well tonight we almost came out as three. Burn that shit in your mind."

Lissha looked over at Bayonna and the severity of the evening began to feel heavy on her heart. She took a deep breath and sat on the couch to gather her thoughts. "We gotta cover every end of this shit," she calmly stated.

"No shit," Treebie said as she sat across from her.

When they locked gazes no more words were spoken. They knew they had to be smart and make sure that from now on they paid closer attention to detail. The also realized that now their relationship would be different. The trust had just taken a turn and it was only a matter of time before one of them would push the envelope. When that inevitable day came more than friendship would be lost.

While the girls disrobed and began putting their gear in black plastic bags, Lissha stood there thinking. She had to admit Treebie was right. Big Zo knew they were hitting spots. If Kiam had told him that he had his hand in gambling houses Big Zo would have told her to steer clear of those particular houses. So if Kiam hadn't told Big Zo about his gambling houses, what else was he doing on the low?

Lissha now wondered if Kiam was really loyal or if his allegiance had grown cold with the rise of the money and the power. She grabbed her phone and walked in the other room. When Big Zo picked up she unleashed the coded report and his icy silence confirmed that something definitely wasn't right.

Chapter 31
Good Times Never Last

Kiam was chilling in the passenger seat, listening to Eyez hum along with a Keyshia Cole song on the radio. She had volunteered to drive back and he hadn't refused. He looked over at his baby and smiled; she was still radiant from their weekend retreat.

She reached over and held his hand. "I really enjoyed this weekend," she said sincerely.

"Me too, baby. We have to do it again real soon, something about being up in the woods brought the freak out of you," he teased.

"I'm always your little freak." She released his hand and slid hers between his legs and grabbed a handful of dick .

"A'ight, mess around and make me give it to you on the shoulder of the highway," Kiam warned.

"Give me some of that back woods *wood*," she replied stroking him. "You can't hang."

"You feel my little nigga, don't you? He hard body." He looked over at her.

"Yes he is. All swole up and ready to take a chick down through there."

"Pull over." It was dark outside plus the windows were tinted. He was game for a quickie.

"I'm not messing with you, Kiam, you already got me walking sideways." She giggled and removed her hand from off that steel before she became tempted to pull over and ride it.

Kiam was looking over at her to see if she was really game but the kitty was sore from all that good lovin' he had put on her. "Look at who can't hang," he boasted.

"Be quiet, baby." She cheesed and reached over and play-punched him on the shoulder.

"For real though, ma, I really enjoyed this weekend. A nigga could get used to that."

"Yesssss," she sang, savoring the memories. She didn't want the weekend to come to an end. To wake up in his arms and receive all of his attention had her floating.

Faydrah glanced down at the engagement ring on her finger and prayed that the fairytale would last forever. All she had ever wanted was to be his wife. The diamond on her finger was his promise to make her wish come true.

Halfway back to the city Kiam decided to get his cell phone out of the compartment between the seats and check his messages. They had turned their cell phones off and left them in the truck the entire weekend so that they could focus entirely on each other.

As Faydrah steered into the fast lane, passing a slow moving Suburban, Kiam powered up his phone and saw a half dozen text messages from JuJu and several voicemail notifications. A line creased his forehead, something had to be wrong. He didn't bother opening the text messages or listening to the voicemails, instead he called JuJu's cellphone.

"Man, I've been trying to reach you since Friday night," JuJu said as soon as he answered. Kiam could tell from the tone of his voice that something serious had taken place.

"What happened?" he asked.

"Niggas ran up in the gambling spot on 117th and St. Clair."

"Who ran up in there, undies?" asked Kiam, referring to the vice squad.

"Nah, it was those Blood Money niggas. Man, they killed everybody in the house, and they took all the spread. Something like a hundred racks."

Kiam's face hardened. "Fuck the money. They killed D-double?"

"Yeah, man, the homie gone," he sadly confirmed." And Lil' Bump too. Bruh, that bitch ass nigga got them in the door."

Kiam's blood boiled as he listened to JuJu give him a full report of the robbery. When JuJu told him what they did to *him*, his whole face washed over in anger. He didn't know who in the fuck the Blood Money crew was but he was gonna kick down every door in the city until he found them. Then he was gonna execute them without trial or jury.

When Kiam hung up the phone Faydrah looked at him out the corner of her eye. She had clearly heard his end of the conversation and she recognized the expression on his face. This was the reason she wanted him to leave the streets. She didn't give a damn about street principles, revenge, and loyalty to people who weren't loyal to themselves. She just wanted him to be around to love her and not wind up back in prison or lying on a cold slab at the Coroner's. That's all she cared about.

Kiam was quiet, which she knew meant somebody was going to die real soon, he was just calculating his moves. Steaming inside, she got off at the next exit. Kiam looked at the gas needle and saw that the tank was three-quarters full. "What you doing, ma?" he asked suspiciously.

"I'm turning around and going back to the resort. I am not letting you do what's on your mind."

"No the fuck you not," he growled.

"Yes the fuck I am."

Kiam reached for the steering wheel and yanked it. Faydrah slammed on brakes barely avoiding crashing head on into a passing vehicle. Her heart was beating fast and her hands trembled. She threw the truck in park and snapped her head around toward Kiam, glaring at him. "What the fuck is wrong with you?" she screamed. "You almost got us killed. Is the streets that fucking important to you." Tears formulated.

"Don't fuck with me right now, shorty," he warned her. He hopped out the truck and stormed around to the driver's side.

Faydrah got out but she sure wasn't getting back in. She took off up the dark four lane road on foot.

Kiam pulled up alongside of her and rolled down the window. "Girl, get your ass in the truck," he ordered.

"Fuck you. You can have the streets." She quickened her pace to a sprint.

"I don't need this shit right now," Kiam fumed as he sped up and caught up to her again. He put the truck in park and hopped out.

Faydrah felt Kiam's fingers brush against her back in an effort to catch her and she kicked into a full gear run. By the time Kiam ran her down he was out of breath and not in the mood for anymore of her shit. He snatched her up, threw her over his shoulder. Faydrah squirmed around. "Put me down," she cried.

Kiam ignored her theatrics, and carried her back to where he had left the truck. He strapped her in the passenger seat and slammed the door. "Play with this shit if you want to," he warned.

Faydrah sat there with her arms folded across her chest as he climbed back behind the wheel. Kiam took off doing ninety all the way back. Neither of them said a word to each other the rest of the drive home.

As soon as they pulled up at her place, Faydrah was out the truck before it came to a complete stop. She ran inside her apartment and slammed the door, locking Kiam out.

With her back against the door and her heart aching, she waited for him to bang on the door and tell her that he had changed his mind, he was not going to seek revenge on anyone. But the only sounds Faydrah heard were his squealing tires and her own sobs. She snatched the door back open to call out to him, but all she saw was fading taillights. Distraught, she closed the door and walked up to her bedroom, wiping at the tears that ran down her face. She fell across her bed then slid to her knees.

Dear God, I only ask that you protect him and those that he encounter tonight. Watch over him Lord, and please hear my prayer.

Chapter 32
Beast Mode

Kiam blocked out Faydrah's emotions, this was not the time for him to be affected by her tears. The only wet faces he wanted to see were those of the family members of the niggas that called themselves Blood Money and flaunted that shit like they couldn't be touched.

His knuckles were white as he gripped the steering wheel and drove through the city with that toe-tag shit on his mental.

One of JuJu's bout it chicks let Kiam in as soon as he knocked. Juju was in his bedroom, sitting on the edge of the bed with an arsenal of weapons at his feet. His mouth was hideously swollen and his right hand was heavily bandaged. Pain medication had him drowsy, but none of that diminished his gangsta, he was ready to ride.

"They handled me like I was a ho. But they fucked up when they didn't kill me. On my hood, I'ma body every one of them when I find 'em," he vowed. The heat in his eyes was intense enough to set the room ablaze.

Kiam laid a hand on JuJu's shoulder and spoke in a low tone so that the girl out in the living room couldn't hear him. "Don't worry, they're gonna die for what they did to you. And it's gonna be painful and slow."

"I'm ready to ride," JuJu said. *"Tonight."*

"I know you are, lil' homie, but fall back for a minute and let me collect some Intel on these niggas, then we'll ride. Now tell me everything you can remember about those Blood Money boys, no detail is too small."

Leaving JuJu's place a half hour later Kiam went over to Lissha's. It was past midnight but he didn't care about the time, murder never sleeps. Muthafuckas had tested the crew's get-down on his watch and that shit was unpardonable.

261

Lissha came to the door wearing a long t-shirt and wiping sleep from her eyes. She looked in his face and saw the blazing heat behind his pupils. He brushed right past her and headed to her living room.

Lissha closed the front door and followed. She already knew why he was there, but she was nervous about how much he had been able to find out. She quickly replayed the events of Friday night in her head. Had they done anything that may have given their identities away? Lissha tried to recall.

Kiam flicked on the light and sat down on the sofa. "Have a seat," he said. Lissha studied his face before complying. Three lines creased his forehead and his jaw twitched.

This muthafucka hotter than fish grease. Damn, Treebie fucked up and now I'm left to face the music if he knows. Lissha instantly regretted answering the door without her strap. Now she had to use guile, act like she normally would with him, and deny all accusations.

"What the fuck is going on, Kiam? Why are you barging in my shit at one o'clock in the morning bossing me around?" she hurled.

He ignored her question and his look hardened even more. "What do you know about Blood Money?"

Lissha swallowed nervously. "Um, I heard of them, they're a stickup crew. Why?" She dummied up.

"Is that all the fuck you can tell me? Do you know who any of them niggas are?"

"No. All I know is that they have a lot of hustlers shook. Why are you asking about Blood Money, did something happen?" She had recovered her poise, it was evident he didn't know shit.

Kiam told her what had happened.

"Wait a minute. When the fuck did *we* get into the gambling business? You doing shit behind me and Daddy's backs now?" she asked, deflecting his attention off Blood Money.

"Fuck you talking to? I'm doing what the fuck I do. And as long as the money is proper you just play your position. I don't answer to no fuckin' body. Big Zo knows my get-down, I'm a loyal nigga, that's why he chose me to run this. Now get your panties out your ass and do something constructive, like tell me anything you can to help me find out who Blood Money is. That's what the fuck you do."

Lissha stood up and smoothed her t-shirt down over her brown thighs. "Since you're so power struck find them yourself. I'm going back to bed. Don't let the door hit you in your ass too hard on your way out."

When she turned to head back to her bedroom, Kiam sprung up off the couch, snatched her by both arms, and spun her around to face him. Instinctively Lissha fixed her mouth to snap, but Kiam went there first.

"Look," he snarled, "this is not the time for your slick ass mouth. Money and lives got took tonight. From this point on, the games stop. Get that through your head or I'ma force it inside that muthafucka. Now take your ass to bed and wake up with a brand new attitude." He shoved her toward the bedroom and walked out the door.

After she heard Kiam drive off, Lissha grabbed her phone off the dresser and hurriedly got Treebie, Donella, and Bayonna together on a conference call. It was imperative that everyone understand that Kiam was on a warpath and there could be no more slip-ups. "That muthafucka is boiling," Lissha kept saying.

"You told us that five times already. Damn bitch, if you scared increase your insurance policy," said Treebie.

"Fuck you," Lissha replied.

The ladies argued back and forth about what, if anything, should be done to thwart all efforts of Kiam's to find out who Blood Money were.

"If he gets too close I'ma put him in the dirt," said Treebie.

Ca$h & NeNe Capri

Chapter 33
A Gangsta's Reaction

Kiam had been turning the city inside out searching for the identities of Blood Money. He offered fifty bands for each of their names but so far no one had exposed the crew.

JuJu was chomping at the bit to get his revenge; he had bought a Tommy gun and a brand new AK-47 with a Larry Bird *extenzo*— thirty three shots. How he was going to shoot either weapon with one hand, Kiam wasn't sure, but he respected his G.

As he headed downtown to a sport's bar to meet with Frank Nitti, Kiam's cellphone rang. He answered the call without identifying the caller. "Bitch nigga, you don't look for Blood Money, we look for you," The caller said then line went dead.

Kiam stared at the blank screen. As he suspected, the call came from a restricted number but he knew that it was authentic because the caller had sounded like he was talking into a wind tunnel or some type of voice distortion device like the one JuJu had described. Whoever Blood Money was, they had just made their first mistake.

Kiam knew that he had them worried, otherwise they wouldn't have made the call. They would have just struck. They were killahs, no doubt, so what was it they made them fear him? He pondered.

He knew that if he found the answer to that question it would reveal their identities.

A half hour later Kiam sat across from Frank Nitti.

Nitti used his steak knife to cut a piece of the rib eye in front of him. "I'm hearing your name loud in the streets," he said, chewing and flashing a fake smile that couldn't hide the envy that was underneath it.

"You must be listening too hard, fam," shot Kiam who was not one to mince words.

"Bruh, you know the streets talk. I hear that Schizophrenic got the whole Eastside jumping. They tell me you got the work for the low, still in the casket. And you got shit sewed up from Miles to Hough, all the way out to EC. You came home and hit the ground running, didn't you?"

"What's your point, homie? You a groupie or something?"

"Nah, nigga, you know better than that," Nitti sat the knife and fork down, pushed his plate back, and sneered at Kiam.

"Get the fuck off my dick and get to the point, then." Kiam's hand slid under the table just in case Nitti didn't let the disrespect pass.

Nitti peeped the move and let his own hands remain on top off the table, palms down. "Damn, Bleed, we go way back. What did I ever do to you to make you come at me like that?"

"Number one, let's not pretend we're close or nothing. Just like you, I haven't forgot about our run in back in the day."

Nitti recalled their old beef as one he still wanted to settle. *Keep your friends close and your enemies closer.* That was how he played the game. "Fam, I let the past stay in the past. Why you think I hit you up? Fuck the bullshit, nigga, it's all about the paper and I hear you're locking shit down these days."

"That's neither here nor there, Bleed. But why you wasting my time reading me my own resume? I already know what the fuck I've done, 'cause I'm the muthafucka that did it. Just say what's on your mind. Time is money." Kiam had did his homework since running into Nitti at the Sunoco station. He knew who the nigga rolled with.

"A'ight. Long story short, you're stepping on toes. And the toes you stepping on are attached to some big ass feet. You ever heard the name Wolfman?"

"Long story short," Kiam reminded him.

Nitti finally got to the point. Kiam listened as he explained Wolfman's offer. When Nitti was done, Kiam chuckled. "Do I look like a worker to you?"

"Don't be arrogant, man. You don't wanna fuck with a nigga like Wolfman," warned Nitti. "Just think about the offer."

"Yeah, a'ight. I'ma think about it and get back wit' you." Kiam stood up, preparing to leave. He looked down at Nitti whose hands were now folded on the table in front of his plate. Kiam chuckled again. In one swift motion he snatched the steak knife and brought it down with force, plunging it straight through Nitti's hand and pinning it to the table.

"I thought about it, Bleed, and that's my muthafuckin' answer."

Ca$h & NeNe Capri

Chapter 35
Time Is Up

Treebie moved up her walkway juggling bags and her cellphone, trying to retrieve her keys. She fumbled with the locks while listening to Lissha angrily insist that a meeting was needed as soon as possible.

"What the fuck happened now?" Treebie was rushing, they had to leave in an hour to make the pickup from Riz's people.

"Bitch, I don't want to talk about it on the phone, meet me at the Winking Lizard out in Independence."

"Way out there!" Treebie held the phone with her shoulder as she slid the door key in the lock.

"Yeah, way the fuck out there," Lissha said.

Treebie stepped inside her house and almost fainted. Wa'leek was sitting in her living room with his arms rested on the back of the couch and a look on his face that said he was ready for a war.

"Oh shit, let me call you back." Treebie dropped her bags and ended the call over Lissha's heated protest.

Wa'leek was eyeing her like a hawk.

"What you doing here?" she asked, laying her phone on the counter and frowning at him.

"What did we agree on?"

"Wa'leek I told you, I need time."

"Well, times up. When I leave this city, you're coming with me."

"That's not happening."

"It's already in motion." He stood up wearing all black, heading in her direction.

"Baby, please. I have something I have to do first," she maintained.

"Yeah I know, pack. Get ya shit together and be ready to roll and none of this shit is up for discussion. I'm about to shake this whole muthafuckin' city up." He peered through those gray eyes and her heart sank to her toes.

Wa'leek turned to walk to the door and Treebie grabbed his arm. "Wah, please. I got a lot of shit on the line."

He turned back around and locked eyes with her. "Like what, running to get that pussy ass nigga's shit from way out in fuckin' PA?" His revelation made her very quiet and confirmed her worse fear, Wa'leek was back in contact with Riz. But what all had he told him.

"Yeah, shocked the shit outta you with that one. I had a sit down with my boy."

"Why the fuck are you going behind my back and getting in the middle of this? This ain't got shit to do with you." She began heating up.

"What the fuck is you talking about? If it involves you then it involves me."

"I'm fucking grown, I don't need your approval, I'ma do me and I suggest you do you. Please stay the fuck out of my business. And for the record, I ain't going nowhere with you." She stood breathing fire.

Wa'leek moved closer to her. Only an inch remained between them. "When I get finished with these muthafuckas, it ain't going to be shit to stay for. I'm giving you an out. Because I promise you this, I never show mercy to my enemies. I love you, but please don't fuck around and make yourself a problem I have to solve," he calmly warned.

Treebie took a half step back. "Why are you doing this to me?"

"Why the fuck are you doing this to yourself? You act like you owe this bitch. You don't owe her shit," he boomed, causing her to jump.

"It's not about owing her, I gave her my word." Treebie's voice sounded feeble under his attack.

"Did she give you hers?" he challenged.

Treebie got quiet.

Wa'leek pounced. "Let me ask you something, and I want you to weigh the question real good. Why is it that Lissha don't go on the pickups? You don't think that shit is a little foul that she gets to sit home blowing Gator while you out there risking your fucking life and freedom?"

Again Treebie didn't respond.

"Yeah, toss that shit around for a little while." He turned and walked toward the door. "I'll be back in a little while so start getting your shit together," he ordered then rolled out.

Treebie walked to the counter and grabbed a glass and a bottle of 1800 and poured herself a drink. As she downed it Wa'leek's words played back in her mind. She hadn't looked at it in that way. But now it was crystal clear. Lissha and Big Zo weren't taking any of the risk but collecting all the dough.

Treebie's phone started ringing, interrupting her thoughts. When she looked down at the screen it was Lissha. "What's up?" she answered, feeling some kind of way.

"What the fuck happened? You just hung up."

"Ain't nothin'."

"Are you on your way?"

"Yeah, I'll be there as soon as I can. I gotta throw my shit in the car."

"A'ight, see you in a few." Lissha hung up as she cruised through the streets worried about why Kiam wasn't answering his phone and what was going to happen if he found out who Blood Money was.

Treebie walked into her bedroom and gathered her road clothes and loaded her guns. Her mind was all over the place. They had to pick up later tonight. Lissha was all heated behind them hitting Kiam's spot. And now she had Wa'leek's crazy ass wandering around the city getting ready to make things worse than they already we're.

"Fuck it," she said out loud as she grabbed her bag, phone, and keys and headed to the door.

On the other side of town...

"Oh, shit! What's up, fam? What brings you to the Midwest?" Gator said with a semi smile as he opened the door for Wa'leek.

"You know how I do, never know where a nigga gonna show up next," replied Wa'leek as he passed Gator and walked right into his living room and took a seat on the coach.

Gator closed the door and followed suit, taking a seat across from him, "So what brings you this way?" Gator said, reaching over and grabbing his cigarette off of the cocktail table and lighting it up.

"Don't do that shit right now," Wa'leek ordered.

"Same old Leek," Gator said as he put it out and placed it in the ashtray.

"What the fuck is going on with this nigga Kiam?" Wa'leek went straight to the point.

"Man." Gator dragged the word out real slow as if he was considering how to respond. "That muthafucka done came out here and took the fuck over," he reported.

"On whose orders?" Wa'leek questioned him.

"Big Zo's."

"And you just let that shit happen?" Wa'leek raised an eyebrow.

"You know how Big Zo do." Gator sat forward and folded his hands, ready to get it all off his chest.

"Yeah I sure do. And I got four years behind the shit that he do."

"Well, he spent three years preparing that nigga to come out here and take the food off the very tables of the people that held shit together the whole time he been gone. That nigga Kiam killing everything that gets in his way.

272

"So what you gonna do, just sit there with your thumb up your ass or you gonna handle your business? What, your gun don't pop off no more?"

"You already know how I get down. I got some shit on the front burner and when that shit finish simmering it's on like a muthafucka."

Wa'leek stood up. "I hope so. I would hate to have to make this trip bloody." He turned to the door.

When his hand touched the knob, Wa'leek stopped and slowly turned back around to face Gator who was right behind him. "Oh, you might want to make sure you put some shit on the fire for Riz while you at it. He told that nigga one of your little secrets."

"What secret?" asked Gator.

Wa'leek smiled. "Happy hunting. I got my own rat to smoke out of a hole. Good luck." He turned the knob and walked out, slightly slamming the door behind him.

Gator returned to the living room, grabbed his cigarette, lit it up and began taking long hard pulls. He sat back down with his mind ran a mile a minute. If Riz had told Kiam what he thought he did, then Kiam had more than a head start. That wasn't good at all, in fact it was deadly.

Gator jumped up and grabbed his gun, tucking it in his back. He threw on his boots and left his apartment to head over to see Wolfman.

Wa'leek sat slouched in his rental car watching as Gator pulled out his driveway. "That was easier than I thought," he said to himself as he pulled off following Gator.

Chapter 34
One Thing after Another

As Kiam drove from one block to another, it was like he was seeing the city for the first time. The air was turning crisp as the leaves threatened to fall from the trees. The pulse of the city was idling at the moment, but at its heart was a thirst that needed to be quenched.

Behind the cloak of darkness that casted a shadow over the hoods, there were strong feelings of poverty, death and despair which seeped from every alley and crevice. The season was changing and Kiam was changing with it. It was the autumn of a new day, the whole way he dealt with muthafuckas from this point forward was going to change.

Kiam was in total beast mode, his temper was high and his patience was short. So much had gone on in the last couple of weeks that it had his mind and spirit in an uproar. The one thing he knew he definitely had to repair was his relationship with Eyez.

They had barely spoken since their argument on the way home from the retreat a week ago. Here it was the Eve of their new day and already he had managed to draw a wedge between them with the very things he promised her he wouldn't let tear them apart.

Hitting the Bluetooth in his truck he spoke out, "Call Eyez."

The voice command dialed her number and he waited to hear her voice flutter through his speakers. "Hello," her soft voice called back to him. Its sound was medicine to his soul.

"Hey you."

"Hey, baby, where are you?"

"I'm on my way to Bw3 on Mayfield. What you doing?"

"Laying here thinking about you," she admitted with a purr in her tone.

"Put on some clothes and come meet me."

Faydrah looked over at the clock on her nightstand. It was 10:15 and she had to be at work at six o'clock in the morning. She started to just tell him to come on over but she knew that they had things to rectify. If he came over she would sacrifice what really needed to be said to satisfy her yearning to have him in her bed.

She decided that it would be best for her to go to him. "Okay, let me get dressed, I'll see you in about thirty."

"A'ight, baby girl, drive safe. See you in a minute," Kiam said as he disconnected the call.

Faydrah rolled over and climbed out of bed, mentally and emotionally preparing herself to have this sit down with Kiam as she wiggled into her jeans.

Once in the car she took a deep breath, turned on the radio and cleared her mind.

Twenty minutes later, she pulled into the parking lot in her red Mustang convertible and parked next to Kiam's truck. Exiting the vehicle she straightened her shirt and hit the locks.

When Faydrah walked through the door Kiam stood up to greet her. Smiling, she walked right up to him and stepped into his arms. Kiam held her for several minutes, trying to comfort her weary mind and ease the tension between them. "Have a seat, ma," he said releasing her from his embrace.

Faydrah slid into the booth and Kiam slid in next to her, affectionately pressing his knees against hers. She smiled at the gesture, but the first few seconds were filled with a pregnant silence as she fidgeted with her keys.

"I'm sorry," they both said at the same time.

"Don't be trying to steal my lines," Kiam smoothly stated, taking her hand into his and bringing it to his lips. "I missed you, Eyez," he confessed.

"Kiam, what are we doing?" she asked as she connected her pretty brown eyes with his.

"I love you, that's what *I'm* doing. I know what it is to have you, and I know what it is to be without you, and that's not even an option. No matter how hard I search, I would never find another woman like you. Hurting or losing you is never my intent." Faydrah listened and blinked back tears.

Kiam went on, staring deep into the windows of her soul. "I made a promise to a very solid man who has given me all that he has left. That man became like a father to me when I was behind the wall. What happened the other night was a direct threat to some things that I'm doing for him so I gotta handle it. All I'm asking is that you don't ask me to let him down. Just let me see this mission through." He begged of her to understand.

Faydrah *overstood*. She knew that with men like hers it was loyalty or death, but too often it was both. "Baby, you don't have to see this shit through." She bit down on her lip to quell the anger that bubbled in her soul every time she thought about what the game did to those that refused to walk away.

"This ain't you anymore, Kiam. All your life you have been taking on missions to save everyone else. But who is going to save you?" She rested her hand on his chest.

Kiam got quiet.

"I understand your need to rule; you're built like that. But baby, these niggas out here have changed. Eight years have passed since you were out here, and with each passing year the game has become grimier. Ain't no code anymore." She paused to swallow some of the emotions that fought to spill out. Kiam looked in her eyes and saw her deep concern for him.

"These niggas don't respect nothing," she continued in a voice that was on the verge of breaking with each word uttered. "I don't want you to be the next man's badge of honor." Her eyes became teary as the thought of him laying in some gutter on a dark street flooded her mind.

Kiam put a reassuring hand on top of hers. "I know, ma, and that's why I'm not sleeping on these fools. Just hold me down until I do what I gotta do, then I'm out. Please, Eyez, I need you."

That was the one proclamation she could not ignore. Her heart just wouldn't allow her to deny him what he needed. Faydrah put her hands on the back of his head and pulled him to her. She kissed him gently on the lips, then pulled back holding his face between her hands and surrendering to his plea. "I'm not going anywhere. But please don't force me to live without you,"

"You have my word. I'ma do everything within my power not to let that happen."

"You better do what you gotta do, and I mean that," she reinforced, then the corners of her mouth turned up again.

Kiam smiled back at her.

She lifted her hand up and flashed her jewelry. "Now that you done put a ring on it, you owe me some *till death do us part*. And I want that to be when we can't tell whose teeth is whose in the little cups on the sink."

Kiam chuckled. "You crazy."

"Yup, and that's why you love me." She stuck her tongue out at him teasingly. It was amazing how quickly he could take her frown and turn it upside down.

"Forever, baby." He leaned in to kiss her again.

"You better know it." She savored the feel of his lips against hers.

Kiam stole another sweet kiss. When their lips parted Faydrah asked, "Where is that waitress? I done got hungry messing with you in the middle of the night."

Kiam looked around then flagged the waitress.

After the last wing vanished, they sat and talked and laughed until Faydrah realized that she had better take her butt home and get some sleep.

"You know I still didn't get my fix," Kiam reminded her as he opened her car door for her.

"You been fucking these streets so hard, you forgot that you had something hot and wet waiting on you," she replied, twisting her lips.

"You talk a lot of shit."

"And I can back it up."

"I got something you can back up *on*," he boasted as the thought of getting up behind that fat ass and making her submit hardened his dick.

"Let's see if your punk ass Cadillac can beat my four horses to the house." She tapped the roof of her car and looked over at his truck.

"You ain't taking about shit." Kiam got a little charged up.

"Well, let's go." Faydrah threw down the challenge.

"A'ight, it's on." Kiam put his fist out and Faydrah hit it. He nodded in agreement then turned to get in his truck.

Out the corner if his eye he noticed a black Cutlass creeping toward them with its headlights turned off. Inside the vehicle were evil eyes and faces half-covered with bandanas. "Eyez get down!" Kiam barked and shoved her to the ground just as loud gunshots erupted from inside the Cutlass.

Faydrah screamed as her elbows scraped the pavement and bullets pelted all around them. Kiam covered her body with his and hurriedly snatched his banger off his waist. When he brought it up, his Nine barked back loud. Boc! Boc! Boc! Boc!

Fearing for Faydrah's safety, he pounced back up on his feet and swiftly moved away from her. The shots from his assailants' guns whizzed by his head as he dashed behind his truck, crouched down and busting back at them over the hood.

Faydrah's screams pierced through the rapid gunshots that clapped in the quietness of the night. Kiam rose up and got hit with two up high. He stumbled back against a car that was parked beside his truck. Heat exploded in his body and hot blood poured from the wounds, but he refused to go down.

Fuck death, I don't fear that shit. If this was how it was written, well, bring that shit on! Either way, he wasn't dying with bullets still in his clip. He was bout to show them why niggas in the streets called guns whistles.

With his left arm rendered immobile and hanging limp at his side, Kiam pulled himself upright and raised the Nine in his right hand. "This what the fuck y'all want!" he yelled out, death-struck. Then he sparked up the night.

Bullets whistled through the air and tattered holes in the side of the Cutlass. The gunmen blasted back, then zoomed away, tires screaming.

Kiam staggered around the front of the Escalade, barely able to hold himself up. He was losing a lot of blood and he felt weak. "Eyez! Baby, where you at?" he called out.

"Kiam!" She was on her feet running toward him. Crying and babbling incoherently. She had feared that he'd been killed.

Kiam winced from the pain in his shoulder when she ran into his arms and sobbed against his chest. Sticky wet blood coated her forehead. "Oh my God!" she cried, realizing that he had been shot.

Kiam blocked out the pain when he heard the sirens heading their way. His head was beginning to feel light but he had to think fast. He was a convicted felon. If the Jakes caught him with a tool he was going back to the feds.

"Faydrah," he groaned loudly, cutting through her emotions. "Take this and get out of here!" He handed her the Nine.

Faydrah understood. She took the gun, hurried back to her car, and got in the wind.

As soon as she pulled off Kiam slumped to the ground and lost consciousness.

Chapter 35
Enough Is Enough

Faydrah sat up in Kiam's bed and stretched her tired limbs. With one hand covering her mouth to stifle back a yarn, she looked over at the empty spot next to her. Last night was the first night in almost two weeks that she had a chance to in a bed and her body was relieved for the much needed rest.

She slung her feet over the side of the bed and walked slowly to the bathroom, moving like an old lady. Her body was still very sore from the close brush with death, and sleeping in a chair next to Kiam's hospital bed night after night only made it worse.

She looked long and hard in the mirror at the evidence of the pain and confusion she had been going through since that night. Bags were beginning to form under her eyes and worry lines seemed to be etched into her forehead. Beyond that, her soul was in total turmoil. Kiam was alive and for that she was grateful, but with all the police attention and having to look over her shoulder, a part of her wished that she had left the past in the past.

Pouring facial scrub in her hands, she brought them to her face and tried to wash away some of the restlessness that wore thick around her eyes. After brushing her teeth, she hopped in the shower in an effort to mentally prepare herself to go back to the hospital.

A fresh shower gave her renewed energy. Humming a happy tune, Faydrah threw on some leggings and a t-shirt and a pair of sneakers. Quickly checking some emails she downloaded some files then packed her briefcase. She was thankful that she had some vacation time so she could look after her man.

As she drove to Hillcrest Hospital to see Kiam, she called in to a restaurant and ordered them some food. When she stopped at a red light she looked down at her engagement ring and suddenly found herself crying. Kiam was her everything and within a split second she had almost lost him.

Faydrah decided that as soon as he got home they were going to have a very serious conversation. Things had to change because the one thing she was not prepared to do was bury the only man that she had ever loved.

When the light turned green, she was still sitting there thinking. A horn honked behind her, drawing her mind back to where she was headed. She drove on, stopped to pick up the food she had ordered, then proceeded on to Hillcrest.

Faydrah walked into the hospital speaking to the receptionist and a few workers that she had grown familiar with over the last week. Exciting the elevator and reaching Kiam's door she became alarmed when she saw that it was closed. Her heart thumped wildly against her chest as fear grabbed ahold of her. Could Kiam's condition have taken a tragic turn since she left the hospital last night? She wondered nervously.

Pushing the door open slightly, she held her breath and peeked through the crack. There was no white sheet covering his head and the bed wasn't empty. Faydrah let out a huge sigh of relief. Of course her baby was okay.

Her eyes widened when she saw the two females from Kiam's crew. *Bang!* She swung the door open causing it to hit the wall and moved swiftly past the women and to Kiam's bedside.

Sitting the food on the tray and her briefcase on the side of the chair, she stood up and looked at Kiam with her head to the side.

Treebie and Lissha were silent waiting on Kiam's lead.

"What are you doing, you're supposed to be resting?" Faydrah asked with her lips drawn tight in a straight line.

"Baby, you know I have to take care of my business," he humbly stated.

"Fuck all that. You need to be concerned with getting better. Those streets and the trash that they produce will still be there when you get out." She looked over at Lissha.

"The streets? Bitch, ain't that where he found *you*?" Lissha piped up.

"Yup, and this street bitch got pussy worth claiming." She held up her hand. "But you wouldn't know anything about that, you got that spend the night pussy."

"Bitch, don't get fucked up," Lissha clacked, balling up her fist.

"Struck a nerve." Faydrah leaned in.

"Fuck you," Lissha spat, feeling herself about to leap on Faydrah's ass.

"No, fuck you."

"Both of y'all, shut the fuck up!" Kiam yelled out, wincing in pain.

"I guess ain't nothing wrong with his balls," Treebie cracked.

Kiam shot her a fierce look.

"My bad," she said, holding her hands up in surrender.

Kiam jerked his head back toward Faydrah. "Eyez, sit down."

She looked down at him and folded her arms.

"Don't make me repeat myself," he growled.

Faydrah looked at him with low eyes and flared nostrils and sat in the chair by his bed.

Kiam trained his eyes on the most hard-headed one in the room. Speaking in a low but stern tone, he said. "Lissha, don't disrespect my woman. You give her the same respect you give me."

"Your *woman*? You better make that bitch respect me." Lissha was hotter than a stolen pistol.

"Bitch, if you want respect you better give it," Faydrah cut back in, springing up out of her chair.

"Sit down!" Kiam ordered.

"No, fuck that. This bitch can get it. I'm tired of all this shit. Your fucked up promise to her father got you in all this bullshit."

"Bitch, you better watch your mouth," Lissha exploded. "Say one more thing about Daddy and I'll take your fucking life." She moved toward Faydrah with hot aggression.

Treebie's arm shot out, restraining her. "No, sis," she said. Leaning closer so that only Lissha could hear her, she whispered, "Always move in silence."

Faydrah was ready to move some furniture. "Bitch, you ain't the only one with bullets," she spat, moving closer to where they stood.

Lissha snapped open her bag and reached inside. "Not now," Treebie said, looking into Lissha's eyes.

"Fuck her. I'll knock her fucking head off." Faydrah continued to rail.

"I swear to God, if I gotta get the fuck up all y'all gonna regret the day y'all met me," Kiam said through gritted teeth.

"I already do," remarked Treebie. "Let's go, Li Li."

"No, y'all can stay. Because I'm done. I'm not doing this shit," Faydrah said, seething inside.

"What?" Kiam boomed.

"You heard me. Let this bitch take care of you." Faydrah turned to grab her bag.

"Eyez." He reached out for her but was restricted by his pain.

Snatching away, she tried to catch the tears that pushed at the corners of her eyes but it was too late. "No, Kiam, I cannot do this."

Kiam was about to apologize but she cut him off. "You want these streets? You can have 'em. But I can't be a part of it," she stated with conviction.

Kiam looked up at her with regret as she slid his ring off her finger and sat it on the bottom of the bed. "You remember this, the very muthafuckas you're loyal to ain't gonna be loyal to you." She walked past Lissha and Treebie. "Go ahead, lead him to his grave—that's what y'all want to do anyway." She purposely bumped up against Lissha on her way out the door.

Lissha stared at Faydrah's back and put her name on her hit list.

Kiam was past heated. He rubbed his hands over his face and thought carefully for a minute before rendering his verdict. Just as he was about to let Lissha have it, his phone went off. He looked down and recognized Riz's number flashing on the screen. "Yeah, what's up?" he answered.

"Nigga, you think I'm the one to test?! I promise you, you won't get away with that shit," Riz blared.

"Hold up! What the fuck are you talking about?" Kiam was lost.

"Nigga, you know what the fuck I'm talking about," Riz accused then went on to explain his anger. Curse word after curse word assaulted Kiam's ear.

Kiam was too shocked by what he was being accused of to go back off on Riz.

Lissha and Treebie watched as the vein in the middle of Kiam's temple got thicker. They could hear Riz yelling through the phone. Then silence. Riz had hung up. Lissha and Treebie looked at each questioningly.

Kiam was breathing heavier and heavier, trying to figure out what the fuck had gone wrong. "Muthafucka!" he yelled out then slung the phone across the room.

Kiam snatched tubes from his body and jumped up out of bed. He walked to the bathroom then grabbed his clothes from the closet and began getting dressed.

The women looked on silently. They could see blood seeping through the bandages on his shoulder. They could also fell the rage inside of him.

"Go get the car," he said as he tried to deal with the pain that was coursing through his body.

Just as Lissha and Treebie hit the door, in walked the nurse. She looked at Kiam and gasped. "Oh no, what are you doing? You can't leave, you're not well," she panicked, pressing her palms in the air as if to stop him.

"Watch me," he said as he put his feet in his boots. Passing the bed he grabbed Faydrah's ring and put it in his pocket. "Have a nice day," he said to the nurse who was standing there with her mouth open as he walked out the door in search of answers that was gonna get somebody killed one way or the other.

Chapter 36
Playin' With the Devil

Kiam sat in silence on the burgundy Italian leather sofa in his living room. His ratchet sat on the marble and glass cocktail table in front of him fully loaded with one already in the chamber. Next to the Nine sat a half empty bottle of Jack Daniels and a bottle of pain pills.

Kiam's dark eyes seemed more frightening with the two week old beard that framed his normally clean shaven face. His left arm hung down by his side in a sling but there would be no doubt after this evening that he was still deadly.

With his free hand he stroked the hair on his face as he looked around the living room at the upper echelon of his team. Lissha sat across from him on the loveseat studying his expression. She knew that something real serious was about to go down, but even her wildest imagination couldn't have prepared her for what she would soon witness.

Lissh could see Treebie in the dining room loading a plate with food that Kiam had laid out. *That bitch would have an appetite at her own execution*, Lissha thought.

Donella and Bayonna sat across from each other in twin recliners with plates of untouched food in their laps. JuJu however chose to stand close to the door. He had already decided that if one of them were flawed, the only way they would be leaving was twisted, wrapped in sheets and black plastic.

Lissha's eyes rotated from Kiam to the Nine on the table, and the half bottle of Jack Daniels. Donella fidgeted with her hands and Bayonna rocked her foot as the silence became thick with anticipation.

Treebie entered the living room and sat down on the other end of the loveseat. She was cool as a breeze with her legs crossed and a heaping plate of food balanced on her lap. She bit into the drumstick then filled her mouth with fork full of spaghetti. "What kind of meat is in this? Ground turkey?" she asked, looking at Kiam.

"Humph," her grunted.

"Whatever that's supposed to mean. Anyway, it tastes like damn jerky."

Kiam didn't comment, he was steady staring her down.

Treebie felt his gaze hot on her face but she kept on eating. She didn't know why Kiam had called them all together; she suspected that it had something to do with the angry phone call that he'd received from Riz the other day, but she wasn't sure. She knew she was strapped and if he was planning on acting a fool she would surely aid in his venture.

Kiam cleared his throat, then spoke with words that were carefully chosen. "I sat and thought long and hard before I called y'all here tonight," he stated a little over a whisper. All eyes were focused on him and there was no other sound in the room aside from his voice.

He looked from one face to the other. "The last thing a general ever wants to do is wonder about the loyalty of his men," he continued as he picked up the medication bottle, popped it open and threw two pills in his mouth.

He poured himself a shot of Jack and locked eyes with Lissha. "I'm going to start with you. My product made it back here, but the money never made it to Riz, his people got jacked leaving the exchange spot. Now unless I'm stupid that tells me that it was set up on this end. You told me that you'd put your life on your crew."

"And unless you have proof that I can't, don't even bring that shit to me," Lissha defended her girls.

Kiam chuckled. "Besides you and me, they were the only ones that knew when and where the pickup goes down."

Treebie stopped chewing and sat to the edge of her seat. "What the fuck is that supposed to mean?"

Lissha held her hand up gesturing for Treebie to be quiet. She sat up and looked him square in the face, the way Big Zo had taught her to face opposition. "Are you accusing me of something?"

"Until I find out exactly what happened, I'm accusing all of you muthafuckas," he said point blank.

"If Riz's people got jacked, why the fuck couldn't the cross come from his end?" Lissha contested.

"That's what I'm saying," Treebie angrily agreed. "And ain't nobody seen Gator's slick ass in two days, how we know he didn't have something to do with it? You need to find out where that nigga at."

"I already know where he's at," Kiam replied matter of factly.

"Well, enlighten the rest of us, please," shot Treebie, impatiently.

Kiam smirked. "You're chewing him."

Treebie gasped and spat out the spaghetti. She cocked her head to the side and looked at him crazily. "What the fuck, man!"

"I skinned that bitch nigga alive, then I ground him up real good," said Kiam.

Treebie slung the plate off her lap and bolted to the bathroom. Lissha, Donella, and Bay stared at Kiam with their mouths open.

JuJu was still covering the door. He was not surprised by Kiam's revelation, he had helped him dice Gator up.

Treebie returned to her seat still gagging and waiting for Kiam to tell her he was only kidding, but the look in his eyes confirmed that he was dead ass. *This nigga craze.* Treebie shook her head in utter disbelief. The others were thinking the same thing.

Kiam looked at them as if to say they hadn't seen shit yet. "Gator was stupid," he said. "He should have known that he would be the first person I suspected. I thought he had something to do with the attempt on my life, but I was wrong. He jacked Riz's people. I couldn't get him to admit it before I ended his suffering, but it don't matter, I know that he was skimming money for years. Riz told me that."

"You put a whole lot of faith in what Riz say. That nigga could be wrong about all this shit," Lissha voiced.

"You got a problem wit' it? Cause if I'm right about Gator having something to do with the jack then one of you had to help set it up." He paused and looked in the faces of the women one by one. He had to admit that they were tight lipped and unified. But in a minute Gator's accomplice would fold.

"I'm gonna give the guilty one a chance to own up to what she done. If you do that I'll show some mercy, but if you sit here and play innocent I'ma do to you the same thing I did to your boy," Kiam promised ominously.

Neither of the girls expressions changed a tad, noted Kiam. "Y'all gon' play this shit all the way out, huh?" Still he got nothing but four blank stares. The silence in the room was profound.

Switching tactics Kiam said. "I give that soft nigga, Gator, credit; he wouldn't tell me nothing. Nah, he took that to the grave with him. But I'ma still find out which one of you crossed me."

On cue Daphne came sweeping into the living room. Four sets of eyes focused on her.

Kiam chuckled and picked his gun up off of the table. He looked at Daphne and said, "Point out the bitch that you saw with Gator when he met with Wolfman."

Daphne locked eyes with the guilty one and did not bat an eyelash as she raised her finger and pointed directly at the traitor. "That's her right there," she said.

To be continued...
Trust No Bitch 2:
Available Now!

BOOKS BY LDP'S CEO, CA$H

TRUST NO MAN

TRUST NO MAN 2

TRUST NO MAN 3

BONDED BY BLOOD

SHORTY GOT A THUG

A DIRTY SOUTH LOVE

THUGS CRY

THUGS CRY 2

TRUST NO BITCH

TRUST NO BITCH 2

TRUST NO BITCH 3

TIL MY CASKET DROPS

Coming Soon

TRUST NO BITCH (KIAM EYEZ' STORY)

THUGS CRY 3

BONDED BY BLOOD 2

RESTRANING ORDER

BOOKS BY NENE CAPRI

PUSSY TRAP I, II, III & IV

DREAM WEAVER

TAINTED

Coming Soon From Lock Down Publications

RESTRAINING ORDER

By **CA$H & COFFEE**

GANGSTA CITY **II**

By **Teddy Duke**

A DANGEROUS LOVE **VII**

By **J Peach**

BLOOD OF A BOSS **III**

By **Askari**

THE KING CARTEL **III**

By **Frank Gresham**

NEVER TRUST A RATCHET BITCH

SILVER PLATTER HOE **III**

By **Reds Johnson**

THESE NIGGAS AIN'T LOYAL **III**

By **Nikki Tee**

BROOKLYN ON LOCK **III**

By **Sonovia Alexander**

THE STREETS BLEED MURDER **II**

By **Jerry Jackson**

CONFESSIONS OF A DOPEMAN'S DAUGHTER **II**

By **Rasstrina**

WHAT ABOUT US **II**

NEVER LOVE AGAIN

By **Kim Kaye**

A GANGSTER'S REVENGE

Trust No Bitch

By **Aryanna**

Available Now

LOVE KNOWS NO BOUNDARIES **I II & III**
By **Coffee**
SILVER PLATTER HOE **I & II**
HONEY DIPP **I & II**
CLOSED LEGS DON'T GET FED **I & II**
A BITCH NAMED KARMA
By **Reds Johnson**
A DANGEROUS LOVE **I, II, III, IV, V, VI**
By **J Peach**
CUM FOR ME
An **LDP Erotica Collaboration**
THE KING CARTEL **I & II**
By **Frank Gresham**
BLOOD OF A BOSS **I & II**
By **Askari**
THE DEVIL WEARS TIMBS
BURY ME A G **I II & III**
By **Tranay Adams**
THESE NIGGAS AIN'T LOYAL **I & II**
By **Nikki Tee**
THE STREETS BLEED MURDER
By **Jerry Jackson**
DIRTY LICKS

By **Peter Mack**

THE ULTIMATE BETRAYAL

By **Phoenix**

BROOKLYN ON LOCK

By **Sonovia Alexander**

SLEEPING IN HEAVEN, WAKING IN HELL **I, II & III**

By **Forever Redd**

THE DEVIL WEARS TIMBS **I, II & III**

By **Tranay Adams**

DON'T FU#K WITH MY HEART **I & II**

By **Linnea**

BOSS'N UP **I & II**

By **Royal Nicole**

LOYALTY IS BLIND

By **Kenneth Chisholm**

Made in the USA
Columbia, SC
04 October 2024

43593573R00178